That Not Forgotten

That Not Forgotten

Editor
Bruce Kauffman

First Edition

Hidden Brook Press
www.HiddenBrookPress.com
writers@HiddenBrookPress.com

Copyright © 2012 Hidden Brook Press
Copyright © 2012 Authors

All rights for poems and prose revert to the authors. All rights for book, layout and design remain with Hidden Brook Press. No part of this book may be reproduced except by a reviewer who may quote brief passages in a review. The use of any part of this publication reproduced, transmitted in any form or by any means, electronic, mechanical, photocopied, recorded or otherwise stored in a retrieval system without prior written consent of the publisher is an infringement of the copyright law.

All royalties from sales of this book will go to The Al Purdy A-Frame Trust.
www.harbourpublishing.com/PurdyAFrame/index.html

That Not Forgotten
Editor – Bruce Kauffman

Cover Art – William Weedmark
Section Art – heidi mack, Milenko Grgar, David Woodward and Meredith Westcott
Cover Design – Richard M. Grove
Layout and Design – Richard M. Grove

Typeset in Garamond

Printed and bound in USA

Library and Archives Canada Cataloguing in Publication

That not forgotten / editor Bruce Kauffman.
Includes index.
Poems and short stories.
ISBN 978-1-897475-89-8

1. Canadian poetry (English)--Ontario. 2. Short stories, Canadian (English)--Ontario. 3. Canadian poetry (English)--21st century. 4. Canadian fiction (English)--21st century.
I. Kauffman, Bruce

PS8255.O5T43 2012   C810.8'097135   C2012-904346-X

The Last Picture in the World

A hunched grey shape
framed by leaves
with lake water behind
standing on our
little point of land
like a small monk
in a green monastery
meditating

    almost sculpture
except that it's alive
brooding immobile permanent
for half an hour
a blue heron
and it occurs to me
that if I were to die at this moment
that picture would accompany me
wherever I am going
for part of the way

Al Purdy,
from *Beyond Remembering*
— *The collected poems of Al Purdy.* 2000

CONTENTS

Introduction – **Editor, Bruce Kauffman** – *p. xvi*

Section I

Artwork: "Snowshoe Moments" – **heidi mack** – *p. 1*

Finding Form – **Gary Wiilliam Rasberry** – *p. 3*
With the Faith of Our Fathers – **Heather Browne** – *p. 5*
Midwinter Thaw – **Felicity Sidnell Reid** – *p. 7*
the magnolia tree – **Jessica Marion Barr** – *p. 8*
Horizon – **Ian Hanna** – *p. 9*
On the Final Lip of Habitable Light – **Ashley–Elizabeth Best** – *p. 10*
butchering – **David Sheffield** – *p. 12*
Belle Park – **D. L. Iffla** – *p. 14*
In Time the Lake – **Gabrielle Santyr** – *p. 16*
You journey across the land – **gillian harding-russell** – *p. 17*
The Unseen Bear – **Carolyn Smart** – *p. 19*
New Light – **Jason Heroux** – *p. 20*
A Fishing Report, Read from a Teleprompter – **Jan Allen** – *p. 21*
Upon Leaving – **Barbara Erochina** – *p. 22*
Haiku for Twenty Ten – **Brent Raycroft** – *p. 23*
Vibration – **Elizabeth Greene** – *p. 28*
The Lost Road – **Eric Folsom** – *p. 29*
Fallen Sparrow – **Gene Rankin** – *p. 30*
Religion on a Monday Morning – **Joanne Light** – *p. 31*

Credo? – **Joanne Page** – *p. 32*
tether – **John Pigeau** – *p. 33*
A Chorus of Severed Pipes – **Kelly Rose Pflug-Back** – *p. 34*
Full Moon in Scorpio – **Kirsteen Macleod** – *p. 35*
The Body Eclectic – **Morgan Wade** – *p. 36*
Just Breathe – **A. Gregory Frankson** – *p. 38*
Paul Kelley, from *Untimely* – **Paul Kelley** – *p. 40*
Easter 2011 – **Diane Dawber** – *p. 45*
Old Wise Ones – **Coreen Covert** – *p. 47*
Common Ground – **Cori Mayhew** – *p. 48*
Evergreens – **Denise Hamilton** – *p. 52*
At Normandy – **David Malone** – *p. 53*
Sunset – **Nicholas Papaxanthos** – *p. 54*
Fault–lines – **Lara Szabo Greisman** – *p. 55*
The Hot and the Bitter – **Ashley-Elizabeth Best** – *p. 56*

Section II

Artwork: "The Lake Will Never Forget Us" – **Milenko Grgar** – *p. 59*

Breaking Cages... – **Eriana Marcus** – *p. 61*
Dreaming of the Dead – **Carolyn Smart** – *p. 64*
Milk – **Carla Hartsfield** – *p. 65*
rain – **Bruce Kauffman** – *p. 67*
Kundalini – **Amber Potter** – *p. 68*
I Would Photograph You – **Bob MacKenzie** – *p. 69*
Who Bears Grief – **David Malone** – *p. 70*
La Maison D'Eva – **Greg Bell** – *p. 71*
Walking Percy Street – **K. V. Skene** – *p. 72*
Beats – **Jennie McCaugherty** – *p. 73*
Laura and Gloria – **Kristin Andrychuk** – *p. 74*

Starman – **Laura Dyer** – *p. 77*
this is a story – **Kali Carys** – *p. 78*
The Arsonist – **Lindy Mechefske** – *p. 81*
Old Friends, in the Afternoon, Spring – **Laurie Lewis** – *p. 82*
The Vanishing Act – **Roger Dorey** – *p. 85*
Wedding in the Woods – **Phyllis Erwin** – *p. 87*
The New Father – **Sadiqa de Meijer** – *p. 88*
Iced Tea – **Sage Pantony Irwin** – *p. 89*
Imaginary Passport – **Sandra Alland** – *p. 90*
Napping in the Car – **Sarah Yi-Mei Tsiang** – *p. 91*
Vessels – **Sarah Richardson** – *p. 92*
Field Trip, Artillery Park – **Tara Kainer** – *p. 96*
My Mother's Skeleton – **Ursula Pflug** – *p. 97*
Comfort – **Walter Lloyd** – *p. 101*
Cobourg, Night – **Stuart Ross** – *p. 102*
Boy Encaustic – **Sonja Grgar** – *p. 103*
Benchmark – **Patricia Henderson** – *p. 104*
Poem For Al Purdy – **Michael Hurley** – *p. 106*
The Space Between People – **Lara Szabo Greisman** – *p. 116*
Carbolic in the Maytag, Or Visiting-the-Prison Blues – **Joanne Page** – *p. 118*
The Oldest Living Swinger in Canada – **Jeanette Lynes** – *p. 119*
Shaking – **Eric Folsom** – *p. 120*
Rapture – **Eliot Kane** – *p. 121*
A Thought on That Silver Lining – **Linda Allison Stevenson** – *p. 122*
Jamie – **Andrew Scott** – *p. 128*
Letter Home – **Louise O'Donnell** – *p. 129*
Challenging the Law of Superimposition – **Lynn Tait** – *p. 131*
From Both Sides, Now – **Shane Joseph** – *p. 133*
What Ever Happened to Kevin Smith? – **Roger Dorey** – *p. 138*
The Family Business – **Morgan Wade** – *p. 141*
A Poem About Tom – **Laura Dyer** – *p. 146*
the pressure – **Kathleen Moritz** – *p. 147*
foetal escape – **Joshua Jia** – *p. 148*

So Good to See John in Kingston – **Ruth Buckley** – *p. 150*
there was no time – **John Pigeau** – *p. 152*
First Day on Queen's Campus – **John Lazarus** – *p. 154*
Motion – **Joanne Walton Paterson** – *p. 155*
Night – **James D. Medd** – *p. 156*
The Rum–Runner's Daughter – **Joan Wilding** – *p. 157*
Delayed Flight to Dallas – **Ashley–Elizabeth Best** – *p. 159*

Section III

Artwork: "Lakeshore Road in Winter" – **David Woodward** – *p. 161*

Untitled IV – **Denise Hamilton** – *p. 162*
Of Stars and Sleeves – **Clara Langley** – *p. 163*
Remembrance of Rueben Ash – **Diane Taylor** – *p. 164*
Here – **Carolyn Hei-Kyoung You** – *p. 165*
Remembering – **Gloria Taylor** – *p. 167*
Illuminated Moments – **Eriana Marcus** – *p. 168*
Mentality – **Hugh Walter Barclay** – *p. 171*
On the Bus to Toronto in April – **Jan Allen** – *p. 172*
January Eighth on the 401 – **Eric Folsom** – *p. 173*
Cracked Lips – **Jennie McCaugherty** – *p. 174*
port hope boy – **David Sheffield** – *p. 176*
Jar–cracks–are–not–sane – **Christine Miscione** – *p. 177*
Pebble – **Joanne Light** – *p. 178*
Pontypool – Land of Reflections – **Honey Novick** – *p. 179*
the end of traffic – **John Pigeau** – *p. 181*
Abandoned – **Kathryn MacDonald** – *p. 184*
Anthem – **Lara Szabo Greisman** – *p. 185*
The Last Wave – **Lee-Ann Taras** – *p. 186*
Wolf Suit – **Kelly Rose Pflug-Back** – *p. 188*
Sometimes a Dead Poet – **Laurie Lewis** – *p. 190*

city memories – **Joshua Jia** – *p. 191*
wood – **Gina Hanlon** – *p. 193*
Great Horned Owl – **Carole Tenbrink** – *p. 194*
The Blue Church, Prescott, 1933 – **Carla Hartsfield** – *p. 199*
Black-letter Stammer – **Gary William Rasberry** – *p. 200*
Sonless – **Diane Taylor** – *p. 203*
Peace – **Joanne Light** – *p. 204*
in the city – **Kathleen Moritz** – *p. 205*
Ashes – **Kathryn MacDonald** – *p. 206*
Sambaqui – **Kirsteen MacLeod** – *p. 207*
Jiibay or Aandizooke? – **Leeane Betasamosake Simpson** – *p. 208*
Mountain View – **Norma Chakrabarty** – *p. 211*
With This Ring – **Ruth Clarke** – *p. 213*
Where – **Sandra J. Walton** – *p. 216*
Seeing – **Sarah Yi-Mei Tsiang** – *p. 217*
Olga – **Sonja Grgar** – *p. 218*
You Know Who You Are – **Steven Heighton** – *p. 219*
My City is Full of History – **Stuart Ross** – *p. 220*
As if Leaves Could Hide Invisible Beings – **Ursula Pflug** – *p. 221*
The Ghost of Rice Lake – **Veronica J. Atkinson** – *p. 225*
Bereft – **Walter Lloyd** – *p. 226*
Stealing Affinities – **Tara Kainer** – *p. 227*
The Basket – **Philomene Kocher** – *p. 228*
small – **Carla Hartsfield** – *p. 229*
cage – **Bruce Kauffman** – *p. 231*
"Original Sin" – **Anne Graham** – *p. 233*
We are what came before us – **Denise Hamilton** – *p. 234*
Here is a man deep in sorrow like an underground river – **Carolyn Smart** – *p. 235*
Religion – **John Donlan** – *p. 236*
Once in Favour – **David Malone** – *p. 237*
Flood – **Elizabeth Greene** – *p. 239*
un sospiro – **Joshua Jia** – *p. 240*

Section IV

Artwork: "Frontenac Sky" – **heidi mack** – *p. 243*

What Your Words Do – **Rose Deshaw** – *p. 245*
My Poem Falters and Fails – **Vivekannand Jha** – *p. 246*
Limestone Blues – **Patricia Sullivan** – *p. 247*
The Wood of Halfway Through – **Steven Heighton** – *p. 248*
News From Another Room – **Steven Heighton** – *p. 249*
Under Construction – **Susan Olding** – *p. 250*
A Tail for Our Times – **Martina Hardwick** – *p. 252*
Moving Day – **Michael Casteels** – *p. 254*
In Honour of My Visit to Paris – **Terry Ann Carter** – *p. 255*
Waiting – **Gloria Taylor** – *p. 256*
Safe At Home – **Anne Nielson** – *p. 257*
Kraken – **Gabrielle Santyr** – *p. 258*
you live here – **Bob MacKenzie** – *p. 259*
Merida – **Carole TenBrink** – *p. 260*
Urban Meltdown – **Jennie McCaugherty** – *p. 261*
A Body in the Field – **Lauren Hearnden** – *p. 262*
Kingston Calendar – **Jeanette Lynes** – *p. 269*
Elegy For the Pines of Lakeview – **Louise O'Donnell** – *p. 272*
Old School – **Lucy Barnett** – *p. 274*
Bill of Sale – **Brandon Crilly** – *p. 276*
The Voice Within – **A. Gregory Frankson** – *p. 280*
Schism Dreams – **Matthew Shultz** – *p. 283*
P4W – **Greg Bell** – *p. 285*
Monteleone – **Gene Rankin** – *p. 287*
Trees (Ontario, Canada) – **Kathy Figueroa** – *p. 291*
snow – **Gina Hanlon** – *p. 293*
Hemingway, Greene, Steinbeck and the Other Guy – **Shane Joseph** – *p. 294*
Getting There – **Tapanga A. Koe** – *p. 298*

Poem – **Sandra Alland** – *p. 302*
There is a Lake – **Tim Murphy** – *p. 303*
If I Could Only Tell Him – **Sonja Grgar** – *p. 304*
The Wind – **Michael Casteels** – *p. 306*
My Canoe Paddle – **Matthew Sinclair** – *p. 307*
Not Lovers in Lake Ontario – **Veronica J. Atkinson** – *p. 308*
Walking on Lake Ontario – **Theodore Christou** – *p. 309*
Slow Exit – **James D. Medd** – *p. 310*
Tired Dance – **Gary William Rasberry** – *p. 311*
With Limits in the Misted – **Kin Man Young Tai** – *p. 312*
Bits – **Clara Langley** – *p. 313*
Birch – **Kelly Rose Pflug-Back** – *p. 314*
camping on colonel – **Theodore Christou** – *p. 315*

Section V

Artwork: "Rock and Flow" – **Meredith Westcott** – *p. 317*

Winter Crescent – **Patricia Henderson** – *p. 319*
Missing – **Sarah Yi-Mei Tsiang** – *p. 321*
Untitled – **Mieke Little** – *p. 322*
Your Voice – **Walter Lloyd** – *p. 324*
(Untitled) – **Mansoor Behnam** – *p. 325*
Grey – **Matthew Reesor** – *p. 327*
Insomnia at Summer's End – **Carolyn Smart** – *p. 328*
Monsoon – **Kirsteen MacLeod** – *p. 329*
The Reading – **Tara Kainer** – *p. 330*
Little Cat – **Sage Pantony Irwin** – *p. 331*
September – **Amber Potter** – *p. 332*
This Heart Against Reason – **Tim Murphy** – *p. 333*
Chilly Winds – **Rich Tyo** – *p. 334*
Migrations – **Leah Murray** – *p. 336*
Camouflage – **Jason Heroux** – *p. 342*

Pluperfect intensified: Trip West '78 – **gillian harding-russell** – *p. 343*
Tufa – **Bethmarie Michalska** – *p. 345*
Voice of God – **Jennie McCaugherty** – *p. 347*
The Meeting – **James D. Medd** – *p. 349*
Fourth Avenue – **Roger Dorey** – *p. 350*
Near Sydenham, winter – **Theodore Christou** – *p. 351*
Taking Inventory, Garden State – **Joanne Page** – *p. 352*
Four Seasons in a Hospital – **Michael Casteels** – *p. 354*
Season: – **Kin Man Young Tai** – *p. 355*
What Crows Say – **Sadiqa de Meijer** – *p. 359*
Black Knight – **Anne Graham** – *p. 360*
Migratory Animals – **K. V. Skene** – *p. 361*
Pre–Winter Bleak – **Gary William Rasberry** – *p. 362*
Lotus – **John Donlan** – *p. 363*

Section VI

Artwork: "White Pine" – **heidi mack** – *p. 365*

Index of Previously Published Work – *p. 366*
Index of Author Page Listing – *p. 368*
Editor Bio – *p. 370*
Author Bios – *p. 371*
Cover Artist Bio – *p. 388*
Artist Bios – *p. 388*

Introduction

As editor, I've had the pleasure of being the first person to read and absorb a vast number of submissions to this collection of poetry, and short and micro-prose from a wealth of writers. That reading experience – quite humbling. You will find, contained within, the eclectic voice and heart of a vast number of poets/writers who have, or have had, ties to a prescribed area. My heartfelt thanks to all of those who did contribute, and It would have been incredibly wonderful to have included all submissions here, but herein – the best of the best.

As this anthology was conceived in the summer of 2011, the call for submissions went out with the following as its mission statement: "The book's focus is to be a collection of work from writers with ties to an area along the north shore of Lake Ontario, from Kingston to Port Hope and north to Highway 7. Its mission is to paint, with an eclectic brush, reflections of, reaction to, hope within – pieces of ourselves found, pieces of ourselves lost here in this place. The book, more than thematically specific, will be a collage of voice and style from poets and prose writers, who either still or at some point in their lives, shared this place, this soil."

This anthology was purposely set up without specific theme to allow for as much a diverse interpretation of that mission statement as possible, and drew in a tremendous volume of some very wonderful work. Within these covers you will discover the work of one hundred and eighteen written word contributors, and many with more than one piece. Within this anthology you will also discover in that work a gamut of emotion, life-interpretation, story and voice.

A call for submissions for cover artwork went out after the call for written work closed. My thanks for, again, both the number and the diverse wealth of artwork submitted. Artwork arrived in the form of a number of genres. Gracing the cover of this book is artwork by William Weedmark, entitled "The Light".

The book's roughly 400 pages are purposely sectioned into five quasi-thematic pieces. The work within each section loosely "connects" with other pieces therein. In line with the initial mission of this anthology, the sections are untitled and separated only by artwork from the remaining artists shortlisted for cover artwork.

Bios for all contributors, poets/authors/artists, appear at book's end. Included in each bio are the page numbers of this anthology in which their work appears. Admittedly in an untraditional fashion, bios are arranged alphabetically by contributor's first name rather than last. A last piece of artwork does introduce this section, as well.

Again, my heartfelt thanks for the generosity of spirit and heart coming out of this community, and for the wealth of incredible work received. Response to both calls for submissions was both beautiful and heartwarming. It was truly a pleasure working with a vast array of quite incredible authors, poets and artists.

To you, as reader, I simply say "Sit back (for a long time) and enjoy".

Bruce Kauffman,
Editor

Snowshoe Moments
heidi mack

Gary William Rasberry

Finding Form

Of course this is how it must begin:
standing on any green hill
at the mercy of all blue rivers,
reinventing the colours of sky.
Three perfect ravens.

Waiting for the moon
to find a form for the planet's giving way:
shade born out of light.

As a matter of course,
the palette gives and receives
in combinations until the body
is no longer a body.

Whisper the incantation
as it was given, as breath.

Walk around the canvas three times,
counterclockwise for luck and momentum.

Wind the world up until
it spins on spit and sweat
and the bloody pitch of a fallen

pine aware of nothing but
the first drop of rain repeating
itself—three times counterclockwise,
putting the hex on cliché: *out of the blue*

words fall on open fields,
plant themselves and wait
for the world to imagine itself

out of a seed or run its course like an
avalanche down a garden path
ripping up colour as it goes.

Heather Browne

With the Faith of Our Fathers
"See you in the river of my dreams." —Sterling Browne

i.

with the faith of our fathers take the narrow passage,
enter into Morton Bay. Throw an anchor
and let your vessel play the wind
as you face Rock Dunder, turning into its bald cliff-face.
Ask of this out-cropping: Is it magnetism or mere wind

that makes one's vessel drift? Or a kindred spirit which
makes one leap sixty or more feet into its
cold depths? Or swim when the moon lifts
into the red-rimmed eye of the loon singing
all the dark night the old song of your beginning?

ii.

this present river, the Styx, a widening
of the Cataraqui, and flowing south.
In white October its marshlands alight
with swans, with wings scissoring the shore,
shifting the airs. When you drop

from the flat reaches of Upper Brewers,
Lower Brewers, it is a managed fall of
past engineering genius. You are delivered
into an inner harbour—difficult to calculate its breadth—
and there you are: shocked into awakening.

iii.

"See you in the River of my dreams," he said,
and a Snowy Owl appears—his imperial bearing
no dreamer could mistake— on a bull-
dozed hummock, rock and ice commingling.
By a fence a donkey brays. His call goes on

while above his ears a wind turbine spreads wide
its three- pronged benediction: Father
Son, and Holy Ghost. On a March-bright afternoon
the little birds rattle like Sunday papers
in the copses near a road named Concession.

Felicity Sidnell Reid

Midwinter Thaw

Golden bones finger the mist of a mild midwinter.
Articulated skeletons, the willows whip their arms
Against the snow.
Water, crackling free, still runs between the white and dun,
Cleaning soft, beige, sandy edges, honing hollows
For its eddies.
Flirting ruffles, the water swings toward the hairy bank,
Deep-dappled, brown-beige, fringed with whiskers.
The ripples turn.
Bushes haunted by the ghosts of leaves, stiffen to their
Rooted stems, in the shadow of those potent,
Tall, dark trees.
Across the snow the footprints tumble; meet, mix, scatter,
Disappear. The rumpled, binding sheets are sliding off.
Half-warmed,
The live earth shakes its hair; promising but passing
Night-mares to those who can believe the clamps of
Winter undone.

Jessica Marion Barr

the magnolia tree

if you look carefully
and for a very long time
you may notice that
the magnolia tree is rotating
dancing its own orbit

it was dancing butoh
before humans walked upright
the magnolia tree
sighing petals
soft as piglet ears
luminous as pearls

in its veins tiny glaciers
left trails of silver

it turned toward magnetic north
and then turned again

breathing as the seasons breathe
living with the world
in its peripheral vision
the magnolia tree
turns

Ian Hanna

   autumnal sunset orange
    zest and maple brown syrup
     glows delicious amber in deep water
      blue sky distant rusty goose honk trumpet
       song asymmetric wedge shotguns slow motion
        south towards next summer gold moment fades
         to colourless dark gathering like soot along opposite
          H   O   R   I   Z   O   N
         to colourless dark gathering like soot along opposite
        south towards next summer gold moment fades
       song asymmetric wedge shotguns slow motion
      blue sky distant rusty goose honk trumpet
     glows delicious amber in deep water
    zest and maple brown syrup
   autumnal sunset orange

Ashley-Elizabeth Best

On the Final Lip of Habitable Light
Tim Lilburn

Sky and landscape
drawn together in gray tones,
fused in frozen solidarity.

We wanted to dance
pictures in the snow
without getting wet and
skate on ponds concealed
beyond ridges and trees.

Learning the world
in one trip,
traipsing along trails,
snow sinking into the
tops of our boots.

Wolf pups *yip yipping*, snapping
in the backyard,
deer trotting on the concrete slab
Papa made before us,
while we were still a dream.

Daylight foraging, mineral digging,
determining spruce from pine,
moose tracks from elk.

Dogs down in the barn holding
excited conversations with dogs
miles down the road.

As long as it was wild
and we didn't have to gut it,
the limbs of the trees
still danced raw-boned, clanking
like a loose ship-in-a-bottle.

The night descended
like a wave of black paint
just after 4:30, just before 5.

With the sting of the cold rising
off our faces,
we went home to eat in wood
heated tender folds.
Somewhere there was still a
hockey game on to watch.

David Sheffield

butchering

late in the summer
that my grandfather died
leaving a green tobacco can on the shelf
long grass in the ditch along Gosford Road turned
dry and brown

the sun ground its familiar way south
ending a season of boy play that
swung from rough ropes in
dusty, abandoned hay lofts and
leaped without fear
before we had regrets

they, that unruly collection
that added up to a family and
made out an artless existence on
a farm at the end of the road, lost
to liquor and forgotten hopes
grape jelly on stale, white bread, a
kitchen lacking the touch of a mother

I walked past the house
running my fingers along the tail fin of
a dark blue Fairlane parked on the grass
Hank Snow on the radio, the steel guitar wept
through the car window

a barnyard oak tree played witness
to one final ritual
one dying, carnivorous ceremony
performed for an intimate audience by
grey stubbled men with pulleys and ropes
who immersed a pink fleshed
hog carcass, limbs spread wide
into boiling water
a steel barrel baptismal font over a wood fire

immerse, emerge
with dull-edged knives scrape bristle from hot skin
again, plunge, withdraw
the insides, the life force
slumped in a washtub

lying on a hospital bed
crisp sheets, body still, eyes un-opening
on the morning that he died
my grandfather walked the laneway
between fields
between split rail and gnarled apple tree
his feeble voice naming the cows at chore time

I stand alone under the oak tree
the carnal beast hangs
casting its last shadow like a crucifix

D. L. Donna-lee Iffla

Belle Park

Trees getting to the root of the matter:
That's what the sign says,
As if black willows and balsam poplars
were consciously on a mission.
Trees at work, taking on the gruesome ground water.
Taking it and holding it in plant tissue,
they euphemistically say,
So others don't have to.
Some kamikaze career.
No wonder the leaves of the newly planted saplings
Look to me like they're waving goodbye.

Kids skateboard there, guys golf
Near a mountain of garbage
That must, methinks, be melting
Under the genial grasses.
Ducks and geese lie down on the greens,
Or scatter out to the bay.
An osprey carries a fish
       Headfirst, like a scaly submarine,

Their nest a crown of thorns atop a telephone pole,
More salvage than salvation.

The tannery, the woolen mill, the factories
No longer working at the waste we made,
But another ghost still stands at the entrance:
A totem pole growing out of turtle island
With bear paws climbing to its summit.
A hope for healing
Only trees can understand.
Out on the water, scullers
Pull for speed at half light
Beneath pink clouds like commas
In the big blue question that echoes
Over Belle Park—that long leachate
        Running out to the Cataraqui River–

Who pays for what we do?
                We do
                        We do
                                We do.

Gabrielle Santyr

In Time the Lake

The lake is simmering cold today
with its pale fogs swirling and rising:

lifting like a chilling steam
from the cool cauldron's
vestigial chowder
of raw flesh fallen
in crystalline flakes
off pared to the marrow bones
that sink to the bottom
and rest hollow there
compressed into memory's hold

Tomorrow the lake will be frozen
in time
forgotten the ghosts
of its unfathomed past

a mirror reflecting the pristine
blue present
hard in its knowledge
of certain cold truths
about unending skies and
passing desires
that cloud the thin ice
of its diurnal presence

But today and tomorrow are
one and the same
in that they shift
become fickle as mist

No longer the core
where we once thought they'd be
permafrosted and sure

gillian harding-russell

You journey across the land
for Gwendolyn MacEwen too

that has always been there though you don't
always trust what others have told

you about landmarks, routes to follow
destinations. Though

you've been warned, you cannot in your youth
and magnificence always picture what lies

ahead after this second remove
from childhood left behind in a small village

by an historic river, a dam with weirs that thresh eels
in a silver waterfall slithering inside waves

that trail seaweed, and so you think you might have
moved on to the future in coming to the organ shapes

of ocean-backed lakes shaped like a heart and
pair of lungs flying (or is it the swing of a kidney

and stomach emptying?) you cannot see to the other
side of the lake, at present an intense blue haze

that changes with the weather. An explorer, you find
yourself, stepping up to this shale-shanked cliff (eroded

in geological time so the land where that other
might have stood lies underneath the lake's hard shine

and turf of this campsite) on the cusp of discovering, not
what you expected (like him, before you, with his dreams

of crossing into China, with its fine silks and tea)
but, instead, you arrive on a blue and green vacancy

with the lushness of Paradise and the amplitude
of youth extending antique and spacious as

possibilities. Still what monsters and wondrous
sea creatures below quivering lips of waves, restless

widening circles, talking black oracles
of lake storm or uttering

breezy blue nothings as they meld and
eclipse one another, when a coot swims out

like a clown, with a cockeyed tailspin
or a long-legged heron stands elegantly embroidered

on the far point of your retina. (Its cameo preserved
in brain tissue even thirty years later —)

Carolyn Smart

The Unseen Bear
after Henri Cole

Who are you, black bear,
that you can turn your face from me
with such indifference?

Twice a day I cross your path,
see nothing but your litter,
the granite boulders tossed
to mark your hunger.

Perhaps it is my own desire:
the avidity of stimulation,
tart bite of apple pulled
down from the tree,
the smell of you still fresh
within the branches,
stripped and clean.

Jason Heroux

New Light

Late July morning, new light
flashes through elderly clouds

today's infant newspaper
pronounces its first word
war

dainty insects
from the eighteenth century
challenge daylight to a duel

trees revise and fix the wind's acceptance speech
a shiny language sprayed with brilliant pesticides

Jan Allen

A Fishing Report, Read from a Teleprompter
for Gary Kibbins

Your words bring no relief.
Here, speech is submission
        in a quiet room
smelling of paper and electricity
before a map pocked with lakes,
        lost bays
        and empty peninsulas.
An idiom of water and weather
        of the possibility of simple acts
            of limits and lures and reports of success
and the day's first strike a fluttering flash of gills
        red
            divorced from all sentiment.
One more way to murder longing,
one more premise of salvation
        with spoons shimmering
        in olive green depths,
rendering thought in scrolling parts
that are
        a ripe withholding
        a form of humour
        a stone in my mouth.

Barbara Erochina

Upon Leaving

The rising red sun spread
into the length of horizon,
skin pulled taught over a bent elbow,
began the ten months that we moved through our
home like magnets, enticing and resisting in turn.
The colours stretched, strayed
and then cracked, as we kept watch,
God's paintbrush dry on edge of canvas.

Setting before having ever fully risen
we missed the entire day,
too exhausted to mourn
the sun's descent in the west.
I pulled my hips away from yours,
transplanted myself to Toronto.
But bones,
knowing origins
still ache
unhinged from providence.

Brent Raycroft

Haiku for Twenty Ten

Unseasonably
and so a sign of the times
warmer air moves in.

Earthquake in Haiti.
The tremor that reaches us —
heavy planes above.

That strong fruity smell.
Even out in the country
you wonder: poison?

Women attacked in
"the country north of Belleville."
Some Wing Commander.

Orange star rising.
That's Mars, named for our Terror.
We watch him closely.

Murderers held near.
Some wish they could kill themselves
but we don't let them.

Ash in the sky lanes.
Once more we hope for fair winds
as when tall ships sailed.

Glance left: "Save the farms"
sprayed on the backs of road signs.
No crime to agree.

Passing a transport
stacked high with crowd-control fencing.
See how it all fits?

A hole in the earth
beneath the Gulf offers up
what we wanted, free.

In cottage country
world leaders have their quick swim
for which roads are closed.

The space station arcs
faster, brighter than the gods
but already gone.

The Queen in the dark
at least 'til the gennies start.
Canucks, busting cool.

The Kalamazoo
stained with Canadian crude.
Not just passing through.

Investigator
found whole after all these years.
But not what she sought.

The flood continues
out of the Himalayas
closer with each death.

The fire continues
from the Rockies to Moscow
closer with each breath.

I have no long gun.
Once there was a twenty-two.
But where is it now?

Thirty-three miners
finally get home from work.
They're saved, but not safe.

Killers spoil my fun.
Not to mention what they've done.
Let's put on music.

Loud whistle, deep roar.
A plane as big as a ship
banks, under control.

Elizabeth Greene

Vibration

The simplest way to soar
to outer space. If I sing "Skye Boat Song"
or you play Mozart's "Sonata in C Major,"
we're already half in another world,
with its own time, language, rules.

In the gym turned concert hall,
gongs are attuned to New Moon,
Full, Mercury, Venus, Mars, Saturn, Pluto.
Struck, they throw circles of sound
to our cells' core, affirm
we are linked to everything on earth
through heavens.

I thought the music of the spheres would be
brighter, more like Scarlatti,
less like Beethoven's growly underside.
But when David Hickey plays those gongs,
I hear planets' crashing energies,
immensities of space between stars.

We stumble into the night, dazed by vibration.
The full moon whitens the blossoms, glitters
the water, sends out its song, expecting us
to send ours back through the April night.

Eric Folsom

The Lost Road

Canoeing in spring's high water, we shipped
      half the Salmon River over the gunnels,
      dodging rocks and haystacks,
      wet feet, wet asses.
Dick cracked the stern seat right off,
      laughed and said: fibreglass and resin,
      it would be an easy fix.

The bravado of one good love poem
      at the beginning, another at the end,
      that's the cliché I know, but it isn't so.
My wife had just had a miscarriage,
      and I was side-slipping in some chaotic field
      of limbic arousal, running off to play with others.
      The past today seems a labyrinth of water.

Twenty-five years on, the Milky Way above us,
      stars falling up like August snow,
      the billions recede in the black water of sky.
On a meadow by the Salmon's banks, we gather as friends
      of another couple, celebrating their anniversary,
      I marvel at the brokenness of memory.
How the river washes out roads, my love,
      carries every word we never took back,
      even carries words we never said.

Gene Rankin

Fallen Sparrow

fallen sparrow in the field – who sheds a tear for you?
your songs of yesterday forgotten
                         – but they wanted something new

we're drinkin' down liquid barley –and smokin' northern lights
a toast to those who went before – we'll never see those sites
of deep clear lakes and skies of blue – of forest vast and green
a toast to those who went before
                         – a toast to "what might have been"

fallen tree in the forest – who sheds a tear for you?
your shade brought comfort to my soul
                         – but they wanted something new

golden meadow once so bright – who sheds a tear for you?
the children laughed and played all day
                         – but they wanted something new

clear blue lakes of sapphire hue – who sheds a tear for you?
a magic world of fish and loons
                         – but they wanted something new

fallen sparrow in the field – who sheds a tear for you?
your songs of yesterday forgotten
                         – but they wanted something new

Joanne Light

Religion on a Monday Morning

I walk to the altar of stone
and take my confession
where the spring unceasingly flows;
kneeling to fill the urn,
I drown this priestly burning.

My communion is by the side
of a country road,
a tapestry of spring hues
hangs before me.
The hymns are bird songs,
long memorized.

I look to the east
and a round orb
rises to the flutter of new plants.
It died for no one,
but lives each day—
a steady resurrection for the seeing.

And lowering my head
to the humble spring,
I drink from this chalice,
whose mystery from some deep dark rock pool
I can never fathom.

This church is all around me—
its stained glass morning sky.

And God is here in the wind.

Joanne Page

Credo?

Have you any brief with belief?

For god long ago
up there in his sky temple
draped in a (surely)
borrowed dress,
arms raised
the blond balladeer
belting last call
one long endsong
into/for (minor guesswork)
the spangled night meanwhile
one eye cast upon
songbird falling
other eye elsewhere.
Meaning: watching
over everything
all.

And then?

Lost interest.

Who?

Both.
No, questions arose.

Nature, for a time.
Her sky, limestone and prairie, river,
the usual, boiling with the usual

And next?

Now I search poems,
sort through stanzas,
after rapture.

John Pigeau

tether

tether me to something safe
on the earth in the pleasant wind
i walk under awnings, close to buildings
beneath tall, leafy trees
i am flying up & out
into the cold vacuum of space
without you,
without knowing—
without
support

do you see?

can you ever hear me?
my lungs contract
the big dark starry sky
squeezes my chest
like a belt
the
cold earth disappears beneath
my boots
& i plummet
into boneless,
airless space
so please tether me
to something safe
a tree, a car, a woman
a desperate kite
flown high above an autumn park
where children are playing

Kelly Rose Pflug-Back

A Chorus of Severed Pipes

When I was a kid, I threw a stone
into the moon's reflection
and saw it break into a thousand sharp pieces.

It was dark, and the world sang to itself
to keep from being frightened.
Wheat stalks sighed under the thresher's blades,
a chorus of severed pipes.
The crickets and frogs kept time with one another;
I wrapped my arms around nothing
and waltzed circles through the corn rows
adrift in the harvest's beaconless sea.

I kept all the pieces I found
in a sack in the barn
where the pigeons battered, frantic in my chest.

Sunrise flicked its laughing tongue
through the interstices between gap-toothed rafters
and I knew that I could never make it whole again;

all those tarnish-bright shards
carried away in the silt of stream beds
winking at nothing
from the thatch of magpies' nests.

That's why there are still dark patches on the moon.
That's why the animals
still call out to each other in the dark,

bullfrogs' throats stretched fat like pearls
while the crickets rub their thighs and sing.

Kirsteen MacLeod

Full Moon in Scorpio

You are so tired of it,
finally give up
the struggle and
lie on your belly
to breathe your way through

How this tide always swells
and recedes in you, my darling,
water pulled through light and dark
tossed up on weedy shores
bodies from the wreck

Old wounds of the deep
surface, I caress your back,
our bed a ship
your release has begun, love,
it floods in, bathes us
in a pool of gold light
full moon in Scorpio

Morgan Wade

The Body Eclectic

Though we cease as we now are, what we are never ceases.
  - Paragraph 22, Chapter 1, Book 14, The Good Book
I am an acme of things accomplished, and I am an encloser of things to be.
  - Song of Myself, #44, Walt Whitman

This molten coil, a spark from vulcan forge;
today it glints from iris flecks.

An ancient droplet, thawed from comet frost,
perspires, now briny, from this pore.

An atom and even two from first fruit
remain sown deep within my loins.

The iridescent traces of proto-wings
are trapped in these amberous strands.

The fin that ruddered a leviathan
is stretched, to scale, between my toes.

Original cooking fire residues
endure in smudgy fingerprints.

Antique papyrus scratched with soot is now
this article of carbon here.

The whetted iron cusp that sliced at hot gates
abides and stains my marrow red.

Genetic matter thumbing down silk roads
infects and galls my bladder black.

The sodden keels of oak-ribbed caravels
reduced to flotsam in this knee.

The sulphur belched from crude musket mouths
ignites the strife inside my gut.

Electrons that once crackled Franklin's kite
are thrumming up my spinal cord.

Memento mori, ions in my teeth
decay much slower than I do.

These particles are borrowed, every one of them,
and they must be returned.

This speck from my appendix flap
will decorate the final brittle bloom.

This bit of gristle near my hip
will help propel the inter-stellar craft.

This synapse, remade into wire,
will broadcast the truth, twenty decades late.

A clutch of my component parts
will stay behind, mute observers of the last

dramatic sunset, reconciled
to unlit vigils held on cooling shores.

Yet others, in this freckle swirl,
will ride forever, hitched to cosmic dust.

I coalesce, I last a while, and then…
I'm immortal.

A. Gregory Frankson

Just Breathe

i want the land we live upon one day to open up
to the western horizon so i can watch as you spill
the colours of your passions every night onto the canvas
brush stroke thickness devours the way you kiss my lips
consumed in the flavour of the moment –
this love acceptable as a sacrifice Abraham would make
upon the altar erected for the purpose
the dagger sharp piercing of protective skin
false in barricading us one from the other
when all we wish to do is graft our skin onto each other
i carry you full in my belly accepting no term except
eternal gestation of the connection birthed the moment
my lungs first exhaled in your presence
just breathe just breathe just breathe just breathe
bold internal dialogue unmatched by the
twitching twittering words i spoke
because even in our first conversation in flesh
i knew we were matched
until there are no words needed to pass between us
for you to know
my mind – to you it's a Bible spilled open at Beatitudes
and just as holy for you've memorized me
book, chapter and verse before you ever cracked
the spine, and you quote me
with every eye glance, touch and embrace
our tongues share the Word elevated between us
like pillars of fire leading the lost home
to the Promised Land through the wilds of the barren desert
cross seas parted precisely and perfectly
peer into your precious pupils perilously perched
between perdition and paradise –
cuddle confidently into the curl of me
comforted in the crucible of our common created connection
and feel my heaving chest balancing

your head atop my shoulder like an egg in a spoon – and note
the way i hold steady and protect you from harm
for there's never been anyone more precious on my arm
be still, inhale deeply with me the spirited breath of tranquility
and know that spectre lost the desire to travel any further
and has made a permanent home with you and i.

Paul Kelley

Paul Kelley, from *Untimely*
to the memory of Osip Mandelshtam and Dorothy Livesay

i.

That sudden, muffled sound
of a leaf breaking loose from the tree—

it rides the air to hardened earth
for a leaf's eternity.

ii.

On a breath the dragonfly alights,
the old river barely touches its banks,

all the cities of the world churning
in machine's teeth and towers,

dragged everywhere by the whine
of invisible engines, history's hungry junk,

no escape, no return, no elsewhere,
when heart is ashamed of heart.

iii.

The leaf takes the river away,
around the next bend and the next,
laughter assigns the voices
(girls giggle, boys hoot),
the target invites the whirring shaft
into its room.

Lay your head on this truth:
no rising night needs you, swimmer,

and you do not belong to blame
for the emptiness of the membrane
you have made your home.

iv.

When the angels cease their sobbing,

you will find your "peace"
in the mouths of masters and warlords,
and your "freedom"
will fester from their abuses—

on earth, no heaven,
in heaven, no halt
to the torture
called the end
without end,

when the angels have ceased their sobbing,
all has vanished, nothing remains
but space, stars, a song
to be sung anew
by voices more human
than human voices have ever been.

V.

Here lays the stone that wants to be lifted,
to sing the memory of the gone, the forgotten,
marked here the names, the span of days,
the breadth of no more.

Far below us, the stone is sweating
in tunnels dug under the sea.
Above us sinks the laughter, below sinks the scream.

Here lays all water and a body can say:
reach us in this darkness with a spectral light,
for we have been to hell
and have to report
that it is only half-finished.

vi.

Beneath the honeyed sun,
or under the salt of stars:
that is my location,
somewhere by somewhere,
by anywhere you could name,
my thoughts, my words, and me
on the loose, no fixed address—

find me, I am far north of my feelings,
waiting
for the waiting to end.

vii.

A stalk of thorns rises,
climbs by light to light—

reliable,
your only ladder.

Diane Dawber

Easter 2011

James Williamson and Kate Pickett
have proven
by respectable statistics
that the Golden Rule is best for us
most surprisingly
rich and poor alike.

The strongest men
have gone off to war and been killed so often
while the weakest women have died in childbirth so often
that roles are having to reverse

On a personal level
it has taken a healer working in three paradigms
to find and remove
the sword piercing my own ribs.

The grandchildren are coming
eggs have been hidden
containing not chocolate or sweets
not in this century
but puzzle pieces and some of the eggs
call out electronically
"I'm hiding. Come find me."
Fine religious sentiments for the occasion.

There are no lilies
but icicle pansies
daffodils in a black resin urn
and an extravagant pink hydrangea
for the favoured guests.

There is turkey, locally grown,
suitably organic i.e. free of chemicals
balanced off by imported asparagus
probably force fed any number of nasty things
but
with eggs from down the road
and lemons from some far-off pristine tree
I have just managed to make meringue nests
scraped clean of over-browning
and filled with the yellow pudding.

At great carbon expense
four generations assemble
in the misunderstandings and cross-purposes
of family love.

The rock has split in many places
but the tremor has passed
and the sky is either clearing or falling.
Potassium iodide might be required.

Astrophysicists now say
the universe is expanding faster and faster
instead of slowing as expected.
They do not express opinions on whether
we are speeding away from or toward
the Unknown?

Logic
a god of infinitesimally small
but infinitely many
steps—
feeding on information—
is about to grow into The God.

Toss me another statistic
before I inhale the intoxicating fumes
and prognosticate.

Coreen Covert

Old Wise Ones

Old one I miss you on a quiet afternoon, wisdom and
        thoughts filtering through the country tunes.
Beadwork at your side and a pencil in your hand
        sharing the world as only you understand.
Elder man precious to us all,
        we know u heard the spirit call.

Older one sitting in the rocking chair wrinkles so deep
        from your smile there
I was once a child in your arms snuggling up.
You are my Grandmother sharing all your loving charm
        rocking away in your great grandchild heart.

Grandfather and man who for many years worked
        the fields and carried the traditions
        of watching the yield

Feeding and hunting animal for meat and hide
Family as only you could provide
        Praying to the Creator the season was right

English woman drifting through my mind,
pictures of you pouring tea and offering goodies
        baked from a woodstove of many kinds.

Old ones I love u so, precious you are
and you carry the knowledge of ages past
bricks of the foundation where we can grow and stand.

        Your words like a memory burnt inside of my head.

Cori Mayhew

Common Ground

i.

Sun rises, painting a rosy
patina across the city.
Light and shadow play,
skipping against walls and windows.
The ball in the sky leaves a pale
yellow residue on city streets.
It bounces against buildings.

Across the street, the shadow side
draws its own light. Images
glance off glass, splash colour
shot with silver streaks.
White light.

A fellow dances in front of a
large plate glass window.
Crazy Man, reflecting upon himself
in the middle of life.
We neither stop nor hardly notice,
too busy, too self absorbed
going from here to there. Now!

Consider a missed opportunity passing us by.

ii.

Big city churches on shady street corners
have withstood time, heavy weather, reform.
Their spires beckon us to come.
Many are higher than tree tops. Solid
and stoic, wrapping us in community, they
weave old teaching and new doctrine,
a reminder that change and challenge lie before us.

Old stones whisper the past and offer the future.

iii.

The itinerant photographer comes
each year to take the children's pictures.
They and the pony age
by the same incremental time span.
The beautiful little boy poses
on the saddled, small pony.
He might be four, or five, blond
and has blue eyes. He looks out
from those eyes confidently, expectant,
life around his perimeter.
But look closer, a scab
scars his forehead. His
bully brother Billy has hit him again.
Behind, clapboard from the old house,
paint peeling. Chicory
in bloom, the weedy flower
softens hard dirt by the door.
There is no front yard.
The house steps out
onto the street. The width
of a sidewalk saves it
from being run over.

iv.

Light draws squares and rectangles as
it travels, climbing buildings and
meandering back lanes and alleys.
Like shape changers, its beam crawls along
eaves' edges, moves into triangles
or parallelograms that define
old and new architecture. Evening
casts dimpled shadow on our limestone chronicles.

v.

The marina is closed for the season.
Boats line the shore.
Yachts with masts stepped down
rest in their cradles, covered with tarps.
They cower against weather, leaving
long mauve shadows laying
across the deserted park .
Stillness is broken by waves
running with wind to escape the harbour
before freeze up.

The flag snaps and pulls at its tether.
It exudes urgency to take flight before
ice locks things down for the winter.

Denise Hamilton

Evergreens

If you wish to be followed
Run from a crowded room
To an empty street
Where the one who finds you
Will listen till both ears ring
But it won't change a thing
About your mother's illness
Or they way you second guess.
It's not all sad though
There is light around the edges
And high above
the skyline made of ever greens.

So crawl home, crawl back to me
To bed, where you can rest your head
On my lap and tell me
What you wished you hadn't seen,
High above those evergreens.
But you are better for it
Your eyes carry more
Your shoulders, less.   Instead maybe you mean? –

Home is just an adjective,
It's never been tangible noun to me
Wherever I could find a street to flee
See the light or warm my feet
Was home enough for me.

David Malone

At Normandy

For a time that evening
we rode horses that,
large and powerful and black,
thrilled to the salt sea air
and the sound of the crashing waves
as they bore us
and because we'd not ridden before
and so didn't know how to stop them
(nor were there reins, even, for our hands)
we went at a furious pace
and at times his horse was in front
and at times my horse was in front
and as they gave way one to the other
we who clung to their sweat-soaked necks
and propulsive bodies
looked to each other now in terror now in rage
while asking ourselves how O how
would all this fury stop
when suddenly of their own
the horses simply stopped themselves
and turned to go back more slowly,
more quietly, more calm,
over the long way we'd come
but in deeper darkness now and a beginning rain that,
as it fell, washed us all –
man, beast and terrible debris
tossed from the littered sea.

Nicholas Papaxanthos

Sunset
for Jason Heroux

Clouds
rush

to escape

the sky's
endless

cutting
board

the sun's
pink knives

Lara Szabo Greisman

Fault-lines

And for a smaller, smallish town
Tattooed in fault lines:
military, academic, prison lines so stand in—
Mind your step, your steps in the choreography of
Who goes when, where
Your first year there is always hard they say, I said, I say
Watch your back since there, right between
Your spine and your ribs, Cushioned next to nerves and veins,
A compass, the arrow showing the way to home
spins.

Then you'll leave on sea legs, going/returning to where ever,
To places in Capital letters
Places where it's hard to explain why a smaller, smallish town
Why a place stratified with tensions and fuck ups, tears and tares
Where around every corner, it's just a smaller population see,
but there-where each event in the city is linked
to someone loved by someone loved by
And the sequins are glued on by hand.
Where stars become people again
Where people become stars
And successes are gilded in pride, in warmth,
in let's do this again
Where clapping spells out thank you
and where it means it.
There, right there.

Take the 401 to a small-time southern Ontario town,
Just a little outta Toronto. Sure.
It's that too.

Ashley-Elizabeth Best

The Hot and the Bitter

A tune on the water full of sky,
our boat drawn to rocky outcrops
as he handed me an egg-cup of whiskey—
the hot and the bitter.

With finality he said, *That's it,
we'll have to sell.* I thought
I would hide the skiff under the
cabin, or the dock, but then
remembered my fear of ever-growing
dock spiders and water snakes.

Roaming the shore, always
stepping into the same lake,
not wanting to pull in the line.
To keep it this way just a little longer.
We are shouldn't be allowed to skate this
body's firm coolness, the water resistantly
beating against the hull.

Papa named the forest walls,
each tree so different from the next.
Choppy waters made me wish for
stubbly grass. He laughed and said
I had to wait out the duration and
pee over the side of the boat.

When I was little he hid his amusement,
now I am old enough to know better. A whining howl
at the edges, we wolf-watched. Papa felled the timber,
replying mournfully, a dissonant cry from a watery world.

We drifted through that view, this body's country
moving at the day's end, waiting to get caught
white-faced in this man indifferent place,
all we can give is a gift of blood on stone.

The Lake Will Never Forget Us
Milenko Grgar

Eriana Marcus

Breaking Cages
    the illuminated moments
    of the dancing cat and the song bird

She
moved like a cat.
    and contained the same wild independence

her hair, spun around her like a dancer . . .
head held high, always, like a proud white horse.

one green eye, one blue
    she shot an 'I dare you gaze' upon the world
for those she loved:
    a secret code – head tilt, wink, cat smile
so quick that many would miss it but in that flash s
    she shared her best secret

Yes.
    in every moment, every move, her life,
her dance, she designed; no one, nothing, would interfere
    with her own choreography.
She
held true to herself and those she loved.
and
with that wink and cat smile; that secret she shared;
that suggested that she knew something others were missing
She sure did.
She knew how to Live.
From within my cage
i watched her
the vibrant determination and originality

a living example of a free woman.

I wanted that. Her Love. I wanted my life. . .
whatever it could be.
      I broke the Cages
and barely out, fluttering clumsily for years . . .
One day
She told me:
"you are gorgeous"
                the first compliment i would ever trust.
because i knew she was speaking of my Free Spirit
that I was setting loose upon the world.

She could have been a shooting star
      living so much and so brilliantly with a power of
      more than ten other people could try.

In her 29th year, I sat with her every day.
Illness had taken the dancer from her body.
But she still held her own design, the pride of the white horse,
the wild and mischievous cat; the grace and
wisdom of a swan flowed from her fingers; her
"I dare you" that came from her eyes and voice.
      The cat smile became contagious.

When I asked her if there was anything she wanted,
      she replied: "I want you to love yourself".

One night I whispered in her ear;
      "I love you so much, please fly away
      so that you can dance again."

The White Owl circled my head three times

i knew that she was free.

It's been 16 years, and not one day goes by, that,
especially when I remember to hold my head up
when I walk . . . that I know that she is with me.
I thank her every day for showing me how to live.

Now, in my own dance . . . there are certain things
I will never give up:
      dark chocolate, black coffee, cigarettes,
Lemon tarts on October 31st.
         purple and green, collecting scarves . . . and
the continuing search for the perfect pair of red shoes

Carolyn Smart

Dreaming of the Dead
for Richard Rilkoff

Last night you lived in a two floor apartment, in the centre a circular stairway. As we climbed up I touched your soft jacket and pulled you near; I knew it was the last time I would ever see you and I felt my mouth reach out to yours, just touching, over and over. The men you lived with looked at us, at me, and I could see their pity, thinking what's she dreaming of? but we moved further up the stairs and on the upper floor there was an indoor garden with furniture and trees, how lovely I said, when did you manage this in the midst of your long illness? all the time yearning to hold on to you who I would never see again. You've been dead eleven years this December, I remember your smooth clean face, your shining hair, the hours it took to get you out the door most nights. How I want all of those simple things back, the sound of you washing your dishes, trying to find your keys, singing along with the radio as you turned to open the door, leaning over in the bright doorway with your beautiful clothes to switch off the lights before heading out, the brief days still waiting for us beyond.

Carla Hartsfield

Milk

"When the last moon burns low, and, spark by spark,
The little worlds die out along the dark . . ."
                                        Marjorie Pickthall

I'm filling up with clouds.
You have, inside yourself, encased
that high moon in a starless,

western window. Silence
has loved me through many lifetimes,
multiple anxieties over what

kind of relationship waits upon
your locked doorstep. There's
no such thing as emotional logic.

The phone rings, an e-mail pops in.
Your latch snaps and spark by spark,
my tears burst over

porcelain, stung cheeks.
Break-up scenario five hundred and forty-nine,
we take our unfathomable world

into ourselves and down it like
frothing milk. My lips,
untouched for days, press

and search for more
transmutable energy. For too long
I've floated between room dividers.

Sometimes they are elegant, silvery
clear drapes of longing. Sometimes
they are hung so weakly, little holes

start opening, dying out like
Pickthall's worlds, and moths
flutter and chew, cause

arrhythmia, screw up our hearts.
Can anyone second guess addictive love?
Manic and angry, straight

like a bullet's murderous thought.
More room dividers
installed like pace-makers,

charged up with sex,
setting off alarms inside
and between our bodies. We fly

toward that last moon,
transfigured by a quest
for calm, authenticity.

It balloons and ignites,
luminous rice paper.
Burnt and burning, you skim

my hot skin, breathing
more little worlds to replace
those collapsing.

Bruce Kauffman

rain

you, carrying
the love
    of children
watching sides
      disappear but
      edges sharpening
          grow

you feeling years
    of years

fearing the coming
      too soon or
      too late or
      too long with
          worlds sliding
          walls falling
              behind you

you, watching and
now questioning
      all things as you
      feel the earth roll
          beneath you

you, who ran
through the streets
      the pastures
      as a child
you
now just learning
      how to crawl
      on this new water
          of time

Amber Potter

Kundalini

Calloused hands, rough fingers
Feel good on smooth skin
In dim shadows, yellows become blues,
Oranges become reds, and fire
Created licks sacred corners
It's easy to blur sight and sound
When eyes are filled with tender longing
And the music of limbs winding together
Is played to the beat of quickening pulses
The tear of perspiration starts to trickle down
And finds a home where
the back ends and beauty begins
Losing all sense of the world
Bodies rise and fall in the
Ocean tide of Bliss
Ideas of love and fancy are for mere mortals
Ecstasy like this is meant to be
Tasted by the lips of Gods
And with each undulation, the moaning song
Of Ancestors primitive rises in the dark.
Answered by the crack and break of the
Climactic sunrise, tearing through the sky
Like Blades of Burning Steel
Holding on for fear of falling
Into primordial darkness
The quickening ceases to end
In a web of
Salt, Sweat, and Soul

Bob MacKenzie

I Would Photograph You

I would photograph you in just that way,
you reclining among the windblown grain,
the sun winnowing its light through your hair,
your cotton summer dress soft in its light.

You would be resting there in the sunlight
gazing up the hill at that warm farm home
inviting you to come when you're ready
like that shining city you see in dreams.

I would add colour to this photograph,
clover perhaps or daisies in the breeze,
and bright paint on that old grey house and barn,
and add a bright print to your cotton dress.

I would photograph you in just that way,
lit by sunlight in a world of flowers
where songbirds sing and the sun seeks you out
but, most of all, I would photograph you.

David Malone

Who Bears Grief

Despite the blood on his hands I love him,
and on visiting day we embrace.
Not that there's isn't grief, because there is, and shame,
and the awareness too
that another doesn't have what I have,
marred though it is.

For the grief she must feel –
grief that, hard though I tried,
I know I'm responsible for too.

For my son is *my* son;
and just as he can't wash his hands,
neither can I.

Greg Bell

La Maison D'Eva

In the morning we get ready together.
Sun bleeds through sheers in our bedroom window.
I linger behind, as usual, caress her
lithe arms, slide my hand under an elbow.
I shave, we share the mirror and she talks.
Her eyes are blade blue. Half dressed, in long sleeves,
she blow dries her hair while lightly I stroke
her high, exposed thigh. But she won't believe

me when I tell her she is beautiful,
and I cannot grasp her pulling away,
cutting me off, then wrapped in a towel.
Why, slipping by the lingerie shop today
the statuesque and flawless mannequin
also stretched, I swear, to stop her, my Jacqueline.

K.V. Skene

Walking Percy Street

Alone. Fists jammed in pockets, foot-
steps following
that cat's eyes
pleading and fierce. Yesterday
is another country
full of lives I can't live anymore.

Look, I'm changing direction –
what is, is. As for what was,
only the odd car, indifferent cyclist,
feral cat
disturbs the dark flower of memory:
the sharp angles of your body, scent
of your unlaundered T-shirt, the sneakers
the cat pissed on, that double-handful of pennies
dusting the dresser, battered hairbrush,
goddamn photograph, wedding ring,
long overdue book
and the absurdity of abandoning
everything I've ever been careful for.

The drumbeat of your long stride
turns down Park
behind me
cat morphs into a trough
of village air – there is prey elsewhere

and I'm unravelling you,
making things up:
black cat,
husband/lover –
strange, yet familiar
like my life.

Not lost. Not waiting to be found
until I want to

Jennie McCaugherty

Beats

Foot prints in sidewalk blocks
As the cracks expose life under the stones
A thousand people walk the beats creating the rhythm
In time with the silence
City...day and night alone
The truth hits me like the lie of a lover about to leave
Hard, harder
Hot, hotter
Cold, freezing

Eyes looking forward to what is to come
And in that we are missing what already rests in front of us
Text the words your body longs to speak
Language is but ten percent of understanding
Watch us get lost in letters void of meaning

Broken hearts, broken windows, broken lives
Souls walked past, bleeding inside
Pretend you don't see them and kiss your lover good-bye

Do what they can to end the pain of a life lived without a name
Grey wash makes everything colder
Repeated sightings of human suffering
Hearts close to her, there was no one to hold her
Forgotten is the child she once was
Witnessed is the shell she has become
Buildings reaching for the sky above
As the sun reflects
Broken in the city forgotten love

Look in the eyes as they pass you by
Lost in our minds thinking we know what is right
As we walk past the woman we could all be
If that moment in time were to shift
And in hope we could no longer see

Kristin Andrychuk

Laura and Gloria

LAURA AND ROBERT — 1933

With March snow glistening deep in the bush beyond their cabin, Laura and Robert in their underpants, lie on the sun-warmed granite outcrop. He bends over her, licks her bare breast, tonguing the nipple. He pushes her bloomers off the rising mound and, stroking belly skin, feels the baby shifting beneath his hand.

GLORIA

At three a.m. Gloria sits nursing her new baby. She stares out the dark window and pictures her parents on those sun-warmed rocks. This is her comfort scene.

She was just a kid helping do the wash when her mother told her of sunbathing in the time before David, Gloria's brother, was born. The story came right after the one about a neighbour catching her fingers in the wringer and how they came out flat, every finger broken. Gloria knew where the release bar was and kept her eye on it as she heaved the sheets out of the rinse water and guided them through the wringer.

When she was little she used to call the washing machine Girk-Gock because that's the noise it made. It was the monster that kept her mother all day in the dark cellar when she could've been taking Gloria and her brother to the beach or on a picnic.

It was cold down in the cellar, and when they hauled the copper boiler of wet laundry outside, the sun made the hanging-up part almost fun.

That's what they had, almost fun, like when the wash was finished her mother would make black coffee for herself and milky coffee for her, and they'd sit on the back stoop and rest.

When her mother told the story, she didn't tell that part about tonguing the nipple. As the years have gone by, Gloria has added details. All Gloria's life Laura, her mother, has been working: doing the wash, gardening, cooking, cleaning, canning, and looking after David who's in a wheelchair. Her mother's not looking after David anymore. He died two years ago. Robert, her dad, who died a long time ago when she was nineteen, is dimly remembered leaving for or returning from work, or at home puttering around in the garden. The sunbathing story is almost unbelievable.

LAURA

In the middle of the night, Laura sits by an east-facing window, entirely alone. She's not alone as evening settles over the house. Her ghosts gather – her husband dead twenty-four years now and her son two. Her ghosts don't fade, become more powerful with age.

It's as if she's been sitting by this window for years, like this is where everything was always headed, an old woman in an empty house, waiting for morning.

Gloria and her family are arriving tomorrow with yet another new baby. Laura wishes for one of those signs like they have in hotels, Don't disturb. She'd hang it on her front door. She can't do that. It isn't the kind of thing you can do to your loving daughter. And Gloria is her loving daughter, her faithful visitor. Gloria who sits there smiling at her wild children running through the house, "Like old times, eh Mum?" What old times? There was only Gloria and David and he was in a wheelchair, and Gloria certainly wasn't permitted to run in the house. Like old times. What fantasy is she living?

What possessed Gloria to have five children? None of them even accidents. She's forty-three and still nursing a baby. And always acts as if her mother should be delighted with each new arrival. "Isn't he wonderful, Mum?" What Laura has always felt like saying is, "Look at him, just another screaming snot-piss-poo-dripping baby. The world is filled with screaming babies."

After he was born, David, while the purple lump on the back of his neck slowly shrank, screamed for six weeks solid. She was alone with the wailing baby in that cabin. Rob was away working in the bush. It was The Depression, you took what jobs you could get.

To this day she can't endure a screaming baby, though all the babies she's been forced to listen to since, have been perfectly healthy. A bit of colic maybe or more likely temper, the cry of, "I want, I want." They'll be crying it all their lives.

"I want, I want," while spectral trees marched on the lighted cabin. Such a small cabin, such a dim light, and he screamed and screamed.

Laura Dyer

Starman

There are comets in your hair lover
Falling softly, skimming your
Razor blade cheeks and
Coating your shoulders with dust

I will not love you forever
People don't last forever

But I will love you as I breathe
and when you go know that you are welcome anytime
My ribcage lies ajar
Waiting for you to crawl inside

My man made of stars

Slip into my chest
Cradle its beating contents
Kiss my skinned knees
Wrap me in daylight
So that I may have something to cling to when the night comes

We are all just growing pains

Kali Carys

this is a story

In the world, there's a girl. Sometimes people notice her. Sometimes she fades. She never quite blends in, but...

There was this one time she felt especially faded. Not because anything was particularly sad in her life at the time. She just wasn't the centre of her own attention that night. Which is unusual for her, but it does happen.

You met her that night. With your arms, and your lips, and your eyes, You drew her out of her faded mode. You more than noticed her. And she definitely noticed You. And she noticed herself noticing You. And she wanted You, wanting her.

This is a story, of course. It's completely true, but it's not complete. It's just one girl – this girl You met – turning her Feelings into words. That's what romance is, and she's a romantic girl in some ways. This isn't the whole story. And she can't put all her Feelings into words (no matter how hard she tries, sometimes). But it's all completely true.

This is her story about You and her. She's told pieces of it to all kinds of people. You've probably heard some of those pieces, even though she's shyest about telling You. Also, You've been there for most of this story of You and her. But You have your own story for all the Moments. At least, she thinks You must. She knows You're romantic sometimes too. Plus You're a story-crafter.

She's only crafting this story of You and her tonight, on the back of her setlist, because this is a passion show. Making the lights work, and showing off her legs briefly is fun, sure. But she has bigger Feelings going on. Today, tonight, she's feeling that much more... passionate? And a little tipsy. She's been faded for a week now, hiding in her pain. But now she thinks she might like to be noticed again. Like You noticed her before.

That's how the story starts, and how it's ended up she's telling it now. Listen?

~~~

There's a girl in the world who fades sometimes, and this is her story of You and her. She is a snowflake of unique screwed-upness, like everybody. Like You.

She knows it's true about her. After seeing a play that taught her that line, she had to find quinoa to bring to her host she loves. Four stores and a nighttime adventure around downtown Toronto's worth of had to. While wandering, she was wondering if she should be more concerned for safety than for silly. Sometimes, what she has to do isn't what she knows she should do. Just like sometimes she needs to not have or be something she wants.

You and she sometimes shared thoughts about screwed-upness. We know our own kind, You said in one Moment. Something like that. You are possibly the most screwed up person she loves. Or has loved, or will love. Possibly. She's not that for You, though, You said in that Moment. Then, she thought it might mean she's growing into a more persony person. But now she's fairly sure all people are all kinds of screwed-up. She thinks it's a matter of difference more than degree. Because difference can be exciting. Moreso than familiar screwed-upness she sees in herself every day. She surprises herself sometimes, though.

In a book she's reading now, one character says, "You're fucked up, mister. But you're cool." Another replies, "I believe it's called the human condition." This story-exchange made her think of You. She wants to tell You, You're fucked up – maybe even call You mister for the fun of it. But You know that already. You've told her so. Did You think she ever doubted it? In another Moment, she got the sense You understand her screwed-upness, at least as well as she does. But there's more in her, and more in You, that's fucked up in ways no Moment's conversation could cover completely.

This is one of those Things that's completely true, that she'll keep learning if she keeps being in this story of You and her.

This is a story, and a story has characters in it. They make the Moments that make up a story happen at all. You and she are just two of them. Something she does sometimes is treat life like a story. It's a one of those ways she's romantic. The Someones she loves most, whose stories she's also a part of, are also screwed up. In their special snowflake ways. That's part of what she loves, in everyone she loves. In You.

~ ~ ~

This is an interlude in the story: a Moment of herself-indulgence.
　　She went almost a week without any crying. Almost one in nearly three. She's finding adventures with self, friends and lovers. There's even a glow some see.
　　She's dreaming and scheming and planning her summer. Sorting her work-plans out too. She almost enjoys now this unattached selfhood. Her life's a Thing without You.
　　She isn't less special, less loved or less loving. Still more faded than she'd like. She's teary today, but still so ready to play. Flower of pretty, femme-dyke*

*Some labels are more about sound than their meaning. She just loves many a lot. It may well be something that gets her in trouble. She'd rather indulge than not.

Lindy Mechefske

The Arsonist

The fire
that consumed
Everything   in its path
burned so hard and
with such beautiful
intensity   left me
scattered
levelled
unable to go on.

Bits of me gone
forever
And recovery
a long slow   tedious journey
where hope is scarce.
I fear
another fire
would do me
in.

Where is the promised
phoenix   rising from
amongst the ashes?

And you,
where are you
now?
Having left the wreck
to let the embers die
does your heart ache
like mine?
Or are you hard
at work
stoking your own
ego
igniting sparks
elsewhere....

Laurie Lewis

Old Friends, in the Afternoon, Spring

All dressed up like a lady,
nice dark suit,
I hardly recognize myself,
this day of grief.

This is the time; this is the day
that tells me I am old.
It's not the wrinkles, nor the grey hair.
Not the thinning lips,
the disappearing eyelashes
that bring me to age.
It's this, the death of old friends and lovers.

This must be what I have searched for,
scanning the obits every morning,
wondering who would be the first.
If not Sam, some other person from the past,
another friend, another lover.

Here in front of the door, standing
stiffly in the middle of the sidewalk,
thin, pale, already looking cadaverous,
is an old man who comes to resemble Harold.
Here is his bony frame,
Ichabod Crane on the streets of Toronto.
Staring at the door, eyes intense and fearful.
His head swivels on the stalk.
I watch how long it takes
for my name to say itself in his mind.
Is this what grief looks like?

The door is dark old wood,
deeply carved
with a pattern of acorns and oak leaves.
Sam would have liked that,
a little William Morris
at the Arts and Letters Club.

Behind me, ascending from the big front door,
an old gentleman leans on a silver-topped cane
that matches his own silver head.
A prosperous European businessman,
he seems, struggling up the stairs
in his black coat with a velvet collar.
There is, as he moves,
a moment of seeing a stranger,
of looking at him without memory or connections.
But the fluff of hair, the fullness of face,
something about the jowls,
the way the eyes move ...
And suddenly he is Frank
and could be no other and
all past comes to the present and
I can't imagine that I didn't know him.

We pass the afternoon this way, all of us.
People who shared a level of love
or friendship or acquaintance.
Seeing people as strangers for a moment
until suddenly they become themselves.
The men, except for Harold, heavy,
prosperous, corpulent.
The women lean or plump,
as old as Sam's first wife,
as young as his last girl friend.

Our mutterings drift up to the high ceilings,
settle into the paneled walls,
welcomed by the old mellow wood.
Is this grief?
Bodies planted on the oak floor
stiffly like trees. Is this age?

Among us, the old ones here,
friends and colleagues,
there is little joy.
We know it's only a matter of
time. We try not to wonder
who will be next,
when we will next meet.
We try not to look at each other
with these thoughts.
Is this life?

In memory of Sam we are drinking gin and tonics,
his favourite tipple.
In memory of lunches or parties or afternoons
in his garden or his bed.
The G and Ts don't taste the way they used to.

So I change to Chardonnay,
hoping to improve the afternoon.

Roger Dorey

The Vanishing Act

Only because I am a parent now
Do I understand the "Vanishing Act"
I remember as a kid
My dad or mom taking us somewhere
You know! the park, the pool, the rink
They would look us straight in the eye
And give us the 10 Commandments of Good Behaviour
Then, as we were running away
They would miraculously disappear...
From our sight, from our minds
An even bigger miracle
Was the fact we never, ever wondered
Where did they go!
Did they go to heaven? did they go for a coffee?
And never mind that every time
We went back to check on them
They were always there for us
And when we were gone, so were they
In all my years of academic study
I don't remember reading about the Vanishing Act
And I'm sure I didn't acquire it in my work experience
But one day...
I knew I had it, I just had it!
I must confess
I wasn't very good at the trick at first
But with lots of practice
I became a virtual Houdini
And right now
I am Houdini again
Here in heaven with a coffee
And like a Guardian Angel
My kids are never out of my sight

The only problem the audience has
With the Vanishing Act
Is that I reappear way-too-soon!
The kids say they're never ready
That's how I pull it off!
Coming back when they're not looking

Phyllis Erwin

Wedding in the Woods

Northumberland Hills. A semi-circle of tall pines and cedars, beside a rippling stream, a clearing, boulders of ancient stone. Rays of light from the late afternoon sun. An ideal setting for a wedding uniting two people, nature lovers of kayaking, canoeing, and camping. A judge, a native Ojibwe, officiating. The Anglo-Saxon couple standing in front of a tall weathered grey pine tree, a totem-like image, bare branches stretched out like arms. Classical music coming from the woods, a quartet, clarinet, horns, violin.

Guests entering this magical place from a path through a cedar forest, bright satin bows guiding them to a small bridge and a short climb up the bank of the gently flowing stream. The wedding party, family members, groom and best man, waiting for the bride, her father and maid of honour finally appearing out of the cedar woods. Vows spoken from the heart, exchanging paddles, no rings. A reading from Emily Dickinson's "The Song My Paddle Sings" accompanied by sounds of pebbles being tossed into the stream by young male guests, bored with the adult ceremony.

Back to the civilized world in the garden by the house, champagne toasts to the bride and groom, speeches, buffet, some guests choosing to dine outdoors in the fading light. Afterwards, a bonfire on the hill beyond the house, where a few guests had pitched tents for the night. The newly married couple escaping to a cabin by a beach on Lake Ontario near Port Hope. The moon shining in a star studded sky.

Sadiqa de Meijer

The New Father

Where are her bones? She's fog-eyed, all vowel —
rain could dissolve her.

Everything comes too close: exhaust,
the metallic, mirrored sky

— at night, the wail
under a transport's passing utterance —

even the praising hands
of strangers, even the neighbour's

sunflowers, their ravaged faces
turning to the earth.

Sage Pantony Irwin

Ice Tea

Lemon flavoured ice tea
makes a puddle on a fire rock;
filling, creeping in
until it overflows and
spills out
to water the grass.

The ice is melting.
Drops of yellow liquid push out of the can
and follow the stream
made by the first drops,
who were awarded honorary medals after their deaths
(a few scouts went down
to toss the rewards in the chasm.
Then, like lemmings,
they threw themselves in).

Can'll probably be empty by the time the ice melts,
and my brother, who put it there, will wonder why
I sat here writing poetry,
watching it all drip out.

Sandra Alland

Imaginary Passport

I wanted to play you this tape
of my grandfather

he calls me his wee lassie, praises
oatmeal and Martin Luther King as gods,
curses the Queen at least twice

and aye, he's short and dead but
if you heard the laugh he saved for me

you'd understand how I turned out
so tender
so ridiculous
so Scottish

Sarah Yi-Mei Tsiang

Napping in the Car

Rain's fingerprints on the window,
her breath a soft whistle
inside the car.

We drive for hours, slick black roads
where leaves throw themselves
in front of the tires, roadkill
with all the bright colours
of death.

I remember other cars,
other steamed windshields,
the cramped space of our growing
bodies, the softness of his skin,
rain that anointed us.
We crowned ourselves
golden, fell asleep with the heat
ticking like a parent's voice,
the windshield wipers,
the streaks of slotted light
that meant you were going home.

Pull into the drive, the still road of our backyard.
It's near supper hour now,
my husband's shadow moving across
the windows. There will be tea,
a hot meal waiting. For now, count
the minutes by her slow, round-mouthed
breaths, by the rain's gentle urging.
Let her sleep, a little longer.

Sarah Richardson

Vessels

Old Farm Fine Foods
Out my window
Is my coffee break.
Escaping
Kingdoms
Of articulate
Hazelnuts
Spouting from my fingertips.

Dave
White-haired
Tough
Endearing
Generous.
Mango salsa
Organic milk
And asparagus cream cheese sandwiches.

Sydenham Public School
Stalks my sleep
Hovering over my ear
And children's laughter
Like warm breath too close
Is now my alarm.
Every morning
A father
Grey haired and balding
Holds his daughter in a hug
Hands her a purple lunch box
And waits at the fence until the bell calls her in.
His little girl
Eyes, like owl blinks
Hair like willow curtains
And her voice, high-pitched, like a caterpillar's chariot
I'd thrash my flippers while saying goodbye too.

If I walk down to Lake Ontario
With a blackboard in my hand
I don't draw the wind's travels
Or delete the wind turbines
I pause upon the Island ferry
And drive like "Aya of Yop City"
To the Credit River of Erin, Ontario
Where I once chased minnow's
Below the home of my first lover.
Feet sinking in river- bottom sand
       as thick as decomposing tree trunks.
Chalk doesn't capture the blue of his eyes
Or the wheat on his head- it's like lion's fur.
His heart, a lion.
"You're a lion," I named his heart.
"I, a deer?"
A nod
"You a deer."
So, South African accents
Carved the v's of love
That flew me to Johannesburg
Where I stood outside
The gates of his old home
Me the captive
Never to have seen the baboon that stole his biscuit.

I wanted to be an impala
       but a Canadian deer I remained.
Impala or deer
And a lion
On a beach, a desert, in a safari tent
The two are not friends
Especially not lovers.

My direction changed
Upstream the Credit River
Fuelled by 2565 canoes
Replying that I am not a minnow or a deer or an impala
I am my small town
With large blue bottles
That wait
Hopeful to fill
With underbellies
Of good decisions
And Thursdays of Professors and violin.

There were Thursdays
Professors too
But the violin
I heard the loudest in lectures
      that became my writing time.
The decision
Was made
But I had to catch up.

I am my small town
Sipping on the folk of the Grad Club.
Written on that elegant trim
Of the Victorian room
There is a historic post- script
A pleasant warning
For all writers and readers
Snowflakes
Fall like lilies
And evaporate into pink skies
Of rosy cheeks- the palettes of exhaustion
From transfusing one's poetic soul to another.

Kingston is not just my home
But a plant with many wrinkles.

And I, its photosynthesis
As I write Hazelnut
Here

    My fingertips against computer-

    My computer, a grove
    Each part an aisle
    Each page a tree.
    A word, a hazel nut.

In a cubby of Frontenac Library
On the windowpane
A single acorn
I breathe in the flamboyant fragrance
Of creative risks.

Tara Kainer

Field Trip, Artillery Park

You in the pool. I in the gallery high above
gazing down on you and smiling. (I wish
now I had brought my bathing suit. I could
have taken your hand. Or you could have
climbed upon my back and I'd have borne you
porpoise-like across the waters.) You paddle
at the edge of the pool and smile bravely. I
want my voice to reach a hand across to you
but my words are drowned
in the ghastly green glow of the chlorined pool.

Distorted, distended, sounds float
eerily around the high-ceilinged room
like ghosts. Disembodied laughter, a
slap of flesh against the water, a
squeal of delight, or fear, fades
in and out of the echoing roar of
indiscriminate sound. Language lost.

Now the waves rise from the kicking
clambering children and push you
out to sea. Startled eyes search for me
over your shoulder. Arms thrash, mouth
opens and closes, a fish out of water,
gesticulating silent cries for help.

Ursula Pflug

My Mother's Skeleton

My daughter and I sit in the shade of wild apples, watching tiny garden snails. They are so small one feels a giant watching them, or perhaps as though one has microscopes for eyes. These tiny snails are lost in the vastness of a plank laid across the purple stemmed cacophony of rhubarb.

I gently put the snails back under the rhubarb. "Snails need to be moist and slimy," I tell my little daughter, "or they'll dry out". Rhubarb Hollow is our magic shady place beneath the wild apples. Sometimes I bring a notebook when we come out here to play even though I hardly ever write in longhand anymore, but on the first of June I am still too surprised by green's return to sit in the dark computer room upstairs, even just for half an hour. I treasure this moment because next month or next year Annie won't like this game anymore and because soon I must go inside and resume preparations for our party.

It is our annual Victoria Day weekend camping party. The hours blur by until, just after midnight, I sit with my sister Leni and our friend Margo at a fire in a fieldstone pit, perhaps a hundred years old. We discuss the unknown purpose for this carefully made pit. A large bread oven perhaps, but why so far from the house? Or maybe it's the foundation of a ruined grain silo. The hills are decorated with tents, some glowing like luminous mushrooms. The folks in those tents are late night readers or they're afraid of the dark and think a flashlight left on will keep them safe from wild animals, which there indeed are, especially this far from the house. My black dog Asteroid sits between us, keeping guard.

While other children went to church on Sundays we were marched to the art gallery, having required an equal amount of scrubbing as the churchgoers. We were expected to be very quiet, clean and respectful, as if in the presence of the sublime. My father still has this religious hush when looking at large expensive art books, full of costly reproductions. I feel I know what it was to be raised religiously, yet art didn't become my religion. That was something I was still in the process of discovering, or maybe rediscovering.

At twelve Leni and I spent a summer on a farm near Sudbury. The land was rented by family friend Kerry McFarlane and his brothers, all working in the mines so they could buy land. Often that summer we built bonfires on huge outcroppings of shield rock, and sat around them half the night. We walked endlessly in woods and fields, canoed in rivers that seemed so miraculously different from Toronto as to participate in an alien landscape, one that would require a new language, a new metaphor, to divine. For instance, we saw moose.

My father sometimes mocks my choice to live in rural eastern Ontario, a place which after all isn't important. Not the way Europe is important. It is true the towns are full of empty storefronts and video stores and submarine franchises, lack four hundred year old churches and art museums. At least our own: yet there is a four hundred year old church and art museum nearby, the Nishnaabeg Teaching rocks. One cannot visit them and not feel taught. And in spite of his mockery my father comes and looks at my perennial gardens in disbelief each June. I never let him go home without greens or squash.

My mother is not here; we mourn her still. This is one thing I have learned: to mourn properly is a lifelong task. From time to time I try on her beautiful velvet shoes. I've been saving her nicest size elevens; they don't fit me yet and my feet aren't growing any more. A human's growth isn't indeterminate, stretching through a whole life like the beaver's. Up north, further north in Ontario, she used to sit under the birch trees, doing drawings in such miniscule detail, of deadfall, ferns. She must've had microscopes for eyes.

Later this summer we will go back north, take the Polar Bear Express to Moosonee, my father, my husband, and all our children, his and mine. I should like my children to ride a train before all the passenger trains are gone. Like we did, coming home from that Sudbury farm, with my aunt, the year before my mother died. Eating snack bar food and playing crazy eights all night long while the train rattled and clacked through the forests and swamps of Ontario. My sister and I had never stayed awake all night before, but were brave and persevering, helped by card games and sweetened snack bar coffee. Staying awake through the half-numbed navigation of Toronto's cavernous Union Station, the walk along impossibly bright King Street to eat bananas and cream in a greasy spoon. Greasy spoons don't serve bananas and cream any more; only upscale breakfast bistros for the urban trendy do that. Another thing lost.

~ ~ ~

When it is still night Eleni, Margo and I hear coyotes. What seems like hours but is perhaps only a few moments later we watch the last of the luminous tent mushrooms wink out. Now that dawn is coming our campers feel safe enough to turn their lights off. My sisters and I stand on the hills, the lonely fields far from the house cloaked in pockets of mist, the sky striped lavender and pink. Time collapses and I think of all the years when we were young travellers, staying up around fires, surrounded by forests that stretched farther than the eye could see. We did it in many countries, sometimes together, sometimes separately and for a brief moment all those other dawns, other fires, other journeys collapse into one. What are these, I wonder: fire, night conversation, dawn? They exist to remind us how unknowable and mysterious life really is. The next day you see each other and feel: this one I will call friend forever.

~ ~ ~

I have been living inside my mother's skeleton for twenty years. It's quite roomy and comfortable so most of the time I don't even realize my confinement. As though it had grown, her huge ribcage spread out on these hills like the skeleton of a whale. I remember turning fourteen east of here, listening to spring runoff under two feet of snow on a farm in Lanark County. Kerry sat in shirtsleeves, his jacket beneath him on a melting snow bank, playing the double bass while snowmelt also sang in underground rivulets. A series of phone calls at dusk; Kerry driving a blue pickup to the city; premonition soaking through me like darkening twilight.

~ ~ ~

My mother was born in Europe, where she learned to live for art. But she died here, in a still forested land, sitting for hours under birch trees on Kerry's farm, drawing with a botanical exactness, but also an awe: what is this landscape, what does it say, what are its secrets? My mother came across the sea, all the pain of Europe's war in her pocket. In her other pocket, two seeds, two children. Beneath the truly weird, almost fluorescent green of the forest canopy, up north in Ontario, she planted us, so that we might live.

Decades later we still live in the shelter of her ribcage. The rain comes through, but we don't mind: at night we can see the trails of shooting stars, and the smoke from our cook fires wafts through the slatted bones. I may never find another place to live now.

Walter Lloyd

Comfort

We sat, you sit
curled like a bird
contained and warm
in the nest of my arms
the oceanic pulse
of the oxygen pump
breathing hope.
I rocked you then
like one of my children
I knew nothing else to do
lose ourselves
in the simple to and fro
cloaked over
in the dark of hope
or blind denial
pushed up on the shore
by gentle waves
to comfort you
and me.

Stuart Ross

Cobourg, Night

If I shove the boxes
of books aside, drag
the curtains, crane my neck
just so, I can see the clock
on Victoria Hall. It
chimes twice. My parents
died in another city
75 minutes away. The story
of their lives, as filmed
by Ealing Studios, is screened
on the night sky. Here
it is exotic. Tonight:
the screening. Tomorrow:
the Pulled Pork Festival.
Down below, vines have tumbled
from the brick walls, encumbering
the porch. A green ribbon has
unravelled. I wind it tightly
around my well-sucked thumb.

Sonja Grgar

Boy Encaustic

Empty, arid. No crusty blemishes on my pristine carpet, just a sterile, vacuumed emptiness. My hope and desire blown across the desert into the ape brain of the dunes that stretch out to infinity.

I cannot lie this time. Sugar diet with its false pleasures does not hit the spot anymore. I was hoping for more. I was hoping that the blurred traffic lights would melt in my eyes, and not that I would be christened by the anorexic moonlight as he walked me to the celibate cab ride home.

I kept thinking about the nervousness – his and mine, the only bond floating alive that night, I think. Me rushing to clean the place and to freshen it, incense it, and apotheosize it from the churning cave of fear that would swell any time I thought about how long it's been since a man's foot treaded that carpet, dispelling dust-bunnies back into their secret cocoons.

He was nervous too. The bunny flicker of his misty eyes, the squeamish pleading of his crumpled striped shirt – do not get too close, please... I've already been laid down to passion, you've arrived too late. The train had already sped away.

We sat down at a loud watering hole. There was a little crack in the wooden table, almost like a wound. His fingers perused it blindly, and I tried to imagine what it would be like if they trembled all over my body, after they've managed to hike across that continent of bark that separated us.

What did I want to happen? How did I plan to bridge the gap between my sleepless, chocolate coated cries, and the shy creature before me whose every blink must have been ticking the clock, measuring the time until that last polite sentence when he could bolt out of his seat, and slide back into his fuzzy little nest, high up in the sequoia trees where she-lions do not prowl?

I picture him alone back at his place, and awash in the phosphorous glimmer of the night that traces his delicate pulse back to his lover, the blank page. And I continue to stumble the lowlands below, spewing the red and green of my x-rayed bones, ashamed that he and the world can see their toxic glow drying up the soil underneath.

Patricia Henderson

Benchmark

My favourite bench is haunted.
The ghosts of Kingston sit there.
I see them still when I drive by.
Four spectres. Two young girls at first –
      willowy, bubbly, hopeful, laughing.
Ghosts. But I see them clearly. I do not even slow down.
Other passersby ignore them. Joggers.
Cyclists. Walkers. Dogs. (maybe not the dogs…)
But then, Lake Ontario is so beautiful. Perhaps
      they watch the water and miss them.
Bench hauntings are subtle.
The other two are mothers, watching their young.
It is the girls' first day at Queen's University. Thirty years ago.
They can hardly wait to start their lives.
The bench bores them. The mothers bore them.
The water of Lake Ontario shimmered that day
      so many decades ago.
The bizarre steel beams of the then new artwork
      blocked their view. It is still there too.
The young women are given two handmade sewing kits.
Something from home, something to remember.
They get up and fade towards campus.
So, it is the mother ghosts I see when I drive past.
They sit there still.
They don't see the water, the sunshine, the passersby, the cars.
They watch only the backs of their grown children walking away.
The mother ghosts hold hands. And sit on the bench
      linked by their tears.
I am one year away from sitting on that bench.
No longer the young woman. Now the mother.
A handmade sewing kit will exchange hands.
She'll get up and walk away.

My tears will stain that bench anew.
Ghostly tears will comfort me. I will hold their hands.
Others driving by only will only see the bench.
Some turn, but keep driving
      – a touch of the bittersweet on their lips.

Michael Hurley

Poem For Al Purdy

Things are not
what they seem
nor are they otherwise.
Just look at Al & Acorn for godsake—
both voted least likely
& yet
& yet
still here
still haunting the north shore
still reminding us
where there are humans
you'll find flies
   & Buddhas,
   even ones hiding behind beer bottles
   bluster & bullshit,
   & A-framed
   rather than full-lotus'd.
Who knew?

Some voices speak out
of whirlwinds
others still points
& Al
being Al
not being religious
not being dead
from the neck down
nor gently smiling or conducting choirs
all the time

somehow found himself
fluent in both languages,
found himself willy-nilly
on occasion
plugged into some radiant cosmic dynamo,
some lost kind of coherence,
call it what you will.
He called it
the north shore—
& called it home.

Two guys who wouldn't be caught
dead warming pews
& not always steady on their feet
made space for "mystic" stuff
as Al came to call it
inviting whatever it is
to hunker down
in more than a poem or two
   without sounding like Holy Writ
   like The Lord Almighty or frickin' Moses
but JAZZED by God
Al so juiced he surprises even himself
especially himself
exploring being
bloody well s p i r i t u a l
me, how funny is that
without having ta be bolt-upright refuckingligious
shit!
like that godawful strait-laced Presbyterian terror

masquerading as a mother
rubbing Al 's young nose in Original Sin 24/7
putting him off his feed
til half mort-vivant'd
he found nourishment
in four or five favourite writers—
   Lawrence, Yeats, Blake, Avison—
who snuck an off-tha-wall come-as-you-are spirituality
in the back door
of literalist/fundamentalist Southern Ontario
plus all those out-there folks
he'd get Walter down @ *Wayfarer Books*
to track down:
brain-specialist Loren Eiseley
yogi/shaman authority Mircea Eliade
or them other self-described fools & clowns
able to laugh & pray & belch
at the same time—
   down Easterners like Persian Sufi Rumi,
   Tibet's poet-yogi Milarepa
   Japan's resident Zen loonie "Crazy Cloud."
   Then sat them down
   on the north shore.

In short
the unusual suspects
the other spiritual eccentrics on the block
crazy enuff to be exuberantly irreverent
wise enuff to be wary
of becoming holy assholes
coming on like I AM THE TRUTH
& THE LIGHT.
DO YOU BELIEVE?!

All of them touched
as touched as Al seems to his neighbours
down on his knees
not begging forgiveness for his sins
the bastard
but intent on the moment
   the exact mind-stoppin' enchanting beautiful nanosecond
Roblin Lake water shape-shifts into sparkling baby ice-cubes
card-carrying TOUCHED
by what Tibetans call "Crazy Wisdom"—
not monks by a long shot
but off-tha-beaten track folks
nevertheless in touch
with The Force
the Life-Force
crazy enuff to drink down the spirit of Zen
as it were
wise enuff to throw away the bottle.
Or start bottling their own.
And start passing it around.

Crazy Wisdom's Children
running wild in the country
north of respectability—
that's Al's family
scattered across the planet
& centuries,
& illegitimate at that
unwashed untutored unlettered untethered
unwanted by monastery or academy
Muggles or Main Street,
not outta place in beer parlour
or the outer planets
arcing somewhere over our heads
or the deep space of our hearts
between genius & goofus,

off-tha-grid sage & village idiot,
Hogwarts & Hogtown,
Buddhas & flies—
   that in-between place
   where an Angel might find you
   maybe a devil or two…
   & poems
   those gods & goddesses
   of incandescent moments
   beyond the beck & call
   of the priests of high seriousness read solemnity
   walking their rounds
   in Eastern Ontario   as elsewhere
   pissed off to find plenty to annoy them
   in the likes of Purdy The Irascible
   & His Fellow Merry Pranksters of Poetry.

Gainfully unemployed
the lot of 'em
& farting in their general direction
can't somebody do something?,
sticking it to The Man
but as given to self-burlesque, boondoggle & pies in their own face
as that Middle East fool & fuck-up Nasruddin
Public Enemy #1 of fundamentalists everywhere.
Tricksters & paradox-wranglers
Purdy & his ilk
putting it to us
that without fear of contradiction
we can categorically state
that we can't categorically state
anything
without fear of contradiction,
enrolling us before we know it
in a 12-Step Program
for Recovering Consensus Reality addicts.

Rascals all
stumbling down the magic
mountain with The Zen Commandments
converted on the spot into frisbees,
conducting guerrilla raids
on what Yeats calls
a levelling, rancorous, rational sort of mind
that never looked
out of the eye of saint or drunkard
   unlike Purdy who could peer
   & leer outta both with the best of 'em
   one hand tied to a beer bottle
   whilst leaping sideways backwards ass over electric kettle
   in the most unprefuckingtentious manner imaginable.
   And then some.

Definitely off-the-grid
outside-ye-olde-box Al
much too large
too ungainly
too full of shit & surprises
to rest comfortably
in anything
less than what yer born-again-and-again Buddhist simply calls
"BIG MIND"
"BEGINNER'S MIND"—
   seeing/starting afresh
   buoyed up by the innocence
   the spontaneity
   of first inquiry
   "Everything happening"
   as "In Search of Owen Roblin" has it
   "again for the first time."

Opening to what is
right here, right now,
in this moment,
keeping loose, letting be.
Always a beginner,
always a fool.
The mind empty
of thoughts
of this or that,
past & future,
overflowing with a funky sense
of interconnection,
energetically improving
off the cuff come-ta-think-of-it it-occurs-to-me style
as in "Naked with Summer in your Mouth":
   "Atop boxcars…& beginning to realize
   there is no past & no future
   you're born at this precise moment."

<u>Moment</u>—
the name of the little mag
Al & Acorn start
between fights
to keep their philosophy, their poems, their battles & their bottles
open-ended, off-centre, ex-centric.
Modulating voices in the moment
faster than you can say "Robin Williams"
waxing profound & wacky in the same breath
in a not-at-all-the-same polyphonic stream
of comic consciousness
Al's wry, bemused ponderings
jumping the gap
between comic & cosmic
the ha-ha & tha Aha!

like time-collapsing Einstein realizing
the most beautiful thing
you can feel
ever
is the **mysterious**
knowing the joke's on you
  that tight-assed anxious little you
  caught up in its sad little holdings
  locked into the Control Tower
  afraid to come out & play,
  missing the passing show
  or getting lost in it…

Crazy Al
wisening up
to the presence
of the Presence
within
without you
described thus in his autobio:
  "a shadow self
  I'm trying to get in touch with,"
  "that different part of my brain
  which I called "The Other,'"
  "the other self who lives
  in all of us,
    friend, foe or neutral judge,
  a **doppelganger** of the soul…"

Alias Al
going bump
in the Ameliasburgh north shore night
transposing himself
into Earle Birney or Inuit
pioneer grandpa dead brother birds beasts flowers
w h u d e v e r

consciousness so fluid, so free
it looks out the eye
of heron & tortoise
ancestor & Dorset
no one & everyone
til it dawns on you
be it the view from outer space or inner:
   no difference
   no boundaries
   no yourself
   no self separate
   from the whole
   ball of wax
   Tom Marshall's daisy-chain dance
   everyone interwoven with everyone everywhere all at once——
          T A N D E M O N I U M
& Purdy's words ringing
"Being anything was never quite
what I intended."

Southern Ontario Zen.
Canuck coherence.
North Shore Nobody.
Simply being.
Not being
this & that.
Nobody
special.
Feeling & flowing in & out
of so-called other
people trees rocks fish crows
like you've woken up
inside a Morrisseau painting
changing from nothing to One
a sorta *telempathy*

Going out of his mind
to come to his senses
Purdy getting over himself
contains multitudes.
Which is big of him.
Afloat in the ark of Consciousness
The I That Is We
sees us all
suffering
from a case of mistaken identity
clinging to who we think we are
til the moment we twig
that we're A W A R E N E S S
that we've been inside one another
all along
that the Promised Land
is underfoot
that the universal pokes its head out
of a local grain of sand
& that if you don't have a sense of humour
    it just isn't funny…

But of course
only a crazy fool
would say such a thing
because after all—

Lara Szabo Greisman

The Space between People

I want to talk about the peepholes in doors
And how you can stand
6 inches from someone without feeling their breathing.
And we are gods in these moments
We can dictate the fate, the shape of shy *souls*, with a smile.
Or wrathful, we can trap them in a fish bowl of mental maybe's,
Of our fears.
The *I wish I were's*, the *I could never be's*,
     the *they would never see's*
That wedge under the skin of our humanity —like sandpaper.

    And I find it's always
I and I, not you and I or I and We
    It's always I and I, not you and I or I and We

We think we're all lone rangers on an asphalt runway
    of contradictory dreams.
And it says we can't fly, just skin our knees.
We try to squeeze between the seams of individual assimilation.
But it's easier to talk another person's talk
In this upgrade- better wage-you are your trade- nation.

    And I find it's always I and I, not you and I or I and We
    It's always I and I, not you and I or I and We

But maybe it's no run-way - a highway - a try to be that guy-way.
Maybe we are all standing behind the bars of a social cattle guard.
But we know that rap,
Of someone fucking-up, fail-ing, fall-ing through the cracks-
But if all the *ones* in everyone
Become some
Some who found time to save space in life's line
For a peaceful paradigm.
Some, who got it into their minds to truly emphasize
Our same Smallness.

Then i might not always be

I and I, not you and I or I and We
Not always I and I, not you and I or I and We

And if this peephole distortion fills the right proportions
Of the myths we were told:
about the make your money now –about worth measured in gold.
Then the separation-desperation-sandpaper loneliness-lack of lustre
Are ruptures created to keep us from being whole.

But dependency always has a negative sense,
And these connotations are mitigations forged by fears of impotence.
Fears of vulnerability in union. of being othered. Excluded.
Labelled crazy, weird, stupid.
So we block, duck, cover our confusion : by hiding behind our I.

Always I –I and I– not you and I or I and We.
It's always I and I not you and I or I and We.

And I just want to buy the reflection of a utopian sky.
I want to reach through the fields of shields
Through the space between people.

And no longer be I and I-but you and I or I and We,
No longer I and I but you and I or I and We.

Joanne Page

Carbolic in the Maytag
Or Visiting-the-Prison Blues

Get out the clothes, the bag, the shoes, the socks.
Defold each pleat, reverse all pocket linings.
Rinse lint, disinfect your son and side door locks.
Unhair the brush, decline the Listerine,
toss out the peppermint in its pristine cello twist.
No tablets, capsules, makeup, blemish cream,
nor scissors, clippers, floss, paste or foam.
All beauty products must remain at home.
Launder cottons, lycra, woolly wear,
scrub your coins, forget the teddy bear.
Dry clean yourself, deploy the fluffy towel,
examine shoes and vacuum out the car.
Check your list, go the whole damn hog:
your fate lies in the wet nose of a dog.

Jeanette Lynes

The Oldest Living Swinger in Canada

He parks his ancient Buick on the main drag,
the epicenter, Princess Street, near the banks
and cafés, stone's toss from S & R Department Store
with its living elevator operator who resembles
a dead Bee Gee. Yes, the oldest living swinger
in Canada parks his buggy preserved with love
amidst all this glamour. Weather means zilch to him.
I first saw him on winter's most dire day, walkers
picking their way along Bagot, muttering prayers
into their scarves. His Buick equipped with state
of the art eight-track, windows wide open,
Glenn Miller or Artie Shaw full-tilt. I, too, hurried
across the frozen slush. I was about to tell
a mental health professional nothing good
remained in this world when I noted
the nation's oldest living swinger,
his passion-pit parked, big band cranked,
his bald head tilted back, joggling
to the riffs. His eyes closed,
mouth open, gums aglow,
pink galleries of pure bliss.

Eric Folsom

Shaking

The Plaza, Kingston's downtown strip bar,
Had a sign years back proclaiming *Shaker*s Lounge*
With a star instead of an apostrophe,
Another sign saying simply *Shakers Lounge*,
No punctuation at all.

Management intended a different image,
But I pictured Shaker furniture and broad, plank floors,
Handcrafted wooden pegs on the wall.
When the hymns were done, they hung the chairs,
Got ready for some serious Shaker dances,
Picking their feet up and laying them rhythmically down
In a way that scandalizes Methodists and Baptists.

The second sign, no possessive, caused wonder,
Made me think how even hard working Shakers,
Needed to lounge and linger sometimes,
To lean against a tree and watch the sunset
While someone pours switchel over ice.
Even the strictly religious must have stared
Through the dust of golden hay to contemplate the Maker,
Or tried to imagine the future, our own present
When believers live no more at Canterbury or Enfield,
The beautiful furniture owned by collectors.

Maybe they knew their own thoughts and feelings
Would vanish one day, knew the distant hills
And hazy sunshine would be swept forward,
Just like the wet t-shirt contests, into eternity.
How it doesn't matter at last what parts you shake
Or how hard you shake them,
Only that the clean, fateful course of your trembling
Animates and carries you
Wittingly from here to there.

Eliot Kane

Rapture

Flee from evil,
tormenting my inner self.
The one clawing at the surface.

Don't let it enter the light.

Hide the expression of fear,
This could be too much to bare.
Bury yourself in the darkness.

The light is no longer safe.

I bleed,
yet feel nothing.
Look at my skin:
I pick and pick.

Must we hide?

I sit in silence,
hearing only echoes.
My lungs Pierced,
with endless screams.
I want my heart back in my chest.

We are the forgotten ghosts:
The silent buried.

Aloud, we burn away.

Linda Allison Stevenson

A Thought on That Silver Lining

Hands that fate have dealt have fallen into sickened Chaos
Destiny has foretold a calamity, Death is on the horizon

Memories that linger, Wicked and wished for.
Invisible Imps pull at a soul that is fading and forgotten

How do you see yourself?

Condemned to the unforgiving grave just as life is entered into you
Life is a useless thing,
Ashamed of what becomes us,
apologetic for what we have become, for how we are.
Twisted by intelligence and experience
Nothingness is pure
Burned by beauty, doomed by innocence, always wanting more.

Satisfaction a meaningless grunt
The silver lining has melted in a stars gaze.
Sensory deprivation useless to a planet of zombies
calling themselves the superior race

Conform to individuality,
        be yourself in the midst of a single minded group
Ruler, God and king of a world inside itself, inside you
Sanity is what is made of it, held onto by a tiny silk thread
Escape from yourself, save that last breath, that last smile.

Torrents, rivers and oceans of lies and deception that flow
Truth, a canoe that fell to reality and found itself lost,
        beaten and killed by all that was, is, can be.

Crazy to the point of sanity
Lost in an amazing maze of self-loathing
Eyes glued shut so as to not to discover who you are
Life's little joke, the punch line six feet below

Always alone, how to know another
        when self-identity is washed away
Lost to the one who holds it
Perfect moments of happiness tainted
        by the knowledge of one's self
What about the happy ending,
Life is not a fairy tale

Are you everything you ever wanted?

Evolution brings this species farther from its morals
and deeper into the throws of lucid sanity

Bad acid trip

Loves purity bent and broken by lust
that leaves a bitter sweet itch, better not scratched
When did you fail yourself?
When did it all cease to make sense?
Do you remember when you gave up

I do.

Bruising and beating on the heart and soul, the human condition.

Why try
It's all for naught anyway, fame and fortune won't save you
What if this is all there is, This is it!! No Heaven and no Hell
No Great spirit in the sky, life a cosmic accident
And death being ultimately final, it's on its way.
Not too much longer now

Suicide a great escape
If you only have the nerve, knowledge of what comes after.

Is it better than this?

I wasn't meant to be,

it would ease the pain

Do you deserve all that has been given, refused
        or taken away from you?
The worst thing I ever did, you ever did,
we ever did was

take that first breath

Beauty held inside a demon's grip, a wish of perfection
But if ever achieved,
        still left wanting and hoping for more, for better

New life taken away and destroyed by those who gave it
Ruined by the secrets that are kept and held fast to

Why do you hold onto that love so hard, why do you fight for it?
It's only a trick of the mind, the brain
A release of mixing chemicals, and truly it won't save the day
Jealous of who you used to be, remembering what was,
        scared of what will be.
I am
My strength has failed

Who is better, the host or the parasite?
The host has to struggle and fight for all it achieves,
While the parasite just has to simply exist
Blissfully Unaware!!!!! Happy in ignorance

How dare you judge me, judge others
No one truly thinks they are a bad person

Kill the thoughts that you were ever good enough,
      how can anyone ever be
Do you really want to be here?

Genie in a bottle locked away in childhood fantasies
Always rubbed the wrong way
She doesn't want to come out
Do you ever wander what is REALLY going on?

Happiness is a lie held within itself
If the truth was ever truly known and shown,
      we couldn't handle it
You know you've been lied to,

the question being do you care?

Sink or swim
Fighting the tides, going against the current
      is useless and hopeless
Swim for it, find the existence that you so desperately
      wish for, but eludes you
Sink and find sweet blissful obviation

Trust no one, not even yourself
You can deceive the inner-you better than anyone
      ever has, will, or could
It can always be right inside
Lies of what you know to be true

Heat of hell a better relaxation technique than denial of the heart
Better than rejection of one's self
Giving it all up, giving it all to another, only to have it thrown back.

Phoenix of beauty, colours of perfection
The Phoenix falls from high above for the first time;
      he dared open its eyes to the

Demons breath wilted away the angels wings,
the seraphim's soul was ravaged,
        forgotten by the one she trusted most

He giggled

Goodness never wins

SCREAM!!!!
Soul as black as the depths of infinity
It's too late to fix it. You have broken fate, killed destiny
Isn't this what you wanted?
SAVE ME!!

SAVE YOU!!

Hats off to the ignorant person,

The one who can be blind to it all
The one who can not see the seething pain

If it fails, if I fail, if it doesn't work out this time,
        a refusal to try again
Second coming of nothing, a final hello

Cut me, cut yourself
Make it better; the pain is fantastic, beautiful, and pure
Doesn't that feel better now?
You forgot you were alive, a momentary escape

Smile for the dead, don't grieve for them, as it will soon be you
Their existence, fate has already been realized,   their truth found
Are you a good person, I know more than you do. They told me

Does anything ever truly matter? Can it?
Everything must come out, must fade

Legions of trolls have come to claim what is theirs
So why do you care, or do you. It's all a lie anyway

Life and love are games better left unplayed
There is no prize at the end, you can never win
Play Russian roulette with yourself,
the rewards are greater, the outcome greater

Look in the mirror, who do you see looking back
To you, the stranger in the street is better known
     than that person looking back at you
Truth? TRUTH!!!

Held within arms of steel, melting within yourself,
     into a beating heart.
Tomorrow is a cutting torch. It means nothing.
     Let it go, let it go!!
Where's your irony? All that's needed is a word, maybe a knife.

Strive for greatness, be all that you can possibly be.
And when you find it, when you achieve it,
Turn around and ask yourself why.
The final outcome is the same for you, for me,

for every living breathing beautiful, beautiful, beautiful, thing
It's the same for all

Nothing, nothingness.

I give, I gave, I surrender
A war waged, a fight that could never be won.
A war where everyone loses.

I have nothing left

HOW ABOUT YOU

Andrew Scott

Jamie

Jamie was a fifteen year old boy,
just like all other teenagers,
life and the future ahead of him.
Jamie was to face it with a smiling face,
same smile he had for everyone.

Jamie had potential that was limitless,
energizing personality that shared with most,
participation in new school clubs,
singing and dancing that brought beaming faces.

Jamie is dead,
pushed by others' hands of confused hate,
taunted for knowing who Jamie was,
and for him wearing it with pride,
beaten and bullied into lonely depression,
by others not comfortable in their own shell,
while Jamie knew whose hand he wanted to hold.

Parents that reinforced to keep him strong,
baffled about hate like this in today's world,
the kind that can only be taught,
handed down from the generations,
knowing those hands of hatred,
will not stop until another Jamie is found.

Louise O'Donnell

Letter Home
From Prince Edward County

I want to paint you a picture,
but you paint so much better than I.
Instead, I'll

gather an armload
of stalks from the roadside
wrap them in mists
from the morning fields
tie them with strips
torn from the silver sheet
the moon lays outside my window
each night,

gather a carafe
of old leaf smells,
smell of
red sweet apples and pumpkin musk,
even, stinging sinus clearing
manure smells layered with damp grass.

I want you to meet Debra from
the Milford Coffee Gallery,
the clan from Chapter One,
the best bookstore anywhere.
(Can you believe
a whole section of poetry?)

I want to wrap my arms
around this place,
gather great handfuls
and send it like potpourri
to my dearest friends.

Maybe when January arrives
in her long white skirt
dragging along wind to
scream their opposition
to my frail bits of wood and stone
blocking the path

that's been theirs
since this County poked its rock
above the water,
maybe then I'll send a messenger
to fetch the warm breath
of your encouragement

only maybe

Lynn Tait

Challenging the Law of Superimposition
for Al Purdy

> *and I am angry remembering*
> *remembering the song of flesh*
> *to flesh and bone to bone*
> *the loss is better* – Al Purdy – *Listening To Myself*

I had no poem to write, nothing to offer,
even though buried speechless in the same landscape
may have brought me closer to him.
In his place, my space, land began to speak to me,
childhood memories ingrained with visual clues,
after a twenty year absence I walk thru woods
      behind my house,
find my secret hideaways, the quarry,
      even the raspberry patch.
Everything as I left it only taller,
and I am angry remembering.

Too young. Too young
to travel, what seemed great distances alone.
Family car rides weaving through back-roads – Hastings,
Prince Edward County – it was all the same to me.
I was the Canadian Shield –
a geological landmark that did not belong,
leaving chatter marks in places that should not exist,
a fossil even then, and when I reach his grave site
we enter a convergent boundary – two landmasses
remembering the song of flesh,

the lyric leaching out,
purple milk under my skin,
creeping towards each other
like his blue heron shifts along thin rivers,
closer and closer, flesh
to flesh and bone to bone.

Reading his poems now, swear I was at his side —
know his nurse log, have seen the golden apples
abandoned and white capped.
And though hear his Nature's sighs and calls
and think of death often,
prefer to remember him hung over,
slumped over coffee in downtown Trenton
rather than a renewable resource.
The loss is better.

Shane Joseph

From Both Sides, Now

Part 1 – (The scene – a young man sits at an outdoor table on a farm, writing)

The farm boundary gives me security, it encapsulates my known world. And my family stand watch over me by the fence line in the graveyard that Father created for Papa and Mama. Father joined my *abuelos* in the graveyard three months ago when his crumbling 1940 Chevrolet carrying him, Mother, and my sister Maria, stalled in the middle of the road and was crushed by the petrol tanker hurtling around the bend on the coastal road into Santiago de Cuba. All of them, gone, but they still stand watch over me by the fence.

The only one to get away from the farm was my younger brother Juan. He was the top performer in school and qualified for a friendship mission to Canada ten years ago from which he never returned. Embarrassed officials later told us that he ran away from his hotel room one night in a city called Windsor and was never seen again. No one knew at the time whether he was still hiding in Canada or had slipped over to Detroit across the water in America. I was happy that he had made it to the other side, but I was also envious.

Two years ago, the letters began to arrive, smuggled in by Canadian tourists who had arrived in the resort hotel nearby. His first letter contained beautiful pictures: of the famous Niagara Falls, of lush vineyards, of a tower in Toronto which was supposed to be the tallest in the world. Juan said that he had lots of friends, mostly white Canadian girls who thought his swarthy looks and accent were sexy, and lots of money, and to prove it, there was a hundred dollar bill enclosed. Father did not know what to do with it, whether to cash it in the black market and betray the tenets of the Revolution or to keep it as a testament to the "Capitalist Connection" in our family. And so the note sat in his wallet, pending a decision, which, like everything else in this country, takes a long time to be made.

Mother wrote back, through those same generous tourists who left us with stationery and maple syrup, asking Juan when he was going to come home. He did not reply for over a year. When his answer finally came, it made Mother sob, and Maria went out into the field and did not talk for days afterward. Juan said that he had become a Canadian citizen after a lengthy process called a refugee claim. He was working in a vineyard in a place called St. Catharines and was learning English and hoped to buy his own farm one day. He was not coming home, he said. He had new boundaries now, and with the ability to travel and carry money with him, the entire world was his playground. That letter, along with the hundred dollar bill, was found in Father's wallet on the day of the car accident.

Because of Juan's transgression, we were not allowed to visit him either. It is as if by escaping to another life, we pass through a one-way door, like air through the valve of my soccer ball when I pump it.

I look around my world, this farm, and the door to the house needs new hinges; it hangs to a side and does not close properly. Tomatoes are ripening on the vine and will have to be plucked soon. The grass is overgrown in the field and I need to borrow the baler from my neighbour and stack the barn with hay before the drought dries everything out. In return, I will give my neighbour a few bales for his cows. I also have to see if I can get a piece of piping from the village hardware shop, or from the garage next door – that water tap needs to be fixed, it's dripping too much water. And those tiles on the roof, I am not sure what to do about them; tiles are in short supply these days, like just about everything else – perhaps I'll go down to the artisans village and ask the potter to custom-make me a few so that I can repair the leak in the roof above my camp cot.

Sitting at this outdoor table, where I take most of my meals, write my poetry, talk to my dead relatives, and dream about what life must be outside the boundaries of the tree-line that fences me in, a pang of loneliness grips me. Despite the community I share with my farm neighbours, it is at times like this that I feel that we come to this earth alone and we die alone, even though *Papa and Mama* had died in their sleep, holding each other's hands, and my parents and sister went off into the afterlife together inside a doomed car. This loneliness is also comforting for it has visited me often and is now like a familiar friend. I wonder how Juan, in his cold northern country must feel. Who comforts him?

Perhaps comfort for him comes from his many girlfriends. Another feeling overtakes me, one of trying to win a race but always falling behind, and getting angry about it. I think it is envy, and it has prevented me from writing to my brother all these years. For Mother always said to her neighbours, "Juan may be a rebel, but my Marco has the heart to melt any woman." Alas "heart" seems to have consigned me to carrying on the family tradition of farming, alone, in this family mausoleum that no one visits anymore, while my less endowed sibling enjoys life with girls, money and expanded horizons. But today I will rise above these limiting emotions. Life is too short; those gravestones remind me of that fact. Let me convey my thoughts to Juan in this letter which I hope that the kind Canadian couple at the resort, who gave me the baseball cap and running shoes, will carry and mail for me in Canada.

"Juan, you may have the world at your fingertips, but you are locked out of the womb that bore you...much has happened here since you last wrote..."

Part 2 – (The scene – two months later – a young man sits at an outdoor table on a farm, writing)

Sitting at this table in the yard, I look upon the sad familiar surroundings. This place looks just like one of the many family farms I have passed on this journey, where I was sheltered and fed, where the smiles were generous, the food skimpy, and the discourse on politics and society subdued. Only this farm lacks children running in the dust, the matriarch cooking in the kitchen, dogs barking, and men sitting around drinking rum or just chatting, killing time. This farm is deserted, and has been since I walked through its gate half an hour ago.

Looking at the graveyard, I catch up on the family history

carved into the crude gravestones, a history that I have missed, one I have not earned the right to share in. It tells of those who passed peacefully when their purpose in life had been fulfilled. It also tells of those taken away suddenly, never realizing their purpose—that is, if self-realization is ever possible in this country.

My knapsack holds a change of clothes sorely in need of washing, the last of my Canadian chocolate bars (a very useful "currency" that got me through many bureaucratic bottlenecks), a near-empty water bottle, a letter written in Spanish and bearing a Canadian stamp, and my new Canadian passport – my key to immunity, and lifeline to the outside world that the denizens of this one could never see unless they braved the cold waters of the Atlantic in their makeshift boats and hit the tip of Florida by good fortune.

The places I have visited on this odyssey are full of stories of struggle. I have seen the ravages of hurricanes on houses and hotels left standing along the beaches, the dry arroyos trailing down mountains in which goats forage like gold diggers mining a barren seam, loud posters in the cities and towns proclaiming the 50th anniversary of the Revolution (when does a revolution end?), and abandoned projects from a more ambitious time: Soviet-style apartment blocks, second stories on houses with their roofs still to be put in place, cars rotting on logs for lack of spare parts. There is one such vehicle in a lean-to shed at the back of this farm and it must have a gruesome tale to tell; its tires have exploded and its rear is crushed all the way to the front doors. And yet, there is optimism in that wreck; it reposes on its cinder blocks as if someone hopes to resurrect it one more time in the service of man.

These stories re-affirm my conviction that crazy decisions made on the spur of the moment, are sometimes the best ones. They reaffirm that this trip, reckless though it may have been, was the right choice. That life is a series of choices. One of those stories could have been my story, had I not chosen to write my own.

There is order on this farm. Two full baskets of ripe tomatoes sit by the entrance to the house. The door has new hinges, and wood shavings litter the threshold on the outside. Bales of hay in the barn are neatly stacked while cows roam the field plucking away at loose strands that escaped the baling machine, and the tap outside does not drip unlike in all the other farms en-route. Despite my own impressions of a land in scarcity, the occupant of this farm seems to be in control of his meagre resources. My conscience is relieved. The gap in my life, one that has endured for this lost decade, is starting to mend.

A figure rides in from the field. His chestnut mare looks vaguely familiar, perhaps the offspring of a horse I once rode. The rider is tall, tanned and wiry, his straw sombrero rendering his features in shadow. He dismounts by the well, and using the pitcher, slakes the thirst of the animal before drinking himself. He strokes the mare's nose affectionately while speaking gently to it, takes off its bridle and saddle, and turns it loose into the field. He stacks the riding gear on a rack nearby, returns to the well and drinks more water from the pitcher, and untying his bandana, soaks it in the remaining water and wipes his face. I feel guilty for travelling with a bottle of mineral water purchased at the last store I had passed. There is an unconscious, visceral confidence in this man when he looks upon the land spread before him. He is more a part of it, than I am. That is the cost I paid for leaving.

I rise from the table and walk towards him. As if by sixth sense, he turns and notices me for the first time.

"Marco," I say.

He pushes back the sombrero, and it hangs off his back by its chinstrap pressed against his neck. I see the scar on his right cheek that I gave him as a boy when I threw a stick to hit a stray dog and clipped him instead.

"*Hola*, Juan!" His smile is wide, his eyes wider, his outstretched arms the widest. "You came."

He crushes me in an embrace that dissolves all recrimination. I feel the rough fabric of his shirt, and smell his raw sweat that reminds me of the battle for survival we had fought in this harsh country as children, and which he still fights today. He had chosen to stay while I had fled and lost myself in aftershave and deodorant.

"Welcome home, *hermano*," he says.

Roger Dorey

What Ever Happened to Kevin Smith?

What ever happened to
Kevin Smith?
This question appears to me
In the rear view mirror
In rare moments
Unexpected
Unconnected
To any previous or present
Train of thought
Not even on a parallel track
And I am always
Unprepared and perplexed
Each time it returns
Just as I am now

Why does this question challenge me?
I am not the only one
Who would remember
The beers and laughs
The times we made an ass
Of ourselves
And felt no shame
Swore we would have done it
Again (and again)
And did

Do I see beyond the need
For a good drinkin' buddy?
This was not the sum total
Of our friendship
There should have been
Serious conversations
Though they would have been
Short-lived diversions

We had so much youthful energy
To spend on what
The Big City was selling
And with eyes wide open
It was always open for business
Those times
So far removed
From the need for
Careers
Marriages
Families
Securities
Came to an abrupt end
When our calendars parted ways

Am I gasping to breathe significance
Into a flashback
From a fading history?
Made stranger
Now
Trying to decide whether
It is merely a question of nostalgia
Or the soul needing
To believe in a magic
Lost to lost friends
We walk the line
Fall off at the end
Discovering
Sooner or later life beats us all
We come full circle
Searching for these lost friends
With a private smile
Recall our rise & fall
And return

To the house of order
That does not know
Where to hang
The missing pictures

Is the issue
I can't provide an answer?
Because it is more than simple
Bubble gum trivia
It is a persistent missing piece
That looks at me, through me, to me
Haunting me to resolve the puzzle..

Whatever happened to me?
Am I ready for the answer?

Morgan Wade

The Family Business

There was pure, white light at the top of a tunnel. Exactly as they always said.

I'm dying.

She felt an unexpected flush of euphoria.

Get to the light. Escape the tunnel. Into the light.

But the heat. Suffocating. Relentless. Why so hot?

Elation became terror. And then confusion.

I've always obeyed, haven't I?

She was unsure whether to continue or to retreat.

A shape materialized from the halo above. At first, a crescent moon, a silver luminescence, broadening, cleaving. A smile.

Each shimmering tooth an angel, a rapturous choir standing shoulder to shoulder between two glossy banquettes. Swaying. Clapping. Waxing impossibly wider, shining ever brighter. The sing-song emanating from it, chanting, repeating.

Now getting louder. Less melodious.

Now sharp. Strident.

She felt a sudden, insistent pain in her forearm and the dim walls of the tunnel melted away.

The woman with the heavenly teeth asked her question again, her smile re-ignited, radiating warmth and patience in equal measures.

"How did you feel when you first heard the news?"

Sitting next to Matt, her husband, on the overstuffed couch, she turned her head slowly to face him as the woman leaned in close, interrogating. Matt dug his freshly filed fingernail into her wrist, trying to break through her stupor. The brows above his pale, pleading eyes were gesturing to the woman standing over them. For the first time, she noticed the bottomless pool of a camera lens over the woman's shoulder. And more to the left and right. And the massive Klieg lights suspended from the ceiling, muddying her powdered face with perspiration.

Matt apologized through set lips.

"It's fine," the woman said as she turned to the crew and ran a finger across her throat. "We'll do another take. It's all in the editing. Ready to try again sweetie?"

This time, she nodded.

"Ok," the host said, powering up. "Here we go."

She pointed at Matt's wife and snapped her thumb down.

"How did you feel when you first heard the news?" The woman paused. "That you were pregnant."

The words echoed in the chasm of her head, triggering a slide of its precarious contents. Breathless, she realized the truth, again, with excruciating clarity.

I don't want it.

Renewed gouging at her wrist.

"Wonderful", she mouthed. "So happy".

Matt began to explain how he had been affected by the act of conception, his separation anxiety, how he had felt a part of him was missing.

"Cut!" The smile dropped from the woman's face. "That will do. We'll dub in audio later. Thanks so much."

Matt mumbled another apology as he fed his wife a capsule and raised a paper cup to her lips. The woman waved him away. She was setting up for the next segment. Matt helped his wife up from the sofa and guided her toward the exit. As they left, they could hear the host rehearsing her segue.

"Isn't she precious? So nervous and excited. Carrying Matt's child. Moe and Miriam's record-breaking three hundred and twelfth grandchild! We'll capture all nine months of tummy kicks and morning sickness, sweet reconciliations and hormonal rage. Tune in, you won't want to miss a minute. Now, let's see how Miles and his wife are coping with the arrival of their triplets!"

Later, cradled in the lambskin seats of the stretched Lincoln Town Car that whisked them from home to studio and back, Matt made an attempt at consolation.

"Dumpling. You knew this was coming. I warned you not to take a dose so close to filming."
Matt picked up his wife's limp arm and examined the soft flesh of her wrist. She wrenched it from his grasp, burrowed it into her lap, and turned away.

"Sorry I pressed so hard. You were really out of it."

She put her face closer to the drizzle-greased window. The limo came to a stop at a set of barricades where men in orange vests worked at repairing a bus-sized sinkhole. A huddle of onlookers stared at the car, wondering who might be inside. One of them pushed a battered stroller from the sidewalk fragment into the muck silting the gutter.

"I think you forget sometimes," Matt continued, shifting away to look out at a shuttered high rise, "just how fortunate we are, all of us. The family. How lucky you are."

She realized now, with alarm, that the woman with the stroller was not trying to cross the street, but was heading her way. As she neared, she could see that the woman wore several overlapping coats and a dozen tawdry ribbons nested in the tangle of her hair.

"Matt?"

He gestured out the window to the empty building. "You have opportunities they can only dream of. But you also have a responsibility."

The woman was shouting something, exposing her remaining brown teeth. She stabbed the stroller ahead of her and strained to see inside. Her face brightened. *I know you*, she was saying. *I know you!* The woman yanked and thrust the buggy parallel to the car door, so she could get closer.

"Matt."

"I didn't have to marry you in," Matt was saying.

She peered into the woman's stroller. It was stuffed with rags and shoes, books and cooking implements, dented cans and half-empty bottles. The detritus of a life. Atop the mouldering heap sat a tiny, bald doll with one arm sticking out of a torn frock. Her sparkling green eyes stared back into the car, unblinking.

Matt spoke softly and mournfully into his open palm. "It could have been Madison. *Matt and Maddy.*"

The woman was at the door. Her croaking, crimson mouth spattered at the window. *Congratulations!* With swaddled fingers she fumbled at the handle.

"Matthew!"

One of the orange vests waved the short string of cars across a temporary roadway and the limo lurched forward, scraping past the woman and her stroller. Matt put a hand on his wife's knee and she exhaled. The latest dose leavened her bloodstream and the city receded. Urban landscapes devoid of schools and toy stores, parks and playgrounds, dissolved from view and memory.

Eight months later, a baby pushed through the tunnel of tight darkness and emerged into the glare of the Klieg lights. The child was passed from doctor to host to be held before the bottomless pool.

"The moment we've all been waiting for. What better way to bring our special two-hour, season finale to a close," the host said, waiting for the crescendo, "please welcome..., Felicity, the newest member of the Family Business!"

As ecstasy engulfed the studio audience, the host brought the trembling infant to her anesthetized mother and lay her gently down. The mother's dilated eyes were damp, her upturned face streaked. Viewers took them for tears of joy.

Laura Dyer

A Poem About Tom

Smokers like him
They make love to their cigarettes
Teasing out the smoke that rises from gathered fingertips
Prolong that first inhale, sigh with satisfaction
Working his way up to the climax,
the final drag and then—release.

He will walk away satiated, his desire fulfilled for now
Leaving only in his wake a breadcrumb trail of cigarettes,
the remains of a one night stand.

Kathleen Moritz

the pressure

i fall
asleep with you sleeping too,
skin growing cold

i sit in the dark
waiting

there are raccoons
searching for what we've left behind
scratching at our plastic
doors

there's a moon
and clouds blending with the background of sky
and smearing like milk into a dark mug of tea
and there's me, wound and unwound
rewound
all of it hidden by trees, unseen but for the pressure
of shadows on shadows on faces

i sit up to look over your shoulder
watching you shine a flashlight
into the glowing eyes
of a lost animal

Joshua Jia

foetal escape

hey there bed and wheelchair
and mother is everything going to be rosy
after i go under your wing
and i eat my spinach and meet
spinachgirls when i grow up and become tall and
bullstrong like Papa i know he does everything
right it breaks my heart to see him
come home

hey there white pills with the boring red
striped down the middle like a
Canadian flag will you with
your human body make the sky beautiful
and never say goodbye
"love-don't-leave-because"

hey there stranger-friends who never saw it happen
i'm thirsty and my throat is parched so i can't tell
you how much i care and don't care but
really i know we've set out far past the playground
on one of those pirate ships we used to make out
of paper

outside the window i see paper houses too
they float together like fish in my old aquarium
the sea is being pummelled by rain
and nostalgic motion
sauna-and-fire sparks
thunderclaps as dry as a
funeral drum

but i'm so clumsy with words
what i'm trying to say momma is
every storm has a rainbow at the end
and if you keep massaging my fading
body and giving me those pills
i would be like an angel

Ruth Buckley

So Good to See John in Kingston

John? John Kelly? Here on Princess St. in Kingston !
Who could ever imagine us meeting here?
Can it be fifty years since me met at Expo '67?
I kept that photo of us at the Moroccan Pavillion.
    ... so good to see you John....

Ah, yes, our tender times at Montreal Expo '67.
Unforgettable, intoxicating days and nights.
Our old gang, all twenty-something, small town kids.
Bringing our big dreams to the big city.
Dazzled by a Montreal so over-electrified
by the smorgasbord of international exotica:
seductive aromas of the Mediterranean spices,
rousing oomph pah-pah music in the German biergartens,
peculiar-sounding languages on the streets,
ancient patterns on Algerian jewellery,
mighty melodies of the Russian Army chorus.
    ... so good to see you John....

And us John, how we idled the hours in the poets' cafe
sipping espressos, scribbling verses.
 Do you still write poetry?
And at the next tables, Rene Levesque, Pierre Trudeau.
Political intrigue. FLQ. Edgy talk on the streets.
    ... so good to see you John....

How bewitched we were by the 'French mystique'.
The 'joie de vivre, la musique' on St. Urbain.
 How we harmonized in the Irish pubs,
your tenor, my alto. Do you still sing?
    ... so good to see you John....

And us, John, dancing under the starry sky.
Our song, "Unforgettable." Our hearts bursting, brittle.
Floating in our blissful purgatory... but
no heaven waiting for us.
    ... so good to see you John....

Me? Widowed now. Two fine children.
And you, John? Life is kind? You've lost your Celine?
Goodness, it's midnight. We've chatted for hours.
The café is closing. I must be going.
 If ever John...you'd like a duet in an Irish Pub.
    ... so good to see you John....

John Pigeau

there was no time
For Erin

there was no
economy of words
when I fell for you

we set the city alight
&
dodged the undertow

Joni Mitchell sang a bridge
&
we crossed it
exchanging histories

cruel tiles laughing
&
you won those games
&
not a thing went wrong
&
we drank & we talked
until the sunrise surprised us
we were holding hands
&
that really meant something

a taxi stole you away
for what seemed an endless
time
then dawn brought joy
&
we worked it out

until i fell into you
&
you fell into me
&
we fell into each other
&
there was no time

John Lazarus

First Day on Queen's Campus

My dad, now years dead, walked on these same paths
when younger than my kids,
sat in these ornate halls, in one of those old stone buildings
hollered for copy at the college news desk,
in perhaps this very quad strode through the snow
wearing a bowler and smoking a rakish pipe,
and posed with two friends, young gentlemen in suits
in front of three urinals in a men's room somewhere here,
and there's the playing field where he clowned in a nightie,
a macho frosh unfazed at being hazed,
in shiny blurred greys on thick glossy paper
in big red leather yearbooks
I leafed through as a kid.
First time I'm here.
Applying to teach where he was a student.
I may be too old.

All around, the nineteenth century
stands in the sun, still serviceable.
Funky imposing bright grey limestone,
old red opaque brick,
grand little government buildings
with domes like the bald heads of aldermen.
I wonder how old the concrete on this dock would be,
how old the ground beneath my feet.
A pair of mallards, loafing near the water,
have clearly been there for centuries.
The pendulum of sun on the Great Lake
is what everything else in the world is as old as.
We are all of us —
me, this place, my father dead,
the sun, the lake and the ancient ducks —
all the same age.

Joann Walton Paterson

Motion

Half an hour north-west of Kingston, Ontario, there's a small country cheese factory set beside a family-owned pottery studio and just up from a feed mill. Many a Saturday morning growing up, Mom would drive the three of us girls the fifteen minutes from our place over to the hamlet of Wilton to pick up fresh curds and to watch the factory workers in the bay below mix milk and whey together in huge steel drums, massive mixers moving the liquid cheese about in currents. We'd press our faces against the glass window in the upper-level cheese shop, leaving nose prints, catching whiffs of warm salt.

For years, the same bosomy woman would take our change and hand us our bag of curds. We'd stroll down the road, lean over the bridge and contemplate the rushing or trickling state of the creek, depending on the season, squeaking the soft cheese pieces between our teeth, rolling them over our tongues, licking out the bag. We would linger long past noon.

The walk through the hamlet would take all of five minutes. A park with tire swings, the cemetery with its ivied memorial to local fallen sons of The Great War, the house with toilets and old cars on the front lawn, images implanting themselves within.

Now, even now, I try to squeeze in quick trips to the cheese factory on short holiday weekends home, ask my mother to bring blocks of mozzarella and cheddar when she visits, request care packages of curds or brie sent to the lost places I find myself in. Even still, I kick myself up, up, up on a tire swing into the blue.

James D. Medd

Night

I have seen two eyes in the dark of night
With a bright majestic glow
An angel's face they do belong
And beckon me to know

Closer they come to reach my side
To offer a gift in hand
Then once it rests, placed in my own
I forthwith understand

And last I gather in my arms
The angel's form to keep
And nestle near as close can be
To fall off fast asleep

Joan Wilding

The Rum-Runner's Daughter

I'm a rum-runner's daughter who works the night shift
When the moon is new and shadows drift
and cloak us.

Penelope:
So Sean taunted you, Pa and sneered you're too old!
And claimed your night runs are over.
He said you'd no stomach and your blood ran cold
And dared you to cross Wolfe Island for gold
On a night when the moon gave no cover.
Then dare him to come on the next trip across.
If he won't, you'll have won with no face lost.

I'm a rum-runner's daughter who in all likelihood
will one night be caught with contraband goods
that condemn us.

Eileen:
Pa, the moon will be full on the night of your run
And you'll see the dare as a game to be won.
Sean was angry and drunk when you beat him at cards.
He's vengeful and wants one of your daughters.
Your laugh when he asked you for Fiona's hand
Still burns like an ember when it is fanned.
With you dead he thinks she'll be won.

I'm a rum-runner's daughter who works well at night
In the dark of the moon like a cat with insight
     and purpose.

Fiona:
Pa, you're known in Kingston as a man of his word
with a zest for adventure and fun.
They love all the stories you tell with a laugh.
They wish you success on the run.
Across water or ice you deliver the rum.
And they say it's no crime to find gold where you can:
Wolfe Isle has harsh climate and no arid land.

I'm a rum-runner's daughter who works for the right
Through all of the seasons in the dark of the night
to feed us.

Monica:
You've nothing to prove, Pa; folks know you're the best.
If you're caught who will dare to speak on your behest?
Which of your daughters will you sacrifice;
Her life worth less than a toss of the dice?
Good men in the past have been hanged for much less
Than crossing dark waters with two muffled oars
Holding one's breath as a light searches shore.

I'm a rum-runner's daughter who knows how to roam
silently through these woods that are home
And that shield us.

Kathleen:
Tonight moon-lit bright we set out on a run.
Don't worry, Kathleen; I've a new route in mind
And I've hidden the boat in a place none will find.
We'll make a quick trip and then we'll be done.
One shot hits its mark. Pa looks surprised; then falters.
Don't you know? I cry out. *He's a man of his word.*
He did this for all his daughters.

I'm a rum-runner's daughter who works the night shift
When the moon is new and shadows drift
And cloak us.

Ashley-Elizabeth Best

Delayed Flight to Dallas

He said he was sick the whole way,
puking into urinals and airplane
garbage bags.
I couldn't imagine him
lolling in soiled ways,
heavy in doubt.
Dallas was too far
baking crisp in a foreign sun.

The shield, my home among
the rocks was wetted, pollen
sticking to deck surfaces and car windows.
The trilliums stayed late this year,
hunkering car-spying in ditches.

I don't know if he thinks of me,
all red knees and honking laugh,
spruce needles in my hair and the
faint musk of moss about my lips

But if he did,
it would be lying in triangle beds of bracken fern,
contemplating lumbering further in
to see muskrat reservoirs and
dugouts, following the sweet-sweet
song of warbling yellow birds home.

Lakeshore Road in Winter
David Woodward

Denise Hamilton

Untitled IV

But innocence is portrayed
In the white between the logs
Of my childhood cabin.
And there it will stay
Each summer a reminder
Of the way it existed
And stood so brave,
Asking far too many questions
And pausing far too seldom.

Outside the lake is a growing
At a rate I could not imagine
It is planning on swallowing us whole
So we can see.
Cause outside it's raining
A different kind of rain
A rain of human teeth, and bloody bed sheets
Of overheard whispers, and rotting timber
Of bills to pay and new ways to say
"I'm sorry"
Of busted knees and listen please
To what I am telling:
That log cabin of mine
Has been around a long time
But I only visit in the summer.

Clara Langley

Of Stars and Sleeves

We were young, that was obvious
By the way you had to roll your sleeve
3 times just to hold my right hand
and by the way I twirled my hair
with the fingers of my left

we swam wearing t-shirts
and danced with the lights off
every night we had long talks over the telephone
where I sat in my kitchen
that always smelt of apple crisp
as you whispered into the bell
that you could see all of the stars falling
just outside your window
I'd always swear I never knew
what that meant

one winter midnight,
we took our talking to the street
and it was colder than I thought it could ever be
but still you rolled up your sleeve 3 times
to button my coat and hold my cheeks
then, the stars began to fall above me

Diane Taylor

Remembrance of Rueben Ash

Rueben Ash of Madoc was first cousin to my mother, Mona Kissack of Tweed. At 20, he joined the Hastings and Prince Edward Regiment and went off, claimed by the maw of war.

One day, Rueben's photograph fell off the piano, and the glass in the frame broke. A few days later, the family got the news that Rueben had been killed on the day his photo fell. That was all I knew. Rueben seemed a mythical character in my mother's mysterious family.

Thanks to a story in the November 15, 2010 issue of the Ottawa Citizen, I learned that Rueben married a 19-year-old English girl who, 68 years after Rueben was killed at the age of 23, went to visit his grave in Italy. She placed a wreath with the message, Have I Told You Lately that I Love You? It was their favourite Eddy Arnold song.

Rueben was one of three brothers who joined the Hastings and Prince Edward Regiment that was composed mostly of farmers and nicknamed the "ploughboys". All three married English women and planned to come back to Madoc to farm.

Squibs Mercier at 86 said her heart is still broken and that that is not unusual, because the death of every soldier leaves many broken hearts. Remembering and keeping alive that love should not lessen the feeling for new loves. Inside her still, she said, is the 19-year-old girl who was very much in love with Rueben, the outgoing, confident, guitar-playing farm boy from Madoc.

Rueben Ash, claimed by a chamber of the human heart, has outlived the war and, in a way, is back amongst us.

Carolyn Hei-Kyoung You

Here

I came here
Looking for You
But not quite knowing it

Unsure you were
Really Here
At all

After chasing after You
In Thought
I collapsed, exhausted
Lay down
My doubt
And also heard
It is the crucible of faith

I followed the herd
And lay down
At his command
Whether charlatan or not
Or somewhere in between
Right and Wrong
In this field I found
my Self

Transported to another plane
On the wings of Breath
I found the place
Behind my eyes

Spacious
Open
Where Possibility dwells

Open your eyes
Is that an autumn leaf falling?
Or a fluttering butterfly?

Gloria Taylor

Remembering

All we have are memories
An unfinished manuscript and a life incomplete

I remember my son's guitar
as I recall the concert attended at St. Denis.
Jeff Healey's Band brings sadness
as I listen to the music years later.

I hear the cacophony
of a family in disharmony.
My tears fall hearing Hugo's Jean Valjean in the last scene...
"Bring Him Home".

Harmony is in my mind
although he is gone.
If music be the soul of life,
play on.

Eriana Marcus

Illuminated Moments
dedicated to Debbie and all the Gentle Folk

choosing the Path

in the school, marble steps, oak doors, polished floors . . .
chains of desk to chair and desk again . . .
between the bells and through order and rules
        she moved like a soft whisper
        like a warm autumn wind
    from a season long ago she came . . .
        and wove a portion of her life
through the days.
young girl.
soft brown eyes like a shy doe looked out
from within the mass of wheat coloured hair.
she wore another woman's harvest;
an old calico dress with large hanging pockets
    that once held fresh picked apples.

Even when, after the day, outside the walls,
 they, the others, would gather, taunt
and throw sticks and stones
    she kept her own grace
walking in shoes that like old leaves knowing
    her feet shuffled softly.

and one day
of the sticks and stones (may break your bones)
but names will never hurt you –
    not true – not true
I chose.

I told them to go away, held out my hand
       and asked if i could walk her home
i knew the risk, and freely chose,
for i would rather be the friend
       of the autumn girl.
hand in hand we silently travelled
she invited me in; inside the old brown brick
one would never guess there was
a stream of automobiles outside.
(for) the dust of the street covered the windows;
giving the room a sepia glow of an old photo; no –
       it was more like a master's painting . . .
for what the room contained.

For . . .there was one piece of furniture,
a rocking chair – and seated there was a woman with
       white hair floating past her waist.
nestled and curled affectionately at her feet was a
small wild version of my new friend;
looking out
at me;
from the long skirts of her nest.

The woman in the veil of white hair said
       "Debbie, go get the teacup"

The Tea Cup.

       like the chair, the only one.
       I was a special guest.

I sat cross legged on the floor
and was brought the teacup adorned
with beautiful old flowers
delivered to my hands carefully
so that the chipped edge
would be opposite my drinking lips.

The Lady in the rocking chair said then to me
"thank you"
i waited
"thank you for being Debbie's friend"
i replied, "Thank You, for having me in your home,
I am happy to be Debbie's friend; -
she is a beautiful girl"

"Yes; she is a beautiful girl"

Debbie returned with an ancient hairbrush,
while sipping my tea,
i watched in silence . . .as delicate and graceful
fingers tenderly picked up strands of white hair,
    drawing the brush through
and she could have been weaving lace;
    or playing a harp,
the strings of white, shimmering
in the golden air of the room.

No one else would see what I did that day
beyond poverty or illness
I sat in a room full of love.

worth more than a palace of royal teacups
A rare grace that i got to be part of for that day
one that lives in a room in my heart . . .
                                    forever.

Munnin comes home
Again

Hugh Walter Barclay

Mentality:
A spoken word piece.

The poet begins by waving arms stomping feet swearing cursing with incoherent speech. Then the poet faces the audience to begin by pointing at various members of the audience and asking the following questions.

So, ain't you seen nobody who's crazy before?
And you there, I know it must be tough to be gay.
You there! Rich lady,
you just want to pay someone to keep me out of your face.
Awe pretty girl, you must have a tough life,
remember the day you wore the wrong colour shoes?

The poet leans over as if to pet a small dog and continues.

It's OK puppy, it's OK I won't hurt nobody.
Yes! Yes! I will tell them that, don't worry none.
You there! Doc, what are you doin' to help me, pushing some new pill,
givin' me a shot in the ass, making money on each visit?
You don't want to see a cure.
You don't think a cure is possible,
So what use are you to me?

The poet leans over again to pet the dog.

It's OK puppy, it's OK, we don't need these bastards anyway.

Jan Allen

On the Bus to Toronto in April

The young couple across the aisle is in the form of love
        inscribed by the Y of a shared iPod.
A chocolate bunny leans against the
        splattered window beside them,
its head an open volute, a tattered flower of gold foil
paper trembling before the passing landscape,
suspended stretches of damp brown field.

She strokes his forearm hard with her fingertip
        ruffling fine hairs against
the grain, feeling the ripple of muscle over bone,
the fine, fine slip of skin over bone that is him,
indifferent to the long jolting ride
and the sodden press of sun
        across their shoulders.

Eric Folsom

January Eighth on the 401

Animated weather map, lumbering pastel prediction,
Can you hear an animal sound, a steady lull of water trilling?

Mercy falls like rain, Satan like sheet lightning, and sleet
Sleets like sleet, in layers of single-celled creatures.

The wind backs around the compass, curls in corners;
Makes me wonder is something living under the porch.

Those are pearls that silt the ditches, ice pellets lit by glare;
After twelve hours, I still see the highway when I close my eyes.

I dropped him safely at the airport and turned around,
Mission of Burma too loud, blue lights flashing beyond the hill

Remember when our hearts were young and unintentional,
Doing doughnuts on black ice on the old Stagecoach Road?

Jennie McCaugherty

Cracked Lips

Wake to cracked lips,
Brought to you by the suns reflection off cold hot pavement
Resting under trees as they come
But how often do they come
Cut down by the hands of greed
Every ten blocks they planted a new seed
Breathe the city air no longer cleansed by nature
Now pushed through gas and oil and placed in your lungs to rot
Taste it in your mouth
On my skin

My steps hit her forcefully in the hardness of brick and asphalt
Getting where i am going
Not really being where i am
So i stop and sit
I run my fingers through the grass and then here i am again
Present in my life
No longer stepping in the direction of next time or almost there
I am there in this moment sharing my breath
With the birds that are there
And the trees whom are always there
And the man who is never there
And the child fighting to stay there
Because he knows in his childish wisdom that where he is
Is where we all need to be

But he is pushed into "remember the time, don't do that"
And what about the future
Ever distancing him from himself, from now
It will fade until life is a distant memory
Slightly out of focus
Obstructed by
Should have's
What if's
Pains that seem to linger
All that seems to hinder

Walking towards the future
Ignoring right now
Walking past the pain in the eyes of
People we love
People we cherish
People we cling to
So in tune with the incessant chatter in our heads
This isn't life at all, it is death before dying
But not in that thought out, let go of, good old Buddhist way
But in a we forgot what our hearts are for,
We forgot what we are here for sort of way
Stretch your fingers through the grass
Into the sand
Beneath the water
Drop your cell phones
Turn off your laptops
And your blue tooth
And open your fucking eyes before your waking dream really dies

David Sheffield

port hope boy

you notice a big funeral in a small town
parking lots full, cars parked along the street
the line-up to the casket extended out the door

his sister wept
he was somebody's baby brother
his mother wept
he was somebody's baby

people said things like
understandable, inevitable, a better place,
peace, rest in peace, relief

at this funeral it's hard for a small town to hide its ragged edges
those edges that are part of its own fabric

the woman who couldn't come sober
who came because she knew if she didn't,
she would regret it

the man who borrowed a shirt and wept bitterly,
"this is bullshit" he said, "he was too young"
knowing that he would have to endure the rest of this night,
his own birthday, without his friend since grade six
the poverty of lost companionship
the terror of alone

those who could speak, told of a man
generous to a fault
who offered sanctuary to stray cat people
who worked hard
who tried hard
to quiet the voices in his head, but it was that trying,
in the end, that took him
that finally silenced the voices

Christine Miscione

Jar-cracks-are-not-sane

The white of winter. The glass of your eyes, your lips, the petticoat of your brain in a jar. And Velveteen. Velveteen furbelows & endless crinoline. His chin trembles. Our lips touch. Hands pulling hair like those who came before. The lovers I once had, all the ones who had me. All the feelings of love, the lightness, elation, luminescence, the comedown. Its sugar, its heaps of spice swelling veins. And everything—all of it—in a jar.

My mom kisses it better. She uses profanity to get her point across. Her hair on my head while I'm brushing it. The thickness of her. Then my father, timorous in the background. Quiet & contemplative with no hair to brush. I keep his curiosity in every flicker of my eye-lid, but we never see the same. My feebleness, my switches, my mistakes. I hate that everything I see is rotting in a jar. Wilting frills. Lace rusting and vacuous. And everything under me & clothing me, everything about me hates: words, rhythm, flow. A disease, this drying up everything inside me to petty fabrics. But I've desiccated; I've kissed and told every morning with green tea and an egg. And now it's gone. And now I hate it because I need it. My incurable psychosis. Necrosis of my fingertips typing, my eyeballs seeing. I am the Sunday bus that runs only once an hour. I am scabrous, a dirty bathroom, a mangled hard-drive. I'm difficult to live with. Messy and volatile. I'm me after I have no muse left.

Joanne Light

Pebble

Mom is washing away,
a pebble slipping,
unhinged from the shore;
one of these waves will take her out.

Yet she hangs on.

>I know she's scared, angry
>as a diminishing dot.
>Her worn mountain heart
>clinging to its birth in love
>when it was tall and young
>with its fire and deep tree roots
>   entering.

Wedged in a deep crevice
water refines her further—smooth
for smooth water ahead.

It might take a rogue one
to pull her free.

Her?

I'm the one hanging on.

Honey Novick

Pontypool – Land of Reflections
Kawartha – Anishinaabe: "Ka-wa-tae-gum-maug" - land of reflections

"Pontypool", a Welsh name bestowed upon Kawartha* land,
once populated solely by Anishinaabe people.

Looking through the back window of my memory,
I see an oasis, a place for adventure, acceptance.

A benevolent businessman rented land
to a group of people, Jews, looking to relax, play,
speak the "mameloshn" mother-tongue.

Wood cabins surrounded a cool, welcoming pond,
respite from a week of labouring to earn money.

Today the pond is dust, existing only
in memory, experiences of long ago.

The name, Pontypool, however, is alive.
Even though today it is a wonderful little town,
the name evokes those days of youth, of being young at heart.

Families would rise before the sun,
meet up, fill cars with food, towels, lotion and
drive eastward from Toronto.

In my childhood-mind, it took sooooooo long to get there.

Today it is easily done, there and back.

Fathers left their families on Sunday evening,
an exodus,
returning to the city, then back again Friday evening.

This was the 1950's post World War II Ontario,

still shadowed by McCarthyism
and haunted by Nazism, and in this place
such topics were never discussed in front of the children.

However, while adults busied themselves playing cards,
sun-bathing, "match-making" or planning social activities,
a precocious child could catch snippets of conversations,
as sly looks found expression in several covert languages.

Sixty or so years after the heyday of Pontypool, The Resort,
children and grandchildren of these appreciative Jewish immigrants
gathered at the Manvers Historical Society
to tell tales, remember old friends, express gratitude.

Going back in time, into History, to this time
is a rare occurrence and a privilege given to some.
I am one of the few left given this gift.

These aren't always uplifting pleasant memories,
but, always, significant and important.

John Pigeau

the end of traffic

my head is in a gauzy haze
like i'm hung over or dreaming
in a cloud over the parking lot.
the power has come back on
& i've been thinking how when you died
your mouth was open
& mom & I were watching
a show on the cbc
about a family in the country
who had adopted a deer
& the deer got along wondrously
with the family cat.
it was enough to make you cry,
but then there was a noise missing
like a fan no longer whirring
or the end of traffic,
& i got up & went closer to you
& looked at your twisted mouth
still open, the pale skin on your cheeks
& hands sliding off your bones,
& i said quietly to mom,
"i think she's gone."
& you were.

i recall thinking, as i fetched a doctor
in the hallway, i should hug mom
for she was crying without noise,
standing above you now—
she'd lost her best friend.
she would stop breathing herself
in disbelief, in thinking how could
life have ever been real?
my mother is gone, who will i
talk to now four times a day
on the phone? who will i talk
about because there's nothing else
to talk about & you are my only
friend, besides?
though how could i know
what mom was thinking
she might have been wondering
who in the hell her father was
(a norwegian soldier on leave)
& what had become of him
& what had he looked like,
or lord knows, maybe she was thinking
of all the motels you & she lived in
& all the jobs you worked to feed
the two of you & buy her dolls
or all of all the stray cats she dragged home
after school & you let her keep
if she promised to faithfully get them milk
from the corner store.

meantime, i should have been hyperventilating,
seeing black & white specks in the air,
feeling unreal,
& plunging down seven floors in a vacuum,
but i was standing & breathing just fine
& talking to
a young doctor:
"i think my grandmother just died,"
i said in the same tone i might use to tell
a store clerk i thought they might
be out of bread,
& then my sister was there
& she began to cry immediately
& she said a prayer over you
i could tell,
& then laughed like she was trying
& said, "still with your mouth open"—
& soon after another hospital person
was talking to mom
about funeral arrangements,
& then when there was nothing left
to do but pray & wipe our noses &
pack up all our blankets
& drinks & magazines,
we all headed downstairs
to our separate vehicles
in the eerily quiet morning
like the show was over
& our ears were ringing,
& we'd spent all we had.

Kathryn MacDonald

Abandoned

Curled in the large rocker I watch
as flames waver before rising
in a chaos of yellows and oranges
and burnt sienna, even blue
creating propulsive jazz rhythms
in the stove's black belly

and my mind slips away from this evening
remembering how you taught the art
of woodstove fire-making
placing the paper and kindling just so
and crowning them with logs split small
another day, weeks before the match strikes

filling the air with sulphur.
I lean back against the Morris rungs
drift into reverie, the place not here nor there
where neither body nor mind control
where the little girl inside resides
silent, curious, watchful.

Within, a word rises like the flames
consuming soul like fire wood
and my body quivers then shakes
in the dance of emotion
until exhausted and spent
I huddle among love's ashes.

Lara Szabo Greisman

Anthem

Hear me listen then I'll whisper my hope.
It will happen and has happened before.
It will dawn like progress
Over each new impossible as we discover it's face.
We shine dreams like lanterns
until the lights come on,
Then squint to see empty paper skeletons held up to the sun.

One day all our work and our hurting
All the stands that we make and the shit we won't take
Will be sweet normal freedoms, will need no long reasons.
They'll be victories, legacies, laughter: we won.

The work day has never been 9 to 5 or dawn till dusk,
It has never had sick days or off days or compensation pay.
It's always been stubborn dreamers who forget how to sleep
It's about the dream that leads the way to our faith's giant leap

One day all our work and hurting
All the stands that we make and the shit we won't take
Will be sweet normal freedoms. Will need no long reasons.
They'll be victories, legacies, laughter: we won.

To those who came before, and before the before,
And before they knew we would honour your names:
We are standing on your freedoms.
We can sing because you dreamed of a song. A song.

One day all our work and hurting
All the stands that we make and the shit we won't take
Will be sweet normal freedoms. Will need no long reasons.
They'll be victories, legacies, laughter: we won.

Lee-Ann Taras

The Last Wave

The last time that I saw you
You had embarked on a solitary journey
Behind your eyes, you were stepping over slippery stones
Squeezing through narrow passages,
Trying to navigate in the dark
But mostly, you were picking at old rusty locks
You came upon door after door
All of them closed
The only words left in your mind were
"Open", "free", "go"
I knew you were already away then
And there was no wink that you gave that said, "I'll be back"

Your thin, cool fingers had already begun to fly,
Scissoring in and out, expanding to form bird shapes
Flying up and away
These were your wings
This was your wordless wish
And in the silence of the room, the three of us understood

They say if we live long enough
Or the body is sick enough
We return to much like how we began
A fragile baby self
Seeking only comfort and sleep
I remembered this as I reached out and cradled your head
Smooth as a polished bird's egg
The child rocking the old man who held the father

I could never have touched you like this before,
It would have embarrassed both of us
But at that moment, it was the only form of contact left
I was no longer daughter or even stranger,
I had become, briefly, solace it self,
A vaguely human thread of connection
That your infant mind held loosely in its grasp
Your other hand coiled tight into a fist bunched up by your ear
Just like a baby sleeping

Out of this murky falling away
Of roles and time and years
There was the quiet but steady pulse of the ties of blood
And love

It was time to go
I said goodbye to the ghost in the chair
Your eyes told me again that you were walking in far away lands
And you did not notice my departure
I started to pass through the doorway from your room for the very last time
Suddenly a pull in my belly made me look back
The old man holding my father in the chair
Allowed him to awaken, but only for a moment

I recognized you then
You were there behind your eyes for a brief glimpse
Your arm reached up, out and back again
It was the last wave
And it was your last gift to me

Kelly Rose Pflug-Back

Wolf Suit

What a graveyard this room has tilted into;
an overflowing necropolis of the shed husks of things.
Little decapitated bodies of sparrows scattered everywhere,
like rice after a wedding.

When I play my harp
strange pale-skinned eyeless things emerge from under the double bed,
recoiling again from the brightness of my eyes
which have begun to repel the light like new quarters.

Soon I will lie
awake and blinking in the ground,
sedated by the pressure of tree roots.
When I come to people in dreams
I will be much taller than usual,
stooping under door frames.
I'm not really sure why.
I understand this is the natural progression of things:
we all become ash-gray eventually,
terrified of falling asleep facing the closet door.

On Sundays I limp into town wearing my wolf suit.
I will never touch the only dress in my closet;
it's fabric is cheap and white,
the sleeves made of a silvery substance as thin as cobwebs.
Some time a few years ago
I began to suspect it was meant to be a child's Halloween costume,
although I still tell visitors that it's a dress.
I offer them a look at it instead of something to eat.
There is no food in the house;
my organs were replaced years ago by neat contraptions
built of stained glass
and half-full of coloured liquid
with little wheels moved by tarnished brass gears,
like wind-up toys.

There are days I still look for my bloody, anatomical heart—
it isn't wrapped in grease-stained butcher's paper in the freezer
or drawn around someone's initials
on the wall of a public bathroom.
It isn't on a chain around the neck of one of the girls I see in town
or anywhere else I can think of.

On Mondays I pick up my wolf suit off the floor.
I hang it in the closet and bide my time
picking at the rusty nails in my ankle
as I wait for it and the dress to reach for each other in the dark.

These floorboards are veined with tiny colonies of insects:
I know that soon my bones will be static,
wrapped in the soft bodies of earthworms.
My own trials will be imprinted into the wood-grain of this house
for idle children to watch, in repetition,
while I survey them from gaps between floorboards
with my pink eyes.

Laurie Lewis

Sometimes a Dead Poet

sometimes a dead poet
speaks to me
some rage or melancholy
touches the mute numbness
of my evening
reading alone after dinner
the words of the dead

tonight it's Raymond Carver
long gone 20 years dead

I'm ready to fall in love again
here in my Chardonnay night

but him? american bad boy?
      been there
      done that
      the blues
      the booze
loved that once already
and look where it got me

reading alone after dinner
the words of the dead

Joshua Jia

city memories

she breathes the light fall and it's the empty
silicone that funnels all these wires from my hips
until the tornado is a blossoming
cup of fruit

we turn over the sheets and i put on the suit
and something is playing on the tv although
i can't quite tell what

the car stops and out comes the
hustle and bustle
where is my brother and sister
are they the skyscrapers leading me
to nowhere

have not slept and
there is the Toronto Stock Exchange
and construction over my head
making me pillows and blankets
for me to warm my fears

when i take the cash in
my hands

i see the man i hate

i am a child in a suit
and next thing you
know i am making death
threats

to everybody i miss

there is a light fog that hangs
in my closet
there is a warm breeze that
dusts my hair every morning
there is the past and the cold souls
we've killed and un-killed
only to remember to forget
they are not even alive in our words
when we finally read them in our sleep

Gina Hanlon

wood
for a.

the Indonesian woman sat in the house
and they teased

your foot is pointing at me
and where to put it?

you are eating with your left hand
you are slipping

there is the groom. the tent with the poles
a handful of confetti

he glared at me turning
and shook it out of his hair

he called for several years
on my birthday and christmas

the last card got no response

now there are ten wands in the house after that
the multiplication of wood

Carole TenBrink

Great Horned Owl

She glanced up from her work and looked out the window toward the ancient Maple that towered like a mammoth stalk of broccoli spreading into brilliant fall sky. In the crook of the trunk, where it split into three, her eyes locked onto the likeness of an owl. She could clearly see the mottled grey-brown shape within the light and shadow ripples of gnarled bark.

Amazing, she thought. How did I never notice this shape before? Every time she glanced up toward her view of Lake Ontario, her eyes glued instead on this mysterious shape. Owl pull, child self delight, and adult task focus tussled for several rounds. Then, a moment arrived when her glance caught the feathers fluttering in the wind.

She leapt up and ran for the door. "It's a real owl", she called out loud to the morning air of her kitchen. Child self flew outside and beheld the owl, large, regal and still as a stone. The woman stood respectfully about twenty feet away. All of nature, up to the top of the sky, came to a halt before this magnificence. Transfixed, her eyes stared into this eternal moment. Owl rotated his head toward her; his golden eyes pierced her green eyes, and dug deep into the magma of her core; something primeval stirred; wild ringing began to reverberate inside her body.

She marveled at how the owl's camouflage had fooled her..... and how, in spite of his nocturnal habit, the owl was here, past midmorning.

She could smell wild fall wind off the lake. It tousled the owl's breast feathers into a shimmer and tickled its frigid fingers under the woman's loose shirt, raising goose bumps. She shivered, but stood fast, unwilling to miss a second of the owl's visit.

It's a Great Horned for sure she registered, even in her mesmerized state. He has two tufts of feathers on top of his head, like cat ears. As far back as early childhood, the Great Horned owl's Hooo   Hoooooo   Hooo   Hooo had rung in her ears, always calling her to this dark place within herself. And now, at last, here he was, enthroned before her, inviting her admiration.

When her shivers became uncontrollable, the woman dashed inside, threw on a jacket and tossed the binoculars strap around her neck. She wanted to see close-up, yet maintain a respectful distance. Back outside, she smiled. The owl was still there. Holding her breath in excitement, she raised the binoculars, anticipating what she would see next.

NOTHING. The crook of the tree trunk was empty. No owl. No owl image in bark. No sound to indicate takeoff. The woman whirled around immediately to scan the tree canopy, the whole expanse of sky, eyes darting up and down, back and forth, around and around. No sign.

Nothing. In disbelief, she regarded an emptiness of air. How could a creature disappear in a flash like that, in the split second it had taken her to raise the binoculars up to her eyes? Yes, she remembered, silent flight. The fringe feathers at the front of his wings bestow the power to come and go with not a flutter of sound.

Silent, yes, but not invisible. How could this bird just evaporate, dematerialize? Gone. Visitation over. The woman felt betrayed. The owl had first appeared with such convincing camouflage that she had believed him imaginary. Then, once she'd been taken into his reality, he vanished. She sighed, felt lost.

Nothing to do but go back inside to read about the Great Horned Owl. As she sat there, with the green Audubon bird book resting on her lap, truth dawned. That was the point. Here and gone. The Great Horned had left something stunning of himself in her. The conviction of those golden eyes said so. Staring at the picture, she blinked and blinked, as if she too had nictitating membranes to wash her vision clear and pure. Unbidden, these words came to her....

Claim kinship.
Owl's eye   Deep Well   Womb   Wisdom
Look into your well
Owl eyes   Your eyes   Well of wisdom
Look   Look down inside
Deep   Women's   Womb   Wisdom

~ ~ ~

Winter passed. Mid – March arrived. The sap began to run. Some days the snow began to melt. Near Spring Equinox, the woman and her friend took a walk at the shore to soak up some early spring energy.

From up ahead, she heard her friend call, "I found something."

The instant the woman looked up, she knew. Her friend held the Great Horned Owl. His head wobbled. "Is he alive?" she asked, hoping against hope.

She came close, felt the body. Of course, the owl was dead. They lay him down between them. He was so light. Yes, they whispered, the bones of Great Horneds are hollow. In silence, they brushed their fingertips all over him, felt his silkiness. How else to pay homage to this perfect body that still held its clean wild smell. Her friend murmured, " He was half buried in snow… but can't have been dead more than a day or so". His breast feathers still fluffed out in intricate filigree pattern that the woman remembered from last fall. They stretched out the long wings to admire their strength and length… each one, three-fourths as long as a woman's arm. They fingered the massive talons, sharp beak and elegant tail feathers. They walked back slowly from the shore and sealed the owl in a box in the woman's outdoor shed for the sub zero night time.

Next morning, she went out to smell his fresh, wild smell one last time, to unfurl his wings one last time. She had to decide…. What to do with the body? Could she try to get him to a museum or something? Or should she bury him in a marked grave?

A neighbor came by and said that within the last week, he'd seen the owl standing in her front yard under the old Maple tree. Maybe to visit me again, the woman thought. She felt, somehow, this owl had given himself to her. She wanted to honour that, to remember, to preserve a totem of his presence in her life. When she got the owl back from the taxidermist, he told her two important things: this owl is female and she had a broken wing.

Suddenly several things fell into place. This she-owl couldn't fly! She never flew away that day last fall. She slipped into the big hollow of the old maple tree. She must have lived there all winter, scavenging bits of food from the ground, and that's what she must have been doing the day a neighbor saw her. Spring fever must have gotten hold of this injured bird, so that one day she somehow made her way to the shore. Was it the desperation of hunger, or desire for one last adventure that drove her?

The woman felt a pang of guilt.... If only she had known last fall that her she-owl was hungry. But, if she'd been fed and taken to a vet, then what... Anyway, it's not what happened. The woman had no way of knowing her owl was hurt.

~ ~ ~

With the owl-totem perched on her desk, everything came to silence again. The woman sat for a long while at the window, looking out toward the old Maple where her owl had first appeared and then back to the presence before her. This owl had stayed with her all winter; for five months had known her comings and goings. This thought moved the woman to tears and into meditation. The pattern of breast feathers was more beautiful than remembered; it's like intricate lace. But delicacy is only a camouflage, for a Great Horned Owl is also fierce. With the stealth of silent flight, keen vision and deadly talons and beak, she's able to see a small prey from a great height, then swoop down and capture it totally unawares. This owl had such absolute presence, the woman thought, shown in that way she had rotated her head, fixed her golden eyes on me and stared hard, unrelentingly.

With her penetrating night vision, an owl can discern precise detail in the pitch dark. ...sort of the way, I sometimes intuit what others don't see, the woman thought. She heard again that penetrating voice from childhood. Hooo Hoooooo Hooo Hooo, and again it roused a primal energy within her. Just the sound of a Great Horned Owl out there in the night gave her dreams. She mused how those mysterious lightning truths pierce a night's sleep and suggest deep consciousness rising up. Would humans ever learn to seize this inner cosmos with its power to make us wise? She wondered.

She thought about this owl's prowess. Even with her broken wing, who could ever say she was any less than her whole pristine self.   Her beingness, even in death, commanded respect. The woman heard herself say out loud   "May I know such self assurance; may I stand thus in my indelible being….   And be worthy of this owl totem's presence." Again, the words came….

Claim kinship.
Owl's eye   Deep Well   Womb   Wisdom
Look into your well
Owl eyes   Your eyes   Well of wisdom
Look   Look down inside
Deep   Women's   Womb   Wisdom

Carla Hartsfield

The Blue Church, Prescott, 1933

Champion of misdirection,
I take my cue from Prudence Heward's abstraction,
draw in every stone-grey tone she left behind.

Her church and supporting landscape
project deep asthmatic hues. I cannot breathe;
neither could she. At fifty-one,

Prudence sought treatment in California,
leaving her ghost to squeeze out
desperate hollows like paint from a tube.

The Blue Church is so small and huge,
a Georgia O'Keeffe comes hacking into consciousness.
When I leave the McMichael Collection,

her pressed-out, pressed-down strokes
of cautionless air
press sweet stone clouds above

the minds of undiscovered genius.
Artists love her when she shows herself.
Will her artistic soul reincarnate?

Her paintings languish in storage rooms.
Like that childhood game,
here is the church, here is the steeple,

open the vaults and see all the people—
voyeurs, step in,
join Prudence at her easel.

Gary William Rasberry

Black-letter Stammer

For a 1948 Underwood typewriter that lives in the forest.
Word machine. Black metal creature. Beautiful monster ...

Twenty-two frogs are making love in the south swamp
I swear it's true. Yes, I swear it's true as metaphor

for moonlight or black as the paddle's dip into
midnight where there's no need for push or pull.

Twenty-two frogs are making love, I swear
and the south swamp is a metaphor for directions lost.

Twenty-two frogs and the metaphor is love
making itself known. Love making itself.

Love-making, where there's no need for metaphor
no need for moonlight. Love, where there's no need.

The words are songs. The songs are poems
and the poems are type-written. Type-written and

dead afraid of these metal signposts that point to
where I am not. Type-written memos complete

with cryptic references and existential font. Maybe to be lost
first would suggest a way out instead of worrying

about where the keys are on this heavy metal
acoustic typewriter. Here, the words are type-written

and dead afraid. Dead afraid.
(But never better off dead than afraid.)

A confusion of night with sound
otherwise the gift is completely realized.

A confusion of night with sound when metal strikes a chord
to pattern the owl. It's like a locomotive waking up

the forest. Metal-on-metal: a black-letter'd stammer
hammering the night colourless.

A confusion of sound with night
otherwise the realization is completely a gift.

Afraid of adjusting the ribbon. Touch without touching until
everyone guesses a winner—under the B: bullfrog. black.
blackness.

Earth   Stone   Naked jewellery
Tab-keyed night noises. The odd carriage return.

Tab tab tab. The odd carriage
return.

Dark and darker still, words move downhill to fall below
sunset which has already kissed so many

full and hard and fleeting.
Red and orange stains that remember dying

and a locomotive waking up the forest.
Metal-on-metal: a black-letter'd stammer.

Hammering the night colourless.
Colouring the night hammerless—imagine

being so awake in the forgetting.
I swear it's all true. I swear it's all

true. Especially when there's nothing but
Metal-on-metal, metal-on-metal

metal-on-metal, metal-on-metal-on
metal-on-metalonmetalonmetal …

Could there be more than twenty-two?

Diane Taylor

Sonless

Death, my friend,
You have wombed me
In your still and foetal seas
During countless sonless tides.
But my time has come.
I can feel you pushing,
Your bones are giving way.
I must now summon the strength
To emerge from your tight tunnel
Into the world again.
Adieu, my friend.
The slight light of dawn awaits.

Joanne Light

Peace

After,
I felt stars, like lasers, burning,
sprinkled over me in bed.
God shook out his blanket of them so I could sleep.
I fell in their pieces and dreamt.

I woke up, jumped on my bike and saw Mars ablaze.
Aurora in Campbellton quivered
in the skin sky after war entered me.
I was in pieces then.
I had no prayers to say.
The prayers came later when Mars left Venus
and God came back.

I am peppered with Him now,
fear of Gaia's blanket on fire subsides;
memory of the thunder's wound on ears
no longer in the night room.

The stranger, present, watches and is known.
The dream players are one in me
under a quilt still and warm as a star is poet food,
home forever in my galactic solitude.

Kathleen Moritz

in the city

in the city i chew
sour candies as i drive:
pink-and-yellow,
bumpy with crystallized sugar
so sour they sting my whole tongue
and the sides of my cheeks

in the city i listen to music
with my clutch foot tapping,
popping these candies between my lips.
the shock of them, the burning as i chew,
a shiver down my teeth.
my body can't feel anything else.
after i swallow it takes a few minutes
for the aftertaste to turn sweet

everything in this city is exhaust
and slicked windows.
i pretend to see through them
to fingers tapping on steering wheels
and phrases absently sung with the radio
and all of us nodding our heads as we wait
our turn to go

maybe when the light went green
the moment of hesitation between stopped
and going was from the woman
with the cup still in her hand,
her lips shined and wet from the coffee
that burned her tongue bright.

Kathryn MacDonald

Ashes

Three decades of our signatures
flame as I toss invoices and cheques
into the fire consuming '70s, '80s, '90s
and as I read letterhead and payee names
memories flood of houses purchased
and sold, of farm and home expenses.

Heat rises burning my breath
as I sort and toss, sort and toss
the innocent years into golden flames
the days and nights of passion
for the life we were building
the dreams placed in motion.

Flame engulfs the other side
of your pain, of my grief
reminding me of laughter
as our children grew
brought partners home
then the special joy of grandchildren.

Your beautiful signature burns
but I rescue a few "love ya"
scribbled across envelopes
echoes of what death took
reminders of what is forever lost
as tears smudge smoky cheeks.

The paper trail of three decades
lies blackened as I stir smouldering cinders
momentarily resurrecting glow
but soon all lies dark and cold
within the metal barrel
and my shoulders slump with the weight of ashes.

Kirsteen MacLeod

Sambaqui

It's easy to imagine the feasts
of the Tupi Guarani—
bones of shark and monkey,
oyster shells piled high,
a mountain of hulled, open hearts,
old hungers satisfied.
Samba was "shell"; *qui* was "to sleep"
and where shells sleep was also their tomb—
femurs jut from the sandy midden,
time exposed in layers that speak
in the eloquent language of bones
not of what decays—
but of what endures.
It's hard to imagine my sambaqui
with flesh still on my frame.
Perhaps a hill of mango pits, for desire,
my stone idol, a dog, for devotion,
the pearl ring from my husband, for love.

My bleached skeleton, arrowheads lodged
where my beating heart used to be.

Leanne Betasamosake Simpson

Jiibay or Aandizooke?

All along the north shore of Pimaadashkodeyong
(you might call it Rice Lake)
All along the shores of Pimaadashkodeyong
are those Burial Mounds.
Gore Landing, Roaches Point, Sugar Island,
Cameron's Point, Hastings, Le Vesconte.
Big Mounds. Ancient Mounds.
Mounds
that cradle the bones
of the ones that came before us.

This summer
This summer some settlers
Who live right on the top of that burial mound in Hastings,
Right On Top
Were excavating,
Renovating
Back hoeing
New deck. New patio. New view.

"Please pass the salsa".

This summer some settlers
Who live right on the top of that burial mound in Hastings,
Right On Top
Were excavating,
Renovating
Back hoeing
New deck. New patio. New view.
and they found a skull.

Call 911
There's a skull
Call 911
There's more
Call 911
Jiibay.

Breath.
We're supposed to be on the lake.
Breath
We're supposed to be
Gently Knocking
And
Gently Parching
And
Gently Dancing
And
gently winnowing.

Breath.
We are
Not
Suppose to be
Standing
On
This desecrated mound
Looking
Not looking
Looking
Not looking
Looking
Not looking
Looking
Not looking

Did I see that right?
My skull is in a card board box
in that basement?
My bones are under
An orange tarp from Canadian Tire,
Cracked.
Rattling plastic in the wind.

my grave is desecrated
my skull is in that white lady's basement
my bones are under that orange tarp from Canadian Tire
cracked
rattling plastic in the wind like a rake on the sidewalk.

my body is tired
from carrying
the weight
of this zhaaganashi's house.

Ah Nokomis
This shouldn't have happened.
You're relatives took such good care.
The mound so clearly marked.
Ah Nokomis
How did this happen?
What have you come to tell us?
Why are you here?

Aahhhhh my Zhaganashi
Welcome to Kina Gchi Nishnaabe-ogaming
Enjoy your visit.
But like my Elder says
Please don't stay too long.

From Nishnaabemowin —
Jiibay: a skeleton,
Aandizooke: a being from a sacred story,
Nokomis: Gandmother,
Zhaaganashi: white person ,
Kina Gchi Nishnaabe-ogaming: the big place where we all live and work together – the Mississauga Nishnaabeg name for our territory,
Pimaadashkodeyong is our name for Rice Lake according to Elder Doug Williams, Curve Lake First Nation.

Norma Chakrabarty

Mountain View

Stalled plane
Plunges down
Weighted heavily

With earth-bound men
Lives just beginning
Violently snuffed out
By cruel gravity
Strong metal folding

Two young men
Become lifeless bodies
While a friend
Watches horrifically mesmered
Helplessly waiting for
the siren's termination

A captive viewer
Whose pilot's ambition
Burns in the wreckage
With the incomplete
Futures of epitaphed names

Mourning phone calls
Reliving the pain
Of etched moments
Searching for my shoulder

I hear the
Honest turmoil of
Human emotions unguarded
By walls

Comforting the living
For a loss
That I myself
Connect only with
Stories of broken
Chairs at parties

Though I listen
Sympathetically

My mind wanders
To a quiet cabin
At the edge
Of a lake
In
Solitude

Ruth Clarke

With This Ring

An old wedding ring used to surface occasionally in my jewellery box, flotsam in a sea of trinkets and treasures. It held no romantic or sentimental value for me, I had no further use for the old thing, but for the longest time I was reluctant to let it go. It had been an effective adornment, making its statement: married.

My roommate Katie Baxter had found the gold band under a window in a bedroom she was cleaning when she worked part-time as a char at the Ganaraska Hotel on the river of the same name. When Katie first found the ring, she'd left it at the hotel's front desk, but no one had ever claimed it. A year later, the manager had given it to Katie as inspiration for her and Jeff to get married. Katie had never worn it and tossed it in one of her jewellery boxes.

We used to speculate on its origins: How had this symbol – celebrating a union of love, the circle unbroken, been discarded? Perhaps it had been a symbolic gesture: one of the punctuation marks in an evening of passion, flung in abandon during torrid lovemaking? Or perhaps the verb– to fling –was used as a noun in this tryst and the ring had been a prop to get past reception at the hotel. But we were probably too romantic; maybe the only motivation behind the ring's location on the floor was an accident of gravity: it had fallen off the bureau and rolled across the room.

Part of this ring's subsequent history spans ten years on several continents when two women wore it at different times. However, we wore it while we were single, needing to give the impression that we were married.

Katie and I both loved baubles, and shared our earrings and bracelets, so we draped them on plates and in bowls on the bathroom counter where we could both have access. One morning we were both in the bathroom at the same time. I was packing toiletries for Mexico, and trying to disentangle some beads from earrings, when the wedding band clattered across the counter and bounced to the floor, to rest at Katie's feet.

"That might come in handy on your trip," she said, handing it to me. "It's yours. An amulet to ward off preying men: When they see the ring, they are alerted that another man exists in the picture. At least, that's the first place men here look." I agreed and accepted the gift.

Single women travellers always face approaches by men merely because they're easy targets. Alone. Some women enjoy this kind of attention but I wasn't one of them, and I've had my share of uncomfortable incidents. Times when I'd wanted nothing more than to eat a meal at my leisure, to sip a glass of wine, to read a book, but I'd been interrupted, asked if I wanted company. Made to give some explanation, to account for myself, or compose an excuse. My aloneness seemed to be read as a Welcome sign; young men followed me on the street, wanting to practise their English. I started wearing my Walkman, sometimes not even turned on.

On that trip I'd worn the wedding ring with a strip of adhesive wrapped around the back of it, so it would fit on the third finger of my right hand. Its presence affected an immediate and dramatic change: I felt like I had more room around me; I was able to remove my Walkman and raise my eyes to admire the decor inside restaurants. With that freedom, the ring became a staple accessory in my life for many years whenever I left the country.

Then it retired to my jewellery box for several years, redundant in my life because I was married and wore my own ring. The slim, pale gold band idled in the darkness of my jewellery case until eight years ago when Phyllis, a colleague, was going to a remote region in Zambia for a year to work as an ESL teacher. A few months before she was to leave, her boyfriend, a Swede with whom she'd gone to university had asked her to marry him. They would marry when she returned from Africa, and when he'd finished his doctorate. She had announced her happy news one morning at the office, flashing her left hand before my eyes.

"I can only enjoy wearing it here in Canada for the next three months though," she sighed, fondling the ring. She wasn't going to take the diamond with her to Africa for fear of losing it, or of having it stolen. I offered the wedding ring as a replacement. As soon as she got it, she put it on the third finger of her right hand, the wedding ring finger in Africa.

Two years later, when I'd all but forgotten about Phyllis, a small padded envelope from her arrived in my mailbox. There was a more recent note attached to a letter that had been written six months earlier, when she'd been dividing possessions with her erstwhile fiancé. They were separating after five years; he was going back to Sweden, his true love. She'd been happy for him, and six months later, she was able to be happy for herself.

In the letter she'd written: "I've been around the world with this ring on my finger; it's saved me countless explanations with its unspoken message. I remember travelling to Lusaka by bus for a conference, when I'm sure I looked like fair game for a particularly aggressive man whose eyes burned holes in the back of my head from where he sat behind me. He leaned against my seat back and wedged his fingers between the seats—very annoying. At my breaking point, I turned to face him with my ringed right hand poised, gripping the headrest. I asked him if he was squirming for a reason. He settled down for the rest of the trip. And when I've been distraught, this ring has given my left hand something to play with through day-to-day stresses...it has long ago taken the place of my engagement ring because of its comfort...."

The note on top, written half a year later: "I return this ring, with thanks, and now plan to get on with my life."

Since then I have incorporated the ring and some other gold to have another ring made. Had it sat in my jewellery box until after I'd died, my family wouldn't have given much thought to where this thin gold band has been, how many incidents it has discouraged. With this ring a sense of freedom was provided. Perhaps if they knew the true beginning of the story they would wonder, like me, if the original owner ever had any regrets after that midsummer night's tryst in the riverside hotel room, when this symbol of love had been tossed, abandoned. If there were regrets, may they be calmed with the knowledge that this ring continued to serve a purpose, to make a statement for a long time after it hit the floor.

Sandra J. Walton

Where

Stone-studded beaches,
Waves of silver & white
glistening, shimmering
under dazzling sunlight.

    Where were you when I kissed you last?

Sun blazing
head afloat
adrift in the haze
of
hot summer days

    Where were you when I kissed you last?

Implicit Promises,
A remembrance of feelings,
And words
left unsaid,

Where were you
on that day,
arms tied about the bay?

Where were you
on that day,
that day
when I kissed you last?

Sarah Yi-Mei Tsiang

Seeing

You began summer with a gun,
an air rifle stolen from dad's closet,
the one he aimed at squirrels and cats
out the upstairs window of our bungalow.

Afternoon to ourselves, the oil smell
of the gun and flush of your face, the bright
flash of shells, we conquered small hills
of grass, the swollen ditch of a farmer's field.

Miles of sunlight sky and still you managed
to bloody the breast of a golden finch, a bird
no bigger than a star at night, the suddenness
of its fall, our stopped hearts.

That evening, our daily baths,
and the steam's hot breath on the mirror,
I stood, scrubbed and raw and saw myself bare,
a hatchling, bone-soft.

Sonja Grgar

Olga

Her eyes have known
It all
The silent cry of a
Child who doesn't belong,

The lonesome lullaby
Of bodies hushed to sleep
Where the soul
Feeds a silent storm
All night long.

Her eyes have known
The will to
Make any seed grow,

To snatch it from the gloomy soil
And the hungry rain
And have it reach
For itself again.

Her eyes have known
A wisdom others barely touch
Which seeps from her
Like incensed breath,
Like water that carves
A love letter out of rock.

Steven Heighton

You Know Who You Are

While my friend (the kid
you misconducted—the boy you left
songless in a sexton's yard among the open
doors of dug graves, among which he passed
the rest of a life curtailed, half-
cursed) coughed
and edged toward his solo
consummation, sir, you did zero
but soil other choirboys in your charge, and coyly
charm, flirt with the mothers, eventually
passing some pensive months in minimum—
society claiming its pound of flesh, to quote
just one of your hack apologists (the boy
himself is now an ounce of dust)—
where, I ungraciously suppose, you must
have checked your mirrored face, to rehearse the miens
of remorse, that sanctimonious sideshow,
along with other states of which your choir used to descant
in the superb manner you, a fine teacher, taught well: repent,
for example, or *atone*,
which to you must have sounded too much like alone
(a place where you're saddled with your own soul
and nobody there to perform for, fool
or abuse). Hard time! Tonight, sir, I still accuse
you, who—while earth slowly unstrings a boy
in his *lento* measure of staved ground—
still savours the tang
of August tomatoes, chords of Fauré's *Requiem*
(two years served, in fairway minimum)
and the rectifying esteem of upstanding Ang-
lican pals. So in your pool or Jacuzzi
wallow pink as a gangster, as water
bubbles like laughter, or the last
cantique of boy sopranos
vanished into their lives—bass now, tenor—
or through some colder
one way door.

Stuart Ross

My City Is Full of History

Your tenor saxophone is not my toaster oven.
Your winning smile is not my tax return.
When I opened the door at 3 a.m.
to insistent knocking: a stock of celery,
rocking gently in the breeze.

You see, my city is full of history.
Goes back to before
I was born, or even you.
Mother put me on a toboggan
and gave a little nudge. She
never saw me again. Though
I saw her, every day,
walking by the store window
where I was a mannequin.

At the party:
imitation cheese product,
plus raisins, nestled into
the celery's long curl.
Through the window:
my aunt climbing up a tree.

I have avoided product placement
but play an acceptable
"Shadow of Your Smile"
on my toaster oven.

Ursula Pflug

As if Leaves Could Hide Invisible Beings

Angelique does it alone once a week, winter and summer. In summer she takes off all her clothes, wades through the mud, shoots off into the middle where she can no longer stand, treads water for a few moments, then turns around and swims back. She looks for a grassy spot on which to dry off, one not shaded by cedars, relatively free of rocks and dead fall. She smokes one cigarette before she gets dressed. She likes being naked in nature too much to give it up. Still, the thought always niggles; what if a strange man comes across her lying naked on the grass beside the Ouse, far from shouting distance? Not likely; deer season is in November.

Once when she arrived at the river there was a black bear on the other side, investigating something in the shallows. Angelique knew the bear probably wouldn't cross to attack her, but all the same she ran all the way back. The trail was knotted with dead fall, rocks and roots. She only slowed for breath when she'd reached the back pasture, out in the open again. Her heart hammering, she listened for the dog, didn't hear him. The bear could eat her dog instead of her. That would be okay.

Angelique used to think the bear chased her all the way to the village. It was time to leave the farm, the bear was telling her.

Or maybe it was the fairies.

They were not a thing you saw but a thing you felt. Angelique acknowledged their presence with an organ she'd never known she had, as if a gigantic eye had just been blasted open by their presence. Part mockery, part dare, there they were, hiding under the cabbage leaves. Full of shame, stooped and bent and dirty and poor and tiny and magic and otherworldly, they shaded their eyes with their hands, staring up at this rude giantess who had so rudely interrupted them. "Go away," they said.

But how could she, for it was her garden after all and needed weeding?

They tried to hide under the leaves. It was pathetic really, as if leaves could hide invisible beings which of course they can't.

"We don't want to be seen," they said. "Not yet, and not by you."

"Too bad," Angelique said.

What she meant was, *I couldn't stop seeing you if I wanted. Now that I can it's not like I can put the ability back in its lock box for you must understand that's quite impossible.* Shutting her new enormous eye, her ear, for she couldn't really see them and they spoke not in words but in meanings and feelings sent from one to another and now to Angelique as well by some kind of faerie short wave radio. Angelique stared and stared, felt and felt with whatever the new organ was. Went inside and put on a soup to simmer. Set out dinner for the family. Read the children Tolkien before bed.

Pretending things were normal didn't really work, because as almost everyone knows, you can't go back if there is no back to go to. It had been erased, back had. Permanently. Or so it felt, for they were still there the next day and the day after and the day after that. At times Angelique even admitted she liked it, because at least this feeling of strange and fertile newness was, well, new, if quite impossible and a little creepy but things had after all been boring for longer than she could remember.

~ ~ ~

In the dream she came to a village where a ring of beautiful old houses shared a huge common garden. The garden was wild and overgrown and better because of it, at its heart a deep still enchantment. Angelique approached a house and knocked with a brass knocker and the door opened and she went in and then it swung shut behind her. The door swung shut and then they were there as they'd always been; she'd felt them a moment before they'd made themselves known: a door opening, an eye beginning to open, another eye closing to make way for the first. They advanced from all sides imprisoning Angelique in a sleep so deep and old she knew the door would never open again, she'd never

ever be able to leave. This was a spell as binding as being born: once invoked it could never be broken except by dying. It was over now, everything she'd ever thought life was for was over, irrevocably and forever. A spell as deep as dream, as sleep, no, deeper, a sleep perhaps which had two doors: first, the door into ordinary waking life, now slammed irrevocably shut, and then the other. The one they'd taken her through, locking the first.

And so Angelique and Mort picked up and moved. Angelique built a new garden and planted it and then they came, and there were more of them than there had ever been at the farm. Eventually she got used to them and didn't worry about being crazy anymore and even got to like them and as she did they seemed to change, but it was Angelique who was changing.

~ ~ ~

Since their move she wonders whether men still snowmobile on the Ouse, whether the ice ever gets thick enough anymore. Angelique always went the day after, when their trails had not yet been covered by new snow. Once she found part of a deer carcass on the frozen river, half eaten by coyotes. Farther on, a loose leg, its knee socket gruesomely mobile, which her dog found fascinating. On the way home she came upon a little hunting shack, barely larger than an outhouse, but with a window and a chimney. Angelique was afraid to look into the window. What if someone was inside? And why was she both brave and foolish enough to leave the trail?

Angelique still goes on long walks alone, except on the country roads around the village. The Ouse runs through her backyard now, home to blue herons, snapping turtles, otters and a beaver which, like the Pleistocene Castoroides, is almost the size of a sub compact car. In the village she doesn't have to worry about people raping her or shooting her accidentally, even in deer season.

Smoking; skinny dipping alone; walking off trail; bears: it seems these things don't frighten Angelique as much as they do other women, even if they should. What frightens Angelique is something else. Like Angelique's mother only in England, Virginia sunk stones into her pockets, submerged herself in the first Ouse.

Home from her walks, Angelique removes stones from her pockets and lines them up on the windowsill beside the postcards of her mother's drawings. The stones are not from here, not from now; they tell the story of a different kind of life. Angelique counts the stones sometimes. One for each child, one for herself, one for Mort. Because of this, one day the river's name will have a new meaning, the meaning of a stream that winds its way between worlds.

Veronica J. Atkinson

The Ghost of Rice Lake

There is a place I used to go,
where wild rice in a lake did grow.
The water once a shallow level,
that is, until changed by a devil,
so that a native man did starve.
On a rock, his story carved.

Now some will swear they fish with dread,
praying not to see the dead.
But my heart aches so for the dear,
because his soul still perseveres,
searching for that treasured grain,
forevermore in hope, in vain.

Walter Lloyd

Bereft

She came at me slowly
from across the room.
The gloomy distance
of a thunderstorm.
She kept changing colours.
Her speech sounded hollow
echo in the valley
of her ribcage.
I watched the woman
who used to love me
leave her body
and slam it shut.
so it was wooden
and mechanical
when it told me to leave.

Tara Kainer

Stealing Affinities

Eyes stare

across the lake
through the dirty pane

of perception, smug
in their complicity

making feathers out of pine trees
monsters of clouds

stealing affinities
with light & wind & water

Usurpers of mysteries

I's marking space
measuring out time

squeezing enigmas into shape
that form a grid

over the landscape
rigid & false

as a prison.

Philomene Kocher

The Basket

my heart is a basket
holding
my ruby ring
bits of string —
        some useful again, some not
a stone from the waterfront
a leaf from the park
the last letter I received from my mother
the letter I wrote to my father —
        retrieved after he died
my baby photo —
        wide eyes through crib bars
memories and songs
recent kindnesses
and a thumbtack or two
        hidden at the bottom

Carla Hartsfield

small

This place is so small I must become pure.
My anxiety should go into hiding.

Gradations of small, incremental turns,
peace within inches of nothing.

Under the microscope, past loves
point to obsession, negation.

No room for unwashed errors.

Walls I like. Asthmatic passageways
in the city of small.

Ghost moans, ghost tires scream up and down
the causeway, bone-chilled air of Skeleton Park.

I am liking small. I ride the swings
as if my childhood in Texas brought balance,
a mother who thought I was good.

My father releases me on a Stingray bike,
handlebars tattooed with Batman stickers.

Wobbly, the gravel road can't hold me up,
knees scraped. Scabbing. Scared.

What it means to pick one, two, or more of me
out of rutted psychology, pure limestone.

Hello small, there's only one of us.
Admitting small is such a high.

small is not gratitude,
traceable pattern. Sometimes small
is all I can handle.

It cannot be sewn, ignited, planted
in the undefiled vessel.

small is how I survive between
now and the new moon, an uncovered

manhole breathing lilac-scented air,
wary of combustion, kisses like gunshots,

and a mother who hates small,
wishing daughters were pure

illusion in a field of poppies
bloodied in the aftermath.

Bruce Kauffman

cage

you cage
this bird
    foreign to here

and you clip
    its wing
believing
    she would not
    remember
        tree
believing
    she would
    forget
        the tree
        from where
            she came
    forget
        the seed
        insects
            she used to eat

and you believe
that in the morning
    as she sings

    she sings
        for you

but she sings
      with eyes
      closed

    singing back
    to dew laden
        branches of
        mornings

            before wire

           before wall

Anne Graham

"Original Sin"
Lucy 1990 (three years old) As told to Anne

I'm only three years old, a tiny outward shell,
crouched in the corner, smelling of urine and rank sweat.
Approach, I hide my head, not to protect myself,
but more to protect you, from the stories in my eyes.
I feel they are there, evident for all to see
I must protect you, for they are most hideous.
When seen, you will hate me for the horror and the
dark reminder that such things do indeed exist.

The kicks, the blows and cruel indecencies, all seem
to come – when they look. I see the hate, disgust and lust.
I feel my being engenders such extreme response.
Do I look deformed? Am I an obscenity?
Do you feel the evil, the hatred in my eyes?
I'm small – will I become more evil as I grow?
I must restrain my growth, isolate this hate.

I know if you touch me, you will feel, that awful energy,
evoking from you, swift reaction. Kinetic interchange,
transmitting evil from my soul, which elicits horrified rejection.
So I pull away and hide my eyes – don't touch me
for your own sake, stay away. Yes, for goodness sake.
Leper- like, I should ring a bell, unclean! unclean!
Do not touch me – and yet I need **someone** to care.

Denise Hamilton

We are what came before us

The story line is clear
in the
potholes littering the streets
the swimming pools filled with autumn's leaves
and the cracks found in your childhood home's
foundation.
I frame my records and keep my receipts
maybe one day redemption will come,
when I am looking the other way.

But I know your disposition
as well was I know the ceiling above my bed
you're not going to stay but
you're not going to go too far away
so come a little closer
and roll one the way
your brother taught you
and I will kiss you the way
my sister taught me
because after all,
we are what came before us.

Carolyn Smart

Here is a man deep in sorrow like an underground river
for Jim Lyon

Days surround us like moonlight and the shadows fall down and down.

Here is a man deep in sorrow, a man without hope, who turns to the window and the lake cracks open, this clean and quiet place where in winter silver wolves run down the white-tailed deer. The cry of loons altered when their nestlings take to water, water so clear it is as if one crawls through it to reach the pines beyond. The man would speak of this, with wonder, amongst friends. Now the cats come through the windows and curl about his legs.

This man has reached his end; he opens to the future like a gift. All of it was said: that we were only strangers to this life, and cannot turn a river from its chosen course.

John Donlan

Religion

What must it be like, to lie on the pond
bottom, muck soft under your back,
pale stalks rising all around in the gloom
while you drown?

Drowning is painless, survivors say,
unfrightening, a strangely serene surrender
to memory, and nothing. – And after?
Most people believe

some best part of us will always live:
comforting, but unlikely.
The late sun is glittering off the leaves;
their *hush, hush* is infinitely soothing.

Seeing and hearing are the best part of being here:
they're the way the world's constancy and love
enter us, and convince us this life
is all, and comfort enough.

David Malone

Once in Favour

I was once Solomon's favourite
concubine. He used to ask for me often.
He said what he liked was I didn't try
too hard to please him and that sometimes,
even, I would let him please me. He said
too I gave him insightful conversation.
That was the most gratifying thing....
                              But
now I'm not the favourite. Now he asks
for another. O she's beautiful, all right,
though not in the way I was, and younger –
but docile too, I would say. And it's
because the king's older now, older
and more tired, that he asks for another.
I mean, he doesn't want conversation
anymore. Nor does he need his stature
confirmed by pleasing the one he lies with.
With Israel great as it is, and with
his reputation for wisdom bringing
sojourners to him from every land,
to say nothing of his wealth and sons
beyond number, he knows where he stands....
Still, I miss him. It also pains me to know
that he prefers another. Though this is
what can happen with the passing of time –
I could see for myself I was becoming
less and less what he wanted – still, no one
likes to be set aside. What's more, as
gratifying as it was to be the
favourite, it was as hard for the others,
as they never tired of telling me.
Yet now I'm no longer the favourite
they're even more resentful of me and,
though I understand their resentment, still

there should be a limit to it, or at least
a limit to what of it I should have to bear;
which is why I've sought leave from the court,
sought leave and have just now been granted it
(but O how I would have preferred the king
insist I stay). And I'm not unaware
what this means. There's little an aging
concubine can do — even one who was
once in favour with the king — but what she's
always done, only now it'll be in
places far less grand and with men far less
kingly for whom conversation will count
not at all. Nonetheless it's what I'll do,
and I'll do it because it's the road
rejection takes one down.

Elizabeth Greene

Flood

I and the cats on the couch, sleepy with rain,
till Alan said, *Water's coming in downstairs.*
Running down, I saw water
eddying over the basement floor
Alan bailed, I mopped—the water spread
through the basement, under doors,
around our feet.
We bailed and mopped, mopped and bailed.

This is how Noah's flood must have started,
inexorable rain, flooding basements,
making its way through roofs.
People must have tried to bail and mop,
but water kept coming, filled houses,
churned people, animals, away in the silent tide.

We were lucky. We only had wet floors—
the roof held. The cats upstairs slept,
lapped in the sound of rain.
Downstairs, baking soda, concrobium on the rugs,
promises to deal later with sodden papers.

When water knocks,
it won't be stopped.

Reminder that we, mere humans,
don't call the shots.

Joshua Jia

un sospiro

as i sink into my bed
my pink-red sheets forming a cocoon
i watch a moth
dive
straight into the gaps of my venetian blinds
with one broken wing

i watch it dance for life

i imagine its head carried
to egypt and babylon and japan
before it falls into its
mother's waiting hands

i remember my mother's own words before
she pushed me in a wheelchair
through the diagnosis room

i once imagined that God was a butterfly
and that i had gingerbread hands
and that piano keys were the only angels

i once imagined a world with no wheelchairs
only jet skis and scooters and motorbikes
and a pillow made of squares and diamonds
my left eye would walk for me
my right eye would talk for me

i wished then i could barter my imagination for freedom
i remember my mother telling me
"time will kill everything"
as she massaged the blood back into my leg

and the venetian blinds would turn dark

i feel sorry for this moth
who has
no wings.
no mother.
no time.

Frontenac Sky
heidi mack

Rose DeShaw

What Your Words Do

For twenty-two years, I owned and ran The Idea Factory, an out of print bookshop in Kingston, Ontario. The joy of being sole proprietor is that you can make your own judgments about who gets to be literature, pop others into the fifty cent bin. You are giving a voice a second chance, long after the publisher has pulped the rest.

I have a friend who uses Colin Wilson's big fat books as doorstops, other books to hold his beer and prop up his three-legged bed. If you can imagine the practical place that some of your works will occupy or all of your works will occupy for some, then it is easier to believe that the universe will waft your words directly to those in need of them and let the rest fertilize the dandelions.

None of this involves you as a writer after your book launch, an announcement in the local weekly and a thin line on your resume. No need for an 'author' button on the vest. Just concentrate on putting out there the best words of which you are capable, as far as you can throw them. Then turn and walk away, knowing that the letting go is what writing has always been and always will be. It doesn't matter what form your words take, even just online, no tree laying down its life for you.

Your words go to work, making straight for whomever they were intended. Perhaps they will do so for centuries. Maybe they will change someone's life. Writing and sending out those words is your contribution to the great puzzle of the universe. Through your words and my words, we have a sense of the whole pattern of why we're here. Make them your best words then rest in the possibilities

Vivekanand Jha

My Poem Falters and Fails

I write with ink of blood
To testimonialize and give
A touch of eternity to it
But my poem falters and falls
In the poetry of the world.

I pluck words from
A flowery and ornate garden
And weave a garland of them
To adorn the world
But they trample it
Under their feet
Like they crush the stub
Of the cigarette to prevent it
From catching the fire.

I discover the words
Hidden in the unhaunted
Recess of the mind
And juxtapose them
Like an ideal couple
Of bride and bridegroom
At bridal chamber
And turn my poem on new leaf
But they tilt their stony eyes
And turn deaf ears to it.

I infuse my heart and soul
Into the poem
Thinking it would be
The best and the last of my life
But they simply say:
Since it is the beginning
You would learn by mistakes.

Patricia Sullivan

Limestone Blues

The far-reaching, slow-moving Mississippi River doesn't connect with Lake Ontario in a geographical sense, but every August, the northern shore links spiritually with the famed delta through its music, as the Limestone City Blues Festival hits Kingston. Sixteen-year-old guitar whizzes wail Robert Johnson tunes as if they too had sold their suburban souls to a mysterious devil at a crossroads. Ginger-haired drummers belt out *Back Door Man* with the gravelly-voiced authority of Howlin' Wolf. Tanned women gyrate in front of the stage, flaunting a visceral kinetic link with the music that the rest of us confine to nodding heads and tapping feet. All gather to sweat under the sun in the park across from City Hall, or cool off with beers in Kingston's bars at night, for three days turning one of the original Loyalist settlements into a Canuck-accented branch of the Mississippi delta.

Blues titans like Muddy Waters and B. B. King sang of enduring hard times and hard love. What can be more persevering than the limestone with which this city is built? Kingston's fortunes have waxed and waned according to political winds, industrial priorities, military growth or academic development, but its stone heritage is immutable. In the American south, home of the blues, a more turbulent history permeates every field, every road, every bend of the Mississippi and every frame shack where a bottleneck guitar still rules, creating a rich gumbo that nurtured the music and its message of survival. Howling guitars and rollicking pianos have carried that message far and wide, and every August it washes up on the north shore of Lake Ontario to reverberate against the limestone walls and columns again.

Steven Heighton

The Wood Of Halfway Through
A daughter

Any forest craves torrents
of breeze in noon's steeper blaze: as a glider
seeks thermals coiled into high currents,
each aerial a ladder

into middle air. Appearance
never speaks for marrow. I think I was sadder
before you than friends saw. Now all my *aren'ts*
and *shouldn'ts* recede, I'm the reader

of a tongue lacking the negative mood,
the conditional, and other places to hide.
Who is it loves you, his heart now a lantern

in the dark wood of halfway through? The one
you made solid when he felt himself shade,
who made his way back from the border, made good.

Steven Heighton

News From Another Room

Back in a moment with more coverage of America's new war!
– CNN, 09/14/01

This is simple as simple comes. He refills
your wine glass before you can argue.
There are no "new wars," only episodes
of that same crude, ancestral fever.
But every love's a new thing—feels it—knotted,
frail collaboration. Fill his glass
with those deeper lees.
The foghorn, rusting of rain on park heroes,
low vespers of a glacial river all
give news enough for now. Refill his
mouth with the warm red wine
of your tongue, this is simple
as simple comes.

Susan Olding

Under Construction
Queen's University, 2007

No ivory tower for us. We're stuck in a luxury dungeon
where retractable screen and DVD machine don't drown
the sound of dynamite striking stone only inches from these desks,
and when I tell you to write, it's not nerves
that make your hands shake, it's the earth's
vibrations. Start of term, you're eager, so I sneak
in stuff that no one else will teach—ways to play
with words so writing won't be chipping rock, ways to make words
do your work, but you're not so sure they'd work
for you, so you're surfing the web
wondering what that girl in the next row
said, hoping there's Kraft dinner in the cupboard.

Campus is construction yard. Pipes for a pool,
a parking lot. Mud underfoot. Yards of lumber. Rubble mountains.
Summer's blue skies, glimpsed through
ground-level windows and chain-link
gaps give way to golden leaves, then gritty wind and rain;
blasting will continue, reports claim,
till late November. Between the shocks,
I talk, you listen—or not; try the tasks I set for you
—or don't, and I grade papers. That's the game
and if none of us wants to play, we don't know how
to change it. By mid-term, even the jackhammer's
jolt can't raise an eyebrow in this place. Your eyes glaze,
the body snatchers break in during the break and take
what they can, you tune me out, I try not to see,
we've all become blasé about this broken world.

When I was nineteen, I knew a lot. In fact I knew
almost everything. I grow stupider with age.
To tell the truth, today I wonder what I have
to teach you. So I'm done with lectures,
done with discussion, done with dispensing
advice. But before we pick our way
one last time past the mud and limestone detritus
outside the door, here's a final
assignment. Take this poem.
Count the comma splices, note the faulty
predication, the fused sentences. And the fragments.
Mark it up, analyze its structure, question
its logic, paraphrase the author's thoughts—no—
put it in your own words.
Your *own* words. And when you rise like the living dead
from this antiseptic crypt they've slipped us in, I beg you—
open your eyes.

Martina Hardwick

A Tail for Our Times

Once upon a time, on the shores of an inland sea, lived a merry band of knights in a tiny castle. Since this is a politically correct story, the knights were of mixed gender and species, including in their number one of the canine persuasion. Presiding over this motley crew was a king of noble stature and great erudition. King Editor, or Ed., was ever dogged by his faithful squire, the eunuch Sir Rudolph.

Ed and his crew generously assisted all who came to them out of a devotion to proper diction and syntax. Yet, a shadow was stealing over this northern land. Rumours eventually reached the castle of a terrible monster that destroyed all it encountered, leaving nothing but jumbled thought and weak grammar in its wake. The monster, it was said, could sometimes be appeased by the verbing of nouns: it smiled when it heard of people "gifting". It roared with laughter whenever it encountered "lead" used as the past tense of "to lead".

King Ed and the knights bided their time, knowing that to kill the monster, they had to strike at its very heart. They could not hope to overcome it merely by lobbing commas from afar. The king counseled patience. Sir Rudolph said nothing, but looked deep into the depths of his deep soul, and pondered what he found there, mostly thoughts of stale French fries.

The monster rampaged on, shifting tenses with reckless abandon. The day finally came, however, when it overreached itself. One of the visitors to the tiny castle had become so addled in his wits that he dared to use "impactful". Hearing of this terrible transgression, Ed called his knights together and charged them with the task of slaying the monster, either separately or together. The faithful knights weren't a bunch of dumb bunnies, so they elected to tackle their task as a group. Boldly they set forth with Sir Rudolph sniffing out danger as he went.

Before many hours had passed, the knights and King Ed could hear the monster bellowing and laughing. "R U ready??" it screamed as the merry – now not so merry – band first caught sight of their adversary. "ROFL!!!". The monster was terrible to behold. The knights recoiled in horror, all except brave Sir Rudolph. King Ed, after a moment, moved toward the beast while brandishing the latest edition of the *MLA Guide*. The knights slowly followed, some with copies of the *Little Brown Handbook*, others with nothing but their wits with which to defend themselves.

"You've got to give it 110 percent!!!" hollered the monster. "Mwah haugh hah haw!!! Suck it up! At this point in time, it's a perfect storm!! Har har har!!!" The monster was a master of cliché. The knights realized this would be a nearly-impossible battle; they were no match for the cheap platitude and the easy catch-phrase.

Except for Sir Rudolph. He cared nothing for such niceties. He approached the monster steadily. Perceiving no threat, the disgusting creature continued to hurl abuse at the cowering knights. Sir Rudolph sniffed the monster's left leg, licked it, and then…he lifted his own right leg. "Yargh!!" bellowed the monster. "You rained on my parade, you … nice doggie!!" The monster was powerless to express itself. " At the end of the day, it all comes out in the wash!!" it cried. Sir Rudolph circled the beast, approached its right leg, sniffed, and lifted his own leg again.

King Editor and the knights cheered. Because it lacked the ability to form an original thought with which to defend itself, the monster built toward apoplexy. With an enormous "Skwerumph!" the monster exploded into a million little fragments all over everywhere. The knights cheered again. Sir Rudolph wagged his tail modestly.

King Ed rewarded his faithful knights handsomely for their bravery that day, with a special Dentabone for Sir Rudolph. The knights realized the importance of the work they did for others. As for Sir Rudolph, he never spoke of the part he played in the battle. But he was ever ready to lift his leg in pursuit of a higher cause.

Michael Casteels

Moving day

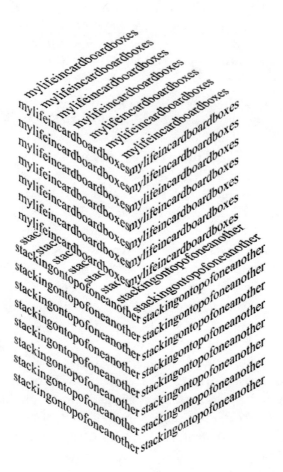

Terry Ann Carter

In Honour of My Visit to Paris

In honour of my visit to Paris
I've decided to name my breasts

Gertrude (the larger one) and Alice
(the smaller one) on the occasion

of a literary tour
which of course will include

the Luxembourg Gardens
the apartment of the famous duo.

In the evening when I am bathing
I look down at Miss Toklas and Miss Stein, whisper

we're going, we're going to France.
And the larger one wants to hold salons

invite writers for plum brandy
artistic conversations.

The smaller
wants to eat hash brownies.

Gloria Taylor

Waiting

W-a-i-t-i-n-g for:
a cup of morning coffee, a bus, a cheque in the mail,
children to grow up, a job, rain to stop, sun to shine,
a friend to call, paint to dry, fever to break, lilacs to bloom,
the car to warm up, a roast to cook, a wound to heal,
leaves to change colour, another birthday celebration.

Waiting for "Hi Mom, I'm home."
My heart sings.

Anne Nielsen

Safe At Home

Mother and I stood at the kitchen door of our farmhouse. We watched, through the green screen door, Rusty lope to the car. Dad sat behind the large steering wheel. Rusty opened the door and climbed in beside him, I wasn't going to let him see me cry. He'd been scouted for pro baseball and was leaving for try-outs.

All the windows were rolled down on that hot August day. Rusty seemed to hang out of the car more than he was in it. He looked at us cross-eyed and made a goofy grin. What a clown.

He cupped his hands around his mouth and shouted over the noise of the car's engine.

"Good-bye mother!"

"Good-bye sis!"

"I'll be back soon."

Mother dabbed her eyes with the bottom of her apron. I raised my hand, blew him a kiss and waved good-bye. The wheels churned up the dust as the car bounced over the ruts and out of sight.

Rusty's career was going well, until war broke out. All eligible men were needed to aid in the war efforts. Rusty signed up and left for Europe. We prayed one day he'd be safe at home again.

~ ~ ~

Sixty years later. Normandy, 2003

I gently caress the white stone with my hand, sun washed from time. Child-like I trace his name with my finger. His facial features still clear in my mind, along with his baseball glove in one hand, a bat at his side, and a dream in his heart. To me, Rusty will always be that innocent young boy of seventeen. A tear slides down my cheek. I've traveled a long way for this final goodbye.

Now it's time to go.

We shall not forget them.

Gabrielle Santyr

Kraken

The lake is a monster: muscles ripple
with the wind across its back
it breathes green sighing weeds, swells,
then pounds the shore it cannot take:

Inside, your belly churns in viscous twilight,
chilled alewives stream and surge
along strange arteries of sepia;
ochre striped bass slide in disguise;
small smelts dodge around your bony clefts;
and hydra hatch among the writhing cilia,
while twitch whiskered catfish,
scavenging your stagnant undercurrents,
consume their weight in macrophages.

Outside, I skip a stone, send
messages across the wrinkled skin,
seeking the bull response,
reach as far as I can go. Eventually
the creature turns,
roars up the beach to jaw me down.

Gut neurons have long memories
so I turn and run. And they
absorb my cries, turn them into
wavelengths of desire and energy:
cacophonies of krakens
let loose on windy nights.

Bob MacKenzie

you live here

it seems you have been here all along
so when I notice you
                          it's not strange
you're just there as you always have been

there are bits of you strewn through the house
fall leaves adding colour to my world
where otherwise there might be none at all

sometimes I see you or hear your voice
you live here
                so long after you called
announcing the end of everything

yet still remnants of you remain here
an old toothbrush
                        a clock you gave me
our music
        our places
                bits of you

I bear your mark and it doesn't fade
I feel you beside me
                      I hear your voice
I see you there at the edge of sight

can true love be erased from the heart
how can I answer what I don't know
how can I know if I did love you

I do know you have stayed here with me
long after you told me we should part
and I see and hear you
                      you live here

Carole TenBrink

Merida

"......my brute, who could
look you in the savage pupils of your eyes,..."
Osip Mandelstam

In Spain I saw Merida, that young girl bullfighter, beaming her resplendent smile on the crowds. She arched her back, stiff as a bow, in that acute invitation only young girls can offer. With naughty black steps, she climbed the ladder, dragging her cape behind her to view the spot where she had plunged the sword, just that soft black dent behind the head, that dark head, with its mad eye and massive bone.

The crowds were ecstatic at how she had done it, so quick a fierceness; her stab had seemed mere touch. She knew how to do it so well; her finger could have done it, found out that delicate point, to the fore of the brute. In the long moment she stood there, the crowds grew tumultuous, enraptured; but then they sighed, uneasy at such diminutive power. Soon, a strange stillness fell.

Everyone slept uneasy for weeks, except for Merida and me. We're celebrating, Bull-slayer, Conquistador, She-who-acts to get rid of bully mentality. We keep watch for what will come, our keen eyes fixed on the paradigm shift. Beasts stir both from within and from without. I hear drums, beating low, coming closer. We don't know how it will end... but I see feminine powered bodies flowing in everywhere, our red and black skirts flaring, gold trumpets blaring. Our velvet rags emerge blood-filled, glutted and rotten with the clear pain our precise fingers release.

Jennie McCaugherty

Urban Meltdown

Walking down our streets, my streets, your streets
I'm having an urban meltdown

I bought into your lies, my lies, our lies for 25 years
For 25 years I couldn't see clear
You taught us of need and control and gave it the name love
As this lie ignites the forest fire of people's ties
It changes the landscape, dark and barren
Leaving space for the new
You taught us of acquiring and called it life
As we quiet our passions and buy what you are selling
Part of us dies a little as she fights to be heard

Eyes blank, lost in the bear-trap of our minds
Risking losing more than a foot
Eyes open, seemingly open, yet we do not see
Our ears tainted with the story line
As we play it over and over and over and over
Step back and you will see it bend the landscape of reality
Until it breaks; exposing the sun in the nights sky
Exposing the lies that you and I buy into without question

So go to college, buy that house,
and marry him or her to lessen the alone
Distracted by the TV selling half truths,
Or the computers still landscape of connection through disconnect
As the emptiness expands fill it with more and more and more
Stuff, control, success
But in rare moments of silence you can feel it there

So turn up the music and tune it out
Until the story-line breaks
Until it gives you far less than it takes away
Eyes opening to the blinding truth at the dawn of your being
Deconstruct it, all of it until only truth remains
Only then will we live unchained

Lauren Hearnden

A Body in the Field

Which cornfield were these stalks. And to which month, in which year did this full moon belong. It had all become similar. The same moon was uncommonly bright and, both nights, a shadow stumbled with Arianna through rows of corn. Despite the light, she only saw vague forms in the dark that bent and reached and caught to tear her rose-printed nightgown. She tripped; Arianna sunk on her hands and knees, the mud sucking her slowly lower. She didn't know why her joints strained and hurt. She forgot which wrists she wore that night.

In a cornfield under a moon, Arianna was young once. She was infatuated there. She walked with mud stained to her knees. There were corn husks caught in her blonde hair until someone ran a hand down her cheek, around her ear and the pieces fell on her shoulder. The moon was bright enough to show her rose-coloured blush.

"No one will find us here."

In a cornfield under a different moon, Arianna was dying. She was old by then. Her hair was too thin to catch a corn husk; her skin was delicate and webbed with scratched from the field, covered in a thin layer of freezing mud it took her slippers. Sometimes, she laughed. She clutched a crumbling bouquet of flowers and she spoke to the corn or to the moon or to the girl she hadn't seen for half a century.

"We can never, never, never ever tell anyone," she said.

Arianna slipped between the cornfields. She collapsed into the mud and tried to remember who had given her the flowers. She finally pulled her hands out of the ground and stared at them; her mouth opened. These hands didn't belong to a young woman. These hands were blue and veined; they couldn't uncurl. This fear didn't belong to a girl worried her parents might notice she was gone. This fear belonged to an old woman, alone and cold in her nightgown, finally resting her head on the ground so each weak breath flecked her lips with mud.

~ ~ ~

Arianna's daughter, Beth, chose a deep blue dress with two rows of buttons on the front for her mother to be buried in. Its cloth was slippery. Beth held the dress with both hands then pressed her face into it and smelled her mother's soap. When she pulled her face away, there were two darkened spots. Her hands tightened within the fabric. Low, grunting sobs caught in her chest, squeezed into her throat. She placed the dress on her mother's neat bed.

Beth returned to the open closet and pulled a yellow, summery dress towards her face and smelled that one too. Then another. Dryer sheets, soap with vanilla, and floral perfume.

The mother that raised her and the mother that didn't recognize her died in the cornfield and Beth knew she cried out of selfishness. She only wanted to keep the pieced of her mother that would have hugged her and pressed into her that smell of soap and perfume, though she was a grown woman then too and the veins were beginning to pop out around her own wrists.

At the funeral, where Arianna wore the blue dress, Beth knew all but one of the mourners. A girl wearing a black t shirt and jeans never signed the book, never sat down and soon disappeared. She would never understand how the girl had known her mother.

The flowers teased with their secrets too. Beth wondered if her mother picked them and travelled to the cornfield half dissolved in the memory of a person.

~ ~ ~

The early morning sky settled into pale grey of immanent winter. The vehicles were stuck because the ground was half ice, half mud. There were cars scattered along the cornfield's thin road: two police cars, an ambulance and the coroner's sedan. Thomas backed his tow truck half a kilometre down the narrow road to reach them. Reston, in his passenger seat, smoked a cigarette with his head turned to the back window to help guide the truck.

The coroner's car was the first they reached, where it sank at a severe angle. Thomas cranked open the driver's side window open as a police officer approached.

"Some mess, isn't it?" the officer said.

"Some mess," Thomas agreed. A small smile drew out the edges of his mouth.

The officer sighed loudly. "A kid called it in, but she didn't say the person was dead. If she just said, 'there's a body in the field' we would have only lost one car, but she said there was a person wandering out here—got a cruiser and an ambulance dispatched. Ten minutes later they're both stuck, then mine when I come to get them and then even the damn coroner."

"A real mess."

"A real pain in the ass. How long do you think this will take?" The officer rubbed his chin. His nose and cheeks were blotchy from the cold.

Thomas made a low whistling sound, "Hard to say. Maybe an hour, not more than two."

The officer looked troubled. "Better get started then."

Thomas nodded. The officer left the window and sledged back into the cluster of uniforms, passed through them and walked into the corn.

"I guess the stiff's over there," Thomas said to Reston.

"Someone probably got run over by a tractor. Probably a real fucking mess," Reston replied.

"Maybe it was murder. If I was going to murder someone, this would be a good place." Thomas backed the tow truck closer to the sedan's bumper.

"Rape and murder," Reston joked, "it's the perfect place. One house, way over there, nothing else for miles."

"Except you get stuck in the mud on the way out and would have to call us." They both laughed. "Want to hook this one?"

"Yeah."

Reston jumped out of the cab and walked around to the back of the truck where the coroner handed him his car keys. Thomas lowered the hook from the cab and Reston attached it to the sedan then threw his cigarette butt away and put the car in neutral. Reston stood beside the car, a hand held the chain as it lifted from the mud with a low buzzing sound. Reston returned to the passenger seat and lit a new cigarette. They drove back with the sedan pulling behind.

"I saw her, the body," Reston said. "They're putting her in a bag."

"What does she look like?"

"Real old. Real fucking old. Not wearing much either. Looks like Grandma got lost."

"Shit," Thomas said. "Hell of a place to snuff it."

"'Shit' is right. She might have ruined mud for me. Once something's been seen, it can never be unseen. And trust me, I saw all of her."

Thomas chuckled. He pulled a cigarette out of his shirt pocket and lit it as the truck slowly waded back down the road. Out of the corner of his eye, he saw a figure among the corn not far from the police vehicles. It was a dark-haired girl in a black rain jacket. He wondered if she lived in the farm house at the edge of the field. He wondered if the police knew she was lurking there.

He didn't think he really cared. The call woke him early and Thomas wanted breakfast. But there was something odd, something memorable in the way the girl watched through the stalks. She popped into Thomas's head throughout the day then slipping away as unannounced as she arrived. Finally, she stashed herself in some overlooked corner of his mind, and returned only populate the rare dream and an occasional delusion.

~ ~ ~

The south field went untended that day. The police knocked on Hal's door just before sunrise to tell him there was a body. He had already watched their vehicles rutting his road through the window while he drank his coffee in the cold dawn.

A body was unusual.

Who was it, he had asked.

They told him they didn't know her identity yet. And that it was likely dementia. Hal pictured his mother near the end of her life. He asked when he would have his field back. They told him her death was likely from exposure and they doubted there would be an investigation. They said he could have it back by the evening. They apologized for crushing his stalks.

Once, Hal was lost in that cornfield. The memory found him

there, that morning, while he spoke to the police like an old friend who had walked silently behind him for the last 40 years, as a presence he never before quite acknowledged. In every direction, there was only corn. He couldn't see to the end of any row. Then it was night and all of the sky was bordered by bent black spears and he cried as he walked. Eventually, he heard his mother calling his name and he ran towards her.

The police left and Hal sat down at the table. He rested his head in his hand and cradled the memory behind his eyes. He wanted to wipe a tear from that lost boy's face just to feel how, once, it was soft.

~ ~ ~

Clementine picked the flowers. She gathered them and pulled leaves from it as she walked. She walked quickly. Her face was warm despite the cold. She snuck out and no one met her. She sat alone in the park for an hour; each second engraved the mistake more deeply into the interior walls of her skull.

When she cut through the cornfield, the moon was bright. So bright, she saw a woman in her nightgown moving through the corn like a ghost in the distance. Clementine forgot her carving as her heart beat to run, but she didn't move. The woman walked towards her smiling.

There was a mismatched purity in the smile because it wasn't a smile that belonged to a senile old woman wandering in her nightgown, but it looked natural wearing her body. The woman pulled Clementine into a tight hug, where she stiffened.

"You brought me flowers," said the woman.

"Uhh..." Clementine raised the bouquet; the woman took it from her. "I... um... is this your field? Sorry, I was just cutting through..." she trailed off. The woman pressed the flowers into her nose and the wind blew her nightgown against her skeletal frame.

"We can never, never, never, never ever tell anyone," the woman said as she pulled her face from the flowers.

"Umm... okay."

The woman became quiet. The lightness in her face

disappeared, emptied in an instant to wilt, replaced by more lines and oblivious age.

"Are you okay?" Clementine asked, "do you want to walk with me?"

The woman swayed in the breeze.

"Oh, there's a house over there. Do you live there?" Clementine asked as she pointed at the farmhouse. The woman didn't seem to hear. Clementine touched her arm lightly; it was soft.

"When I was a girl, I loved a girl," the old woman said finally though her face remained blank. "And I never told anyone. I stopped thinking about her. But, I-I couldn't forget." The woman's eyes moved to Clementine. The smile returned, "I never forgot you."

"You're confused," Clementine said.

"Mum caught me last time. She heard me coming back through the window."

"I have to go, and you should walk with me. My house is just over that way and you can use the phone if you want. I'm sure my parents will be cool with it." Clementine slipped hand into hand and interwove knuckles.

"When I was a girl, I loved a girl," the woman repeated. Clementine her hand, but couldn't move her frail body. "Am I still? Am I still a girl?" her eyebrows crumpled and her lips parted. "Where are we, Geraldine?"

"I'm Clementine. Let's go to my house. I'll show you the way."

"What's happened?"

"You're just confused. Come on, I'll show you how to get back."

"Get back? Get back to where? I want to stay here, with you."

"I have to get home... and it's really cold tonight. You should come with me."

"I never told anyone, Geraldine." The woman smiled again. She squeezed Clementine's hand.

Clementine tugged the woman's arm harder, but their hands separated. The woman continued deeper into the field.

"Ma'am, um, lady!" Clementine called to her, "Walk back with me!" She ran after the woman; she placed a hand on the woman's shoulder and pulled her around. "You should follow me."

"I have to get home now before Mum catches me again. You should get home too."

"You should come with me," Clementine persisted.

"I'll put these in water when I get home." The woman raised the flowers and smelled them again. The full moon was bright enough that Clementine saw a grey-blue tinge creeping into the old woman's cold lips.

Clementine couldn't convince the woman to walk with her, so she left. She went home, crawled back through the window, and lay in bed with open eyes. The boy that hadn't met her and the park she waited in for an hour faded on the fringes of her memory. She thought about the confused woman and row after row after row, and about how impossibly their paths had crossed. She called 911 before dawn and whispered into the phone so her sleeping parents wouldn't hear.

Clementine didn't realize until she returned to the cornfield later that morning that the flowers were never really for anyone else. She tucked the woman's secret away as her own where they could whisper to her at night. Eventually, Clementine stopped thinking about the woman, but she remained close, just slightly out of sight, almost out of mind.

Jeanette Lynes

Kingston Calendar

Spring in Old Canada. Lilacs burly, abundant. Knives twinkle in Skeleton Park. Ladies bare their shoulder blades. The meds are on the move. On Wolfe Island wind turbines churn all day, great white trees that lost their mind to a three-pronged approach. Cool it, Quixote. They're not the enemy. No sense charging at them spear bared. The countryside near Battersea is legion with wild lilacs. Forests of lilacs. Lavender tsunamis, kingdoms purple and white meshed beneath the earth. He drives you there. You feel sure he has chosen this place to ditch you. You are wrong.

    Back in Kingston a man draped in chains exits the wonky high-rise on Ordnance; the ragged half-dressed woman he just left calls down over her balcony rail —

    Thank you for saying I'm pretty!

~ ~ ~

Summer is for corrections. Quarrying limestone can make you a better person, history has shown. Just *thinking* of limestone can make you a better person, Church of the Good Thief a monument to this hypothesis. The bandits who stole three giant potted palms from your dark veranda should handle limestone, a mineral more enduring than crystal-meth. When one has been swindled one dreams of revenge. One sails to Wolfe Island and back and dreams of revenge. One sharpens one's eyeliner pencil and plots payback. One takes it personal, a frond for a frond. Make them pay. So much has been spirited away. Thieves have grown petty. They dress badly, too, the palm-jackers who skulk mere houses away, so close you've heard your parched plants calling out to you, "water, water, water". You picture their captors wringing vinegar from a sponge, a few drops into each blue-glazed ceramic pot. You keep a shard of limestone on your night table. There's a better side to summer, it goes like this:

    Fireworks bouquet the night sky with some frequency.

~ ~ ~

Autumn and pirates flutter everywhere. So vain they probably think this calendar is about them, don't they, don't they? Breeze stiff as a buckram off Lake Ontario buffets the gold tassels on their silly pointed hats. Riffles their ruffles. You don't suffer from pirate envy or any form of garrison mentality. You sally forth in your brocaded disdain. Everyone knows the great profession of plunder has plummeted *splish splash* in a tall latte near you. Pirates have grown soft. They prefer fine wine and ten fingers, makes text-messages much easier, 'r' in particular. The last real pirate lives near you. His crooked little house wears a necklace of weeds petrified with frost, a fist of ruddy sumac fruit some say produces a tolerable deep crimson wine. Fall is all about timing, you walking past his crooked little house just as he bounded out the front door to his truck, unlatched the driver's door with his remaining hand, flashed his hook as he told you, *you are very beautiful*. Compliments fly in Old Canada. Then he gunned the gas pedal, was gone. Real pirates always have someplace they need to be. The hook and the compliment and the snarl of his face threw you off balance onto the frost-heaved sidewalk, donated your left kneecap to concrete. Left you gothic and lame. For weeks the wound bled, at last an expansive scab, gristle foul as Captain Hook's visage. Fall took you down a peg. Who did you think you were?

~ ~ ~

Mittens make you a better person. Skating makes you a better person. Cudgel your blades you cannot skate. He grasps your wooly hand, promises he won't let go. He's not the pirate from summer. He's the one who didn't ditch you back at the lilacs. A dancer on blades with two good hands. This outdoor rink a dome of slow snow and chimes. This isn't the first time you've felt a spinning sensation in Old Canada. The Zamboni driver wears a dark waistcoat, its long tails rippling out behind him like two flags as his circles grow smaller. He completes the big boxy ballet of your country. You sally forth, wobbling on your laced butter knives. Your skating companion steadies you. There are things he fears, ice is not one of them. After awhile you trust him enough to steal glimpses of the wider scene. Cupola. Pillar. Census. Neon glow of Morrison's with its all-day breakfast. Solid things. You aren't really skating; he is the engine gliding you both forth, generous ruse.

Louise O'Donnell

Elegy For the Pines of Lakeview

There was a double execution on my street today.
Though elderly – more than a century I'm told,
and despite last year's amputations,
both victims stood straight, until
the moment their backs were broken,
their bodies dismembered, vertebrae by vertebrae.
Sound of the executioner's blade accosted neighbourhood ears,
Their blood smell surged through open windows,
Yet, none rushed to their defense.
No stay was called for. No placards waved.

Progress marches in heavy boots.

As green sentries towering above a small community
this pair watched other progress exercises:
meadows carved into streets where
structures sprouted as if from seeds deposited by wind,
then, in time, those houses stripped and eviscerated,
reincarnated in other forms, gardens paved as parks for cars.
While birds nested in their hair these sentries watched
children who'd tumbled in their shade, leave
for places once too exotic to contemplate.
Strangers came. Some with thoughts of
slowing down the progress march.

But, the watcher's time had come.
Unrelenting Progress claimed their lives.

Such small comfort to speculate
their bones might form the structure that,
like the phoenix, will rise to take their place.

From my vantage spot
I am confronted with nakedness.
I feel a silly urge to hold a blanket up,
                                          rescue the sky
from the embarrassment of exposing so much blue.

Lucy Barnett

Old School

I live at the top of a big hill. Maybe it's a tiny mountain. You don't really see it from the road, except for the slight slope and the slant of the twisted spruce trees. In storms, there is no debate, as the wind angrily rips across this hilltop, its ferocity making my house shudder. No matter the deluge, the house remains resolute —it's what happens after 145 years of sitting in the same place.

I came here looking for something, straggles and threads of a dream that started a long time ago. It was in Toronto, in the midst a dry and barren summer, that I started to dream of the field. I tried to describe it to friends, getting visions of purple vetch and oat grass, the coolness of twilight dew, a persistent chattering stream. It was as if City-living had started to strangle the juicy elements of my soul and I was parched for a drink of something new.

I kicked around some other fields, sleeping in one, camping in another. I heard tall tales of perfect rivers flanked by lush meadows. And while they were all tempting, they weren't right. And one day, for no reason, I drove to the foreign East and turned my car north. There were softly rolling hills covered in rows of golden husks, mellow barns and placid cattle. I felt like I was a breeze wafting through a picture-book illustration of country life.

It was fall and the countryside was lit in burning jewel-tones. I drove through a few counties and sleepy villages and eventually climbed to the top of that hill and felt at home. It was an old one-room schoolhouse, squat and solid, settled on a few acres of land. No neighbours. No streetlights. Just a perfect field, flanked by gnarled trees and tickled by a little creek.

It was decrepit and charming and made me both love and fear it. I heard violins as I walked into my homely little home. I saw stars as I wandered across my meadow and through a thicket of young beech trees, ravens croaking a welcome. I was dazed and dreamy. In one bold move that I often think bordered on lunacy, I bought it.

It is not an easy road that leads to my house on the hill. Or a short road, for that matter. But the more I traverse this path, I realize how this hard county has nourished me. It challenged my expectations, forced new goals and poignantly reminded me of what I truly cherish. Life here is hard sometimes. That sharpness severs the chaff and leaves just the bright, sweet kernel of wheat. I am left replete with nourishment.

Brandon Crilly

Bill of Sale

The snow was falling straight down because there was no wind. It was one of those beautiful sights that were rare for Kingston. While anyone indoors could appreciate it, the snow was simply a nuisance for anyone on the street.

A bizarre nuisance, considering it was the last week of May.

The Tired Horse was overfull. People were taking extra time fixing their coffee or tea, postponing going back outside for as long as possible. Despite the noise around him, Martin Kearney had no trouble hearing the old man sitting across from him.

"So tell me, why are you having trouble writing?"

Martin sipped his tea, a nervous tick while he pretended to think over his answer. The old man's unblinking stare was polite, but his unchanging focus made Martin anxious.

"I'm having a bit of difficulty tying my ideas together." He gestured to the thick manila envelope on the table, crammed full of paper and several flash drives. "The story's there, but ... I can't find the right words for it, I guess."

"My sympathies," the old man said with a smile that was as polite as his stare. "My own attempts at writing often prove fruitless."

"Doesn't keep you out of the business, though, eh, Mr. Timms?" Martin grinned.

The old man's expression didn't change. Martin took another sip of his tea.

"To business, then," Mr. Timms said. He reached into his trench coat and pulled out a small, blue notebook and a pen. He set the two items down in front of him and then removed his old-school bowler hat, placing it on the table as well.

"Before we complete our transaction," Mr. Timms said, "I want to make sure you understand exactly what is going to happen here. Do you understand, Mr. Kearney?"

"I'm selling the idea for my novel," Martin said. "Your employer gets all my notes and research, I get five thousand dollars."

Martin figured the old man's anonymous employer was some popular or once-popular author, who used up all his own ideas and needed others now to keep his success alive. Or someone rich who wanted to say he wrote a book.

"Do you understand the full implications of this transaction, Mr. Kearney?"

"What more is there to understand? I'm selling your employer my novel."

"You are selling <u>an idea</u>, Mr. Kearney." Though his tone was still gentle and polite, there was sudden intensity behind his eyes. "The story contained within those notes originated in your mind, and is therefore part of your mind. The characters, the setting ... everything there belongs to you more than any physical property. It is something that no one else could have created in exactly the same way. There is part of your very essence in the idea you are selling."

"You make it sound like I'm selling my soul," Martin said. The intensity of Mr. Timms's gaze prevented him from sipping his tea again.

"An original idea represents your soul in many ways."

"It's just an idea for a story. It's not even that good."

"My employer would not be interested if it was not good. An idea is never just an idea, Mr. Kearney. An idea can mean everything."

Martin's eyes narrowed. "Are you trying to talk me out of this?"

"Not at all," Mr. Timms said with a tiny smile. "I am simply making you aware of the ramifications of your decision."

"I'm aware of the ramifications, believe me," Martin replied. He managed to lift his tea again.

"You are not."

The tone of the old man's voice stopped Martin's arm halfway.

Slowly, Martin placed his tea back on the table. Almost in a whisper, he asked, "What do you mean?"

"You are not simply selling the rights to a novel," Mr. Timms said. "My employer and I are taking this idea from you. Once you have sold it to us —"

"What?"

"It will no longer be a part of you." His expression seemed to soften.

"Meaning?"

"It will be stripped from you."

"Stripped from me?"

"In every way. It will be as though you never had it. Do you understand what I mean?"

His soft expression had grown almost sad. Martin stared at Mr. Timms, trying to grasp exactly what he was being told. He wasn't sure what his idea being "stripped" meant, but the more he thought about it, the more he felt an ominous lump in his gut.

He glanced over at the manila folder, holding the contents to his failed dream and the bill of sale that would release him from it, and forced the ominous feeling down.

"I don't know if I understand completely," he said firmly, "but I don't care. I've been trying to finish this novel for six years. That's six years of awkward sentences, useless scenes, and inane dialogue. You've read the initial notes I sent to your employer. Do you know I've spent years just trying to get David and Mariah's voices right? They're supposed to be lovers, but I can't make them sound like lovers. That's what frustrates me the most. And it's just one thing out of dozens I can't get right.

"People don't even ask me about it anymore. I'm the last one to figure out this novel is going nowhere. It's time to let it go."

Mr. Timms studied him for a moment. "Very well," he said.

He opened the blue notebook, scribbled something in it, and tore out the page before returning the pen and book to his trench coat. From the same pocket he pulled out a thin, folded card. He inserted the notebook page into the card and placed them on the table.

"What's that?" Martin asked.

"Something you can open once I leave," Mr. Timms said as he put his bowler hat back on, collected the manila envelope, and stood.

"Wait, that's it?"

"By the time I leave this coffee shop, you will have your payment. It was a pleasure doing business with you."

He turned to leave, but Martin spoke again to stop him. "You said something about an idea meaning everything. Exactly how important is my idea to your employer?"

Martin wasn't sure if Mr. Timms was going to answer. The old man stared out the coffee shop's windows at the strange, springtime snow, and then turned back to Martin, wearing the polite expression from before.

"Your idea will be important very soon," he said. "Let us say it will fill a void following great change."

Before Martin could ask what that meant, Mr. Timms turned and walked out the door.

~ ~ ~

Martin sat there for several minutes, sipping his tea until he realized he was trying to drink from an empty cup. He had the strangest feeling he had been talking to someone, but there was no one nearby.

It took him a moment to notice the folded card on the table. Confused, Martin opened it, noticing the small piece of paper that fell out. He looked at the card first, and his eyes widened when he recognized the scratch ticket and the five thousand dollar jackpot. He looked at the crowded coffee shop, but no one stepped forward to claim it.

He checked the piece of paper. Someone had scribbled two lines of dialogue on it, between a David and Mariah. It sounded to Martin like they were lovers.

Martin put the piece of paper down, hoping the next person who found it would have some use for it. Then he clutched the scratch ticket tight in his hand and hurried out into the snow.

A. Gregory Frankson

The Voice Within

i am Black
my stigma is in my skin
it's visible to everyone
no matter how i look within
i live with it every day
and concealment is not a choice
i have available to help me
when i choose to raise my voice

Black is beautiful
that's how i feel about my skin
a beauty seen by everyone
no matter how i feel within
i think about it every day
and it appears i have no choice
but to have others react to it
when with pride i raise my voice

Black is dangerous
that's how others feel about my skin
a menacing threat to everyone
because of my rage within
i fret about it every day
for it appears i have no choice
but to generate a fear response
when i loudly raise my voice

i was born Black
my identity in my skin
unchangeable to everyone
from without and from within
defines my treatment every day
and leaves me with no choice
except defend my rights with vigour
and that's why i raise my voice

i am depressed
the stigma breaks my heart
invisible to all but me –
the stress this truth imparts
i live with it every day
conceal this truth by choice
this poem the first i have confessed it
when i've chosen to raise my voice

i am beautiful
that's how i feel about my heart
even if it's not the first thing you see
when my inner anxieties start
i think about it every day
but only sometimes have a choice
of when or how my truth reveals itself
when i choose to raise my voice

the mentally ill are dangerous
so others say about mind and heart
a menacing threat to everyone
just wait for the rage to start
we fret about this every day
others believe there is no choice
but to focus on their own fear response
when i loudly raise my voice

we are born as we are
our identities in our hearts
unchangeable to everyone
the strength this truth imparts
defines my treatment every day
and leaves me little choice
except defend all rights with vigour
and that's why i raise my voice

both stigmas are real
in the skin, mind, soul and heart
we dispel dangerous assumptions
when understanding compassion starts
they live among us every day
i am one – so i have no choice
but to ask you to speak our truths out loud
with a single, deafening voice.

Matthew Shultz

Schism Dreams

In the Occupy Kingston tent, a priest came to leave a donation and stayed to hear a poem, which induced her to offer a prayer and a blessing which has now been passed on to you.

Now we've all got these instasatellite-link datachips at our touchtips tapped straight into globopulation's collaborative eye we simulcastingly describe the whole world within our stories perhaps holding it holy but mostly only solely for ourselves we huddle down in sleeper cells torn apart by terror war tripped out by hordes of maniacal gabbling mechanical elves that somnambulate freely through our primal core of aboriginal Dreaming the original bridge between you and me and all the other mes currently at war with all our other selves like batshit crazy rampaging killer T-cells, and

Even as the spurts of this spectacle spill into now and are caught freezing in our photostreams it seems that time is speeding up as we're all reading up and faithfully feeding our hyper-marked-up versions upstreaming to the global cacophony which cackles with glee up-roar-LOL-Anonymously, with various versions of reality encased in echo chambers built of symbolic social memories of varying verity, witness: the degrees of awareness that not everyone's been telling the truth out there, like when a headline wafts by and you almost swear that you can savour the scent that saturates the air like a bouquet of ... Bullshit! and rotten fishy plot holes that burn through the story like hot coals igniting your nose hairs:

like

"It's not a war, just predator drones, precision bombing brown-skinned heathen homes, intelligence indicated they were in possession of black market Russian nuclear nose-cones (we heard it from some barbarian whose name I can't pronounce when we upped the ante on the water-boarding to include a mask, a catheter and a hose)."

or

"The econopocalypse was completely unforeseen, and although we know it's scary emergency measures are necessary, and anyway they're only temporary, and in the long run will benefit everyone (and not just us), so in the mean time try to look on the bright side! chin up! ignore that smell! and just have fun, normality will shortly begin its resumption! ..."

And it does, New Normal settles in and we all get used to a little extra pressure on the chin as the bit gets tightened between pain and sin and we're steered like drafted beasts and once again set apart and against, scouring at the razor-thin margins of the Earth's freshly shaven and oiled skin and scheming to Win it Big on the final human frontier by sewing the brains, eyes and ears of our kin up forever in invisible nets woven of nanotech titanium tethers that feel as light as those tiny feathers clipped to make pet birds that cannot fly.

A planet whose minds glare as one with the all-claiming eye of a cosmic narcissism enforcing the schism between this holomorphic Earthly prism and the will of those it imprisons more deeply with their every self-serving decision binding them with wires pulsing with their own holy inner fire to the strongest will's desire which will be a bottomless ambition for empire that will turn Terra into Mars to build the infrastructure that it will take to colonize the planets for it already wills to conquer the stars!

But, Imperial Entropy is without real reach in those worlds permeated with the empathy of the impenetrably infinite mystery that over gigayears gave birth to they and thee and I and it and me and you and we from the same unity of Sky and Earth, as seeing self in Other-self all can as one mature into a communion of all through all who stand together with spirits tall and wills free whose tears Call upon the wells of creation within them while all of Creation plays with them a game whose greatest nonzero gain is to grow in wisdom in the ways of well serving the flourishing of being for they have seen selfOtherself boundaries to be but the most fleeting of dreams

As are words such as these.

Greg Bell

P4W

Prayed for daylight breaks in
through a cigarette haze,

filters over grounded bodies –
counted on as coffee in the morning.

Her weed-veined forearms
speed-mean and wordy,

hair hacked short
and spiked unevenly;

she is lethargic and heavy
as her long-remembered Daddy.

In language lifted
from slow-reading books

and mentoring cell mates
she's attempting but nervous

across from the impossibly
pretty reporter,

contradicts herself
again and again –

says she's found God in here:
'Man on the range'

and helped himself.
Barred, bored and depressed

she's scarred for life, she says,
lost all hope.

The word hope dangling from the sentence
like a busted phone;

slackening its hold
like a smoke-ring blown.

Listen up: tonight in Prison for Women,
under this incision-pink skyline,

the wounds have re-opened.
And beauty is going down.

Gene Rankin

Monteleone

Monteleone
Where the mountains tumble upwards to the sky

Shall i ever walk your cobbled streets?
Beneath a sun so bright and pure?
The rows of noble Pines
That have gazed down upon the
ancient Roman Legions marching
While soft-eyed Donkeys, ever patient
Plod along under their heavy loads

Tramping through the mountains
In search of tiny, succulent wild Strawberries
Their vines clinging to storied, silent stones
Clusters of Mushrooms hiding shyly behind the trees
Winding mountain pathways
Where black-veiled women
Visit moss-covered shrines in
the secret valleys of their hearts
Flickering candles and quiet tears
Their murmured prayers carried away
Upon the mountain breezes

Monteleone
Where the radiant shimmering summer gives way
To the swirling, biting winter snows
You, my father, so long ago
Wrapt in the fortress of grand-pap's great cloak
Warm and ever-safe
The clack-clack-clack of his treadle sewing machine
As he shaped bolts of cloth into fine, pride-worn suits
And the heart-beat of the casa
Momma-Lucia in the kitchen
The peppers frying in the sun-gold oil
While sister Margaret's shy laughter
Rings like a silver bell

The sun-baked fields of wheat
Smiling Priests sipping steaming Espresso
In the afternoon mountain air
Christ's Crown of Thorns never far
The Nuns like dark wraiths mumbling prayers
Twilight dreams of longing and devotion
The blue-cloaked Madonna ever present
Hovering with her sad, sweet eyes

The trees heavy with fruits
Like the black-clad girls, bare-footed
Their sweet, swollen bellies
Holding tomorrow's promise of life
Dark sensuous eyes like ripe black cherries
Their amber skin glowing like
Mountain-gathered wild honey

And the Gypsies
Selling their charms and potions
Dark-eyed, mysterious, forbidden
Their fiddles singing in the night air
Round the camp-fires
Where the flames dance
With wide-hipped, Raven-haired girls
Reaching up to a Silver Moon
Their Castanets clicking and Tambourines jingling

And the processions
The sparkling fireworks on the Feast of Saint Roc
The hired orchestra playing long into the night
As the ruby-red wine and the Sambuca flow
Like the music

Flower-wreathed weddings
The Dance of the Tarantella
Dark sombre funerals, heavy foot-steps
Over hard mountain road-stones
Shy lovers beneath chaste, candle-lit windows

Monteleone
Where the mountains tumble upwards to the sky
You gave your husbands, sons, lovers and brothers
To someone else's War
Beneath the sullen grey leaden sky
STALINGRAD
Wild-flowers upon empty sad graves

I carry your brother's name with pride
"Eugene"
Who am i to carry that name?
He, who could shape the dark leather
Into the finest of shoes
And who could play a laughing, dancing Mandolin
His Red hair beneath the Italian sun
Fierce pride and loving eyes

A few short years ago
You and i plunged our hands into
The dark, rich soil
of this wintered Canada
And planted the Grape Vines
Verdant promise of a distant future
When a child's tiny hands shall reach up
To grasp the first clusters of ripe grapes

And in the night
Above the city's never-ending pulse
Between the beats of my heart
Sometimes i hear the Mountain Lion's roar
Strong yet plaintive, sad and sweet
Echoing across the miles of ocean
The endless waves marking the long years passed.

Monteleone
The Mountain of the Lion
Where the mountains tumble upwards to the sky

And then that day came
Dark and heavy
As i held your hand
And my Belladonna held me
I watched your life slip away
In little blips on a monitor
All your friends, your family so loved
They awaited you...

I had to finally say "good-bye" to my Pops

This spring, as the snow melts
belladonna and i will plunge our hands
Into the rich earth of this new casa
Casa di Luce
The House of Light
The vines shall be planted
Roses shall climb
Tomatoes for the sauce
Herbs for the kitchen
And in the kitchen
The heart-beat of the casa
My Belladonna
Singing quietly, softly, so no-one hears

Monteleone
Where the mountains tumble upwards to the sky
Hold my Pops in your storied, strong arms
He is home and dreams his dreams
Monteleone
Where the mountains tumble upwards to the sky.

Kathy Figueroa

Trees (Ontario, Canada)

The hills, there, were brown and dry
There were no plants or trees
Only paths that were walked by man
For a thousand centuries

And though the blue Mediterranean
Was edged with pure white sand
Never did I feel at ease
In that distant land

Ancient and grand cities
Bore testament to the history of humankind
But I felt apprehension
For it was a barren world, enshrined

In Paris and Milan
Places, throughout the world, renowned
I looked past each stone and concrete corner
But not one tree could be found

There were no elegant sprays of green
On graceful branches, upheld
For, lost from memory, in the distant past
The last trees had been felled

Replaced with great buildings
Constructs and statues, fine
But all that man can create
Can't compare to Nature's design

Here, in beautiful Ontario
Where many rivers flow
Are towering pine
Tamarack, majestic birch
Spruce and graceful willow

Balsam fir, cedar, sumac
And poplar, with boughs
That shimmer in the breeze
This is why I love my home best
It's the land of many trees

Gina Hanlon

snow

there are two girls standing on a hillside
snow behind the welfare building

and I could deed you all the snow in ontario

I could stick a flag in it
and it would be like the invention of Canada

that's how the deed was won. they simply took it over
and it belonged to them

do you see how simple it is
it is the key bought by hobbes and locke

it is simply an invention of man
do you see all the snow is yours

and the answer was no and yes

Shane Joseph

Hemingway, Greene, Steinbeck and the Other Guy

It must have been a dream. I was on the ceiling looking down at my mortal remains, stiffening by the minute, finger poised to send out a broadcast message on Facebook to my 14,000-plus faceless fans in cyberspace, announcing that my latest book was about to launch, while the paramedics were breaking into my study to take my body away in a gurney.

Then I was floating off somewhere else, in this barren space with no trees, just mist and wide open fields that promised nothing. Three old guys were sitting on the side of a narrow cart path. On nearing, I was shocked to recognize them as my three heroes: Hemingway, Greene and Steinbeck. They looked glum. But most writers do on the dust jackets of their books.

"Is this Heaven, or Facebook?" I asked

"It's Heaven," said Greene the Catholic, a benign smile on his face. "I've tried hard to get here with no help from the Church. But the place falls below expectations."

"It is fiction," grunted Papa Hemingway. "I'm always thirsty in this joint. It's dry."

"It's a movie set," said Steinbeck. "For a low-budget movie. Not one of mine. What's Facebook?"

I realized my predicament. "It came after your time," I said, sitting down beside them.

"Are you a writer?" asked Greene.

"Yes...sort of."

"How many books have you written?" asked Steinbeck eagerly. "I've written so many, I can't even remember. Even my diaries and journals were published after I...er... died."

"About three," I said.

"What do you mean 'about'?" growled Hemingway.

"Well, one was self-published, so that doesn't count, does it?"

Hemingway's eyes blazed. "Who says so? Every goddamn thing you write counts. When people could not get it anymore, I blew my brains out. I didn't want to live with a bunch of morons."

Greene sighed. "I couldn't blow my brains out even when I tried—several times. You can't trust the Russians when it comes to Roulette, you know."

"I got the 'two for one special' with my writing," said Steinbeck. "When I wrote novels, I turned them into screenplays and vice versa. But my stuff was so sad I had to exit the world. They even said that my book about Grapes was obscene."

"You are all so prolific," I said. "You must have written at least 20 books apiece."

"What took you so long to write three books?" asked Hemingway. "You are not exactly a spring chicken."

"I had to work—full time, to earn a living. Among other things..."

"We all worked," Steinbeck said. "I worked in Hollywood as a screenwriter. Hem here was a journalist and Graham...what exactly did you do Graham, gadding off to all those foreign countries?"

"I'm not at liberty to say," whispered Greene. "Governments will fall, you know."

"Well, I worked in software," I said.

"Does that mean—women?' grunted Hemingway. "Were you a pimp?"

"No—software came after your time too."

"Well, what took you so long with the books?" Hemingway repeated.

Just then, a solitary cyclist came wobbling by. He had a long grey beard and narrow eyes. He accelerated his speed as he neared, as if he did not want to talk to us.

"You should speak to him," Steinbeck motioned. "His oeuvre is about as thick as yours."

I recognized the rider. "That's not...."

"Yes," Greene nodded solemnly.

"S-------," Hemingway said in his customary clipped style.

Something bubbled inside me. I recognized it by how I used

to feel when those rejection slips arrived in the mail, some addressed to the wrong person by some clueless summer student who helped overburdened publishers eliminate their slush piles.

"I'll be back," I said to my three amigos and rushed after the cyclist.

"Hey—stop! Mr. S-------?"

The cyclist wobbled to a halt at the side of the cart path and looked back at me like a man caught by his wife while reading a porn book.

"Why the hell did you not publish all those books that you wrote in hiding?" I asked. "You deprived us from reading great masterpieces."

"None of your business," the venerable recluse answered and put his feet back on the pedals.

"No, wait. Do you want know why I could not publish more than the number of books you had out?"

"No."

"I'm gonna tell you anyway," I said, trying to keep pace with his cycling. Luckily, he was so frail he could not travel fast. I jogged beside him, giving him my story.

"It took me seven years to write my first book, seven more to find a publisher and seven afterwards to publicise it wherever I could. I was famous on Google but only sold a handful of copies, because there was so much choice. Besides, people were deferring retirement and working 24/7 to earn a living after the great crash of 2008 devoured their savings – they had no time to read. On average, a guy my age read one book a year—non-fiction, especially after 9/11. And their kids—Gen Y's—were Texting and Twittering – they did not read books. There were more damn writers than readers in my time. Every mother's son and daughter was living long enough that they all thought they had a book in them. I had to repeat my 21-year cycle with every book I wrote. My heart finally gave out on the third round."

The cyclist stopped. "You are giving me a headache with your foreign language. What does Google, Texting, Twittering, 24/7, 9/11 and Gen Y mean?"

"You didn't get out much did you? Did you ever hear about the Internet? That's what started it."

"Oh, that. I ignored it. And all I had to do was go underground and the silly buggers could not get enough of me. I think you tried too hard to get famous. Less is more, you know."

"You had it damned lucky!" I stomped my feet.

"You writers have it tough these days, I think," he said. His words of wisdom tripped off his tongue and hit the ground to bounce back and clobber me on the head.

"And you thought you had issues?" I screamed.

"Well, at least you won't have to bother yourself with all that stuff here." Mr S pushed off again.

"Why do you say that?"

"Because there are no readers here at all! This is a writer's paradise. At least, for me."

He left me standing in that limbo land, pretty much as I had been all my life as a writer. Like my heroes, I had finally created my own reality in Heaven, or Facebook or wherever this place was.

Tapanga A. Koe

Getting There

He appeared in a flash of smoke, coughing and waving it away. I ignored him; I was in a bad place. There could have been a flaming kitten at my feet, and I'd have been hard pressed to scrounge enough motivation to stomp it out.

Betty had dumped me when I lost the apartment, after my father's law firm canned me. Today had brought the letter. I was a thirty-five year old nobody-loser living out of my car. Just to show him how much I didn't give a shit, I took a long haul off my cigarette, burning it to the filter and singing my fingers.

"Bum a smoke?" he asked.

I reached for the crumpled pack inside my breast pocket; the suit's silk lining cool despite the stifling July day. I offered him my last cigarette and reached for my Zippo. But before I could produce it, he stuck the smoke in his thin-lipped, grinning mouth, and it lit.

"What are you so happy about?" I asked of his perpetual grin and twinkling eyes.

"What you got to be so miserable about?" Smoke curled off of his shoulders and with every puff, it gathered behind his transparent face and drifted out of his dishevelled, lime-green hair.

If I squinted, I could just make out the violent streaks of graffiti on the wall behind him. "A philosophical ghost, just what I need."

He took a thoughtful draw off his cigarette. His hair had darkened to navy blue. "You don't seem too disturbed, talking to a ghost."

"You don't seem too disturbed to be dead," I said, but it worried me; maybe my life was a wreck, but I wasn't crazy, was I? I pretended interest in the scuffed tips of my shoes. He grew quiet. So quiet, I thought I'd dreamt it, but when I looked up, he was grinding his smoke under his boot heel.

"Let's go." He pulled at the back of my jacket, lifting me from my seat.

The forgotten pieces of shredded letter snowed from my lap,

joining the carpet of orange and brown pine needles. "What?" I gasped, looking around. Towering trunks stretched up and up, some I recognized: paper birch with its peeling white sheets; pines that scented the air, strung with brown cones; dark-leafed and green-leafed maples; and towering, open-armed oaks reaching wide.

Others, I didn't know the names, but I remembered instantly which were best to climb, with branches that twisted and knotted; and those with bark which grated the palm; and which ones would be laced with webby nests of caterpillars.

"What are we doing here?" I asked the man, who seemed more than a little out of place, leaning against a tree clad in a leopard print vest and now with cotton-candy pink hair.

"Breathing the air." He started through the forest.

I trudged after him. The sensation of boyish awe ebbing as I wiped my sweating palms, trying to recall what I'd eaten in the last twenty-four hours. Could someone have laced the Slushie from Macs with acid as a joke? Was actually passed out in front of the store? "This is messed up, take me back."

He paused. I could hear rushing water. I came to stand beside him at the edge of a cliff. We looked out over the river, its white water bubbling and thrashing around wide, flat, beige rocks.

He observed me through reading glasses perched on the brim of his round nose. Then he pulled a crumpled paper from his pocket and began to read.

"What's that?" I squinted at the back. Dismissal due to negligence… incompetent… seeking damages in the amount of… "Hey! That's none of your damn business! Give it here!"

He glanced up and raised one bushy, unnaturally yellow eyebrow. "No."

A siege of anger came alive in my guts. "Give it!" I lunged for him. He stepped back. Half his body disappeared inside a trunk and then my heart was in my throat as my smooth-soled shoes slid across an outcrop of grass. I landed hard on the side of the muddy slope, slid helplessly down it, and rocketed off its ledge.

I sailed out and up a few feet, and then began to fall towards the crashing river. A wet breeze whipped past my ears. The bluest sky, holding a depth I'd never known, funnelled in through the portals of my eyes. Then, my body slammed to a stop. But I wasn't wet. I looked down; the ground was still several feet below me and getting further away.

"So, what's the deal?" He floated along beside me.

I swallowed my fright. As soon as I woke, I was bee-lining it to the hospital, I had to have eaten something off. "I'm broke, OK? Jobless, disowned, I've lost everything. I'm a loser."

We drifted over treetops now. The sun nestled between slumping hills, casting pink light onto golden rows of wheat. I shrugged best I could manage in my weightless state. My disconnected cell phone fell earthward.

He picked a couple of cigarettes off of a maroon-barked tree with long, thin branches, lit both and then passed one. Below, black highway stretched on and on, cut at irregular intervals with pale gravel roads sectioning fields of leafy crops from those of golden brown stalks. Gentle, grassy swells rose from the Earth, dotted with grazing livestock, farms and bungalows.

We touched down where the highway snaked alongside the river. He kept walking and disappeared around a bend. "Wait!" I jogged after him, heedless of the growing whir of an approaching engine.

He turned and smiled at me, fading out as the sound of squealing breaks registered. I turned and crumpled as the boxy gray Civic swung around, its rear end tapping me and throwing me back. Pain seared in my thighs. I watched from the pavement as the car arced across the road. It stopped with the sound of shattering glass, one taillight breaking on the guardrail.

Life bled onto the pavement and I knew at once I had lost more than just a job, more than a father, even. Now, I truly was a loser, who had lost all.

I roused to a sting in my cheek. A woman loomed over me; her dreadlocks tickled my forehead.

"You OK?" she asked.

I pushed up off the pavement, a phantom whisper of pain tingled, but my pants remained intact. I was back in the littered parking lot.

"I'm fine, I'm fine, I'm fine." A grin split my face.

The looming stranger backed off, concern creasing her brow. "OK, just checking." She shrugged tattooed shoulders, turned and got into a Civic. The engine cranked and she backed up, one taillight bulb shining white through the shattered red glass.

"Wait!" I cried, but the car took off. A paper fluttered to me on the breeze. Clutching it, I gasped: there he was, a drawing, but it was him – with blue hair and bat wings. "Spiderfest?" I asked, reading the poster. "In memory of Warren "Spider" Hastings."

"Check it out!" He faded in, peering over my shoulder.

"Are you going to keep this up?"

"Only 'til we get there," he replied.

Sandra Alland

Poem

I've come in/off the street
to confess/these crimes:

spectacle, serenity
spilling drinks
on my companion
hope, hiccups, homesickness
fingerprints on the wall
bronchial pneumonia
a large
sexual appetite
short and/decisive words
(yes, no, now, never)
hearing the/murmur of
blood in the plaza

unlearning
falling on
my face
being ever/fond of
a fine lad
mushy softness
business replies
secretive poetry
echoing the/sea's every
word

at three I/picked all
the flowers
in my neighbourhood
and sold/them back
to their owners

I have a mandolin
also
and cannot play

Tim Murphy

There is a Lake

There is a lake of fire you have said is set aside for me –
And I thank you from my bottomed heart for pious generosity.
And yet I fear I must refuse your flaming reds for midnight blues
That ebb and flow around/within the land I came to see.

I stood on cliffs above it, though it was obscured by bluish mist.
Raised my voice to the pinprick stars- shook my swollen fist.
"Christ, where is one to fish with me as John was set aside for thee?
Where is the tide to sweep my life before on land I list?"

Stone I thought solid slipped 'neath my foot in foggy depth,
Swallowed by a watered body whose babble took a breath.
Down through thorns and gravel did my soul/ body travel,
'til by darkened pool I stood and prayed for life and death.

Warm as blood within the body, cold as tears that without fall,
In the night I wavered there, watching the lunar semaphore call.
Knowing lateness will cede to dawn and living still is halfway gone,
I built a boat from wood nearby and set to scale the far-off wall.

There is a lake where one may keep a vigil most lonely and stern,
Also wrapped in smog as I, thinking self an only to burn.
Lake is dark with shadows cast- sun will dance its face at last,
And the fiery lake is overhyped – only warm, as some will learn.

Sonja Grgar

If I Could Only Tell Him

Wish I could tell him
That I do not dance with cowards,
That I used to be one for both of us,
That I am enough of one for both of us.

Wish I could ask him
To kiss my scar
So softly
It would melt
The stitches away.

Wish I could ask him
To charm the poison
Out of my breast
With his cotton candy breath

Wish I could persuade him
That I am worth the risk,
That days with me
Would give him
Enough soul poetry
To keep dancing
Long after I am gone,
Like love locked Frankenstein.

Wish I could believe
That he would want to see me,
To hold me
In my truth,
In my tragedy

Wish I could believe that
If I told him,
That he would not
Scream prison break,
That he would not
Sprinkle my heart
All over his icy hands.

Michael Casteels

The Wind

A sailboat
raises anchor,
unfurls white sails,
departs,
like a softly spoken word
from the mouth
of the harbour.

The wind is so old
that it has lost its voice
and at night
it gasps for breath.

Matthew Sinclair

My Canoe Paddle

My canoe paddle
Rests comfortably; an extension
Of my nationality
Pierces through blue gold and holds
That place in my heart
A stroke of my own minds; finest art
Then marks my departure
Into the awe of yonder
Wandering through an open mind
Impartial to the world outside
This time; and this time only
Stoically guiding the line
I resign

Veronica J. Atkinson

Not Lovers in Lake Ontario

I was nineteen the night my boyfriend said he died while trying to take my virginity. We were alone on a sandy beach of Lake Ontario in Cobourg in May.

"I dare you," I teased, shivering with my toes in the chilly water.

"Too cold." Tommy patted the blanket. "Come here and let me warm you up."

"No way." I splashed water at him.

"Oh yeah?" He guzzled the last of his beer, stripped his shorts, and then chased me into the water, until our bodies glided and glistened in the moonlight.

We dunked and splashed each other, laughed and shivered. Then Tommy dove under and tickled my feet, which made me scream and kick. He stopped abruptly.

"Let's get out," I called, searching the black water for him.

A moment later, he brushed against my legs and I screamed again, expecting him to grab me. When he didn't, I nudged him, and he simply floated away. He'd been under too long.

"Tommy!" I grabbed his limp body and hauled him up. He wasn't breathing.

He was so heavy as I struggled toward shore, swallowing water, coughing and sputtering, trying to keep his head up, my toes barely touching the bottom until halfway there. Once, I thought he gasped, but when I looked, his eyes and mouth were closed.

Finally, I towed him onto the sand, where he lay as though dead.

"Don't die, Tommy."

I opened his mouth. No breath. I sealed his lips with mine to perform CPR. Suddenly, he squeezed me in a bear hug and kissed me hard.

"What the hell?" I said.

"You saved me. Now I want to thank you."

"Jerk." I snatched up the blanket and stomped away.

"You kicked my balls, you know!"

I never skinny-dipped with Tommy again.

Theodore Christou

Walking on Lake Ontario

A white expanse of place and time.

Not sweat and blood, but snow.

I dream of cypress trees and rapids; of the Canadian Shield; of scarred cliffs.

I conjure crass waterfalls and foamy stones.

Someone else has trotted here. There are footprints sunken, still.

This lake is only pallet.

Though the white of snow is blank, it remains subject to our many eyes, our many woes, our appetites, our sighs.

I see the purity of ice, though it is cold and sparse. I see myself, downtrodden, frail, reflected in the whites.

James D. Medd

Slow Exit

Enter
Into the current
That moves too slowly
For the fallen leaves
For the broken branches
That want to be
That need to be
Further downstream

Gary William Rasberry

Tired Dance

Eyes see so little: only
postcards from the painted hillside.
Late-October graffiti calling not-so-loud-now
as last week's unbelievable slogans.

I'm writing the Muse
with a salamander's pencil crayon
connecting the dots, trying to stay
between the lines.

I'm writing the Muse:

> *Wish you were here*
> *send words when you can ...*

Meanwhile, blue jays brag about anything
and everything. A sharp-shinned hawk above it all.
Leaves provide fierce impressions
of fire.

And the lake:

a dark mirror determined
in its refusal
to show me
myself.

This might have happened
to you, walking slow in autumnal time,
the tired dance of death measured
out in quiet celebration up the hill to the sound

of a grey wind that stirs black water.
Turn to look over your shoulder
expecting nothing but
the loss of a season you
weren't watching

Kin Man Young Tai

With limits in the misted

A young Cardinal in view transfers a song to the Pine
such a strong voice from a body
less than the size of my hand
another answers, maybe to advise of territory
but in my fancy, a shared joy.
Morning has the light of a sun behind the clouds,
the mist of a soak
the William Baffin has me speechless and blinding
the blaze of the Japanese Willow
Does it end, the coming and going, the ferns living here,
transferred elsewhere, dying.
Question upon question, all easy to put aside
in a walk or gaze
Maybe some other time I may go beyond wonder
to an answer
But like the glories in this backyard, it changes even as I note.
The mist has spread over this roof
giving me the comfort of dream
The Chinese landscape noted by one myopic
from the study of characters
each within with a claim, this much I observe of the revealed.
The cardinal ends this page;
the sun fixes a glow behind the Maple
the kitchen has a meal to finish for others,
so I let a day reclaim me.

Clara Langley

Bits

revisit those old textbooks
and be sure to understand the lesson
on how to divide and multiply yourself
enough times so that everything goes
into a prefect equation
of bits for you
and bits for me.

Kelly Rose Pflug-Back

Birch

When you left I found a book on the shelf
full of drawings of birds.
I cut them out with my scissors
thinking I would make you a halo
if I could teach them to circle your forehead.
I closed my eyelids with masking tape
and walked with my arms stretched out
into the wind-snapped firs
and the white trunks of birches,
convinced that I could find you if you thought I wasn't looking,
still sitting cross-legged somewhere
catching moths with the flame of your butane lighter.

Theodore Christou

camping on colonel by

I cannot bear it:

The creaking of cedar and pine;
The growls;
The stars and the night;
The bottle of fizzy water, and the granola, and the cheese.

It is all too much tonight.

A timber breaks, and we flee. We scour for fluorescence. We.

There was no bear. No wild things creep.
All is silent.

Go to sleep.

Rock and Flow
Meredith Westcott

Patricia Henderson

Winter Crescent

A window saved my life.

Above the treetops. A window. A window and a light.

Saved my life.

There is nothing like the death of a marriage. Nothing
like the smell of pain wafting over the rooftops. It

gives you time to notice details. Like a window.
Like a light in the window.

It was winter in Kingston. I had begun to feel again. No, no.

Not feel. More like an anti-coma. Winter and the trees in
the backyard – grey, cold spindly things. I never slept
during those months. So I can tell you.

The dark shadows moved across the backyards of
downtown College Street.
The weeping willow in winter mimicking my torn and
bleeding heart. That time. A hibernation. Not death.
Something worse. A sitting in. A waiting. Death is better.

"Sit in the pain" they say. Betrayal never killed anyone.
Death of a marriage never killed anyone. That is a lie,
but one must hold on to something.

The moon makes downtown backyards magical. Dark.
Light. Shadow. Never still. And yet –
someone awake in the house behind mine?

Through the scraggly pine fingers of my backyard.
A College Street house window. One light.
Every night one light on.

In my aloneness I was never alone.

A night light perhaps. Keeping the bogey man away.
Could be. There are children in that house.

More exotically, a writer. Words pouring relentlessly
from his mind onto the page night after night.
A woman keening for her lost husband.
A death perhaps. Insomnia.

No matter. The light kept me going.
The life in that window kept me going
after my heart had stopped.

Life was going on. Night after night after night I nursed
the ache in my body, my heart. The loss of a dream on
my pillow. Sitting cross-legged I sat gazing out
into the darkness. A can rolls from a recycling box.
The moon reveals snowbanks.

The light is on. I tell my story to the window.
To the tortured soul in the house behind mine. You are
not alone – I whisper. We know the secrets of the night.
You and I. Pain is not so bad when shared.

Then, one night near Christmas, I arise from the dead.
An Easter out of season. The light never turns off.
I toss and turn fitfully. In and out of consciousness.
Wake up at 4am to catch that God-awful 5am train to Toronto.

And strewn on the trees in my saviour's backyard are
twinkle lights. Something new. Something wonderful.
Fanciful. Death defying. Twinkle lights in the snow.

The light in the window remains. The twinkles remain.
They stay into the summer. And the night they stop twinkling,
it is okay. I would have missed them anyway.

That is the night I slept.

Sarah Yi-Mei Tsiang

Missing

The river is missing its clarity. It hides like a woman, caught undressing. The shame of it. The river has lost the hot afternoon sun. The wind that stroked it absently, like a lover already thinking of someone else. There is no small shiver, no pleasure, despite. There are only these men, in waders. The mud stirred and sifted through nets. The small child, who lies unmoving. The river moves on and on, away from itself. As though it could empty all it was into the ocean, and forget.

Mieke Little

Untitled

When you wake up in the morning,
Here is what I would do for you.

I would tell you that you are beautiful
And that today is all about you,
As every day should be.

So,
I would massage your temples.
Tell you to stop worrying.
Now that you are awake,
Control those thoughts running in your head.

I would massage whatever else was aching.
I hope that you're not frustrated,
Because you are amazing and beautiful.
You are everything to me.
You are going to learn a lot of new things today,
Just like you do every other day.
But you aren't going to live in the past anymore.

New beauty comes out of growth.
Maybe you were quiet when you were younger.
And maybe 'maybe' is a terrible word because it leaves you indecisive,
Like you've felt for so long.
So maybe you weren't so friendly,
But maybe you had the best intentions.
And maybe you were just growing.

You were just growing.

But you were caring and real and truthful
And that is the best that anyone can truly be.

I know that you are always pushing to be better,
To live the life you want.
And it makes you tired.
It makes you want to sleep;
Feasting on your natural excitement.
And I want you to love
And to feel the need to live.

I need you to be you,
And I need you to breathe.

I tell you to please not live in the past.
Please think about all of the positive things
That create your life,
And that you are creating.
I need you to love everything you have learned,
And understand that every moment in your life
Has been leading up to
NOW.
Please do not live in the past.

SO,
When you wake in the morning,
I need you to look in the mirror,
To understand that you are beautiful.
That I am beautiful.

Walter Lloyd

Your Voice

The timbre and cadence of your voice
made me love you.
I sat entranced
listening to your magic syllables.
The empathy and understanding,
The richness of your life experience
sings to me in symphonies,
enfolds my heart
in loving kindness.
I didn't catch a word you said
as you read to me
your shopping list.

Mansoor Behnam

Untitled

I come from night
Where your hair crosses me
For stealing your faith
And your eyes double cross me
For staying faithful

I come from night
Where your finger knots my nerves
At the crossroad of love and hate
And starts the Fourth World War
By pushing my buttons

I come from night
Where truth breezes between us
And lie becomes as sweet
As the last cigarette we shared

I come from night
Where your heat shakes the cup of coffee
And the whiteness of the steam
Makes us two ghosts lost in the fog

I come from night
Where I drop hands and
Shake my fingers as columns of tears
And splash them in the air
Just to make you laugh

I come from night
Where lovers tell lies
And liars tell the truth that I love you

I come from night
Where the beast meets the beauty
Over a fiery waterfall

I come from night
Where the possibility of truth is present in your smile,
But with your lips in the dark
I can see neither

I come from night
Where the shameless lover climbs the fameless tower of suffering

I come from night
Where your silhouette profile eclipses the full moon

I come from night
That ocean of darkness that tides my corpse
Closer to your body for an honourable burial in love

I come from night
That snake unseen
Pouring venom in my ear

I come from night
Where the wolves settle and ask for your permission
To syncopate our love
By their untimely screams

I come from night
Where I cried wolf and nobody believed me.

Matthew Reesor

Grey

White meets black where light retracts
down dimly lit back stairs
no longer in use.

Still beyond the conquered stone
shaped and raised by snow-aged
hands to serve, join and mark honour.
Here the wizened and wounded
hide beneath storm smeared skies
forlorn and lost by sea.
Self assurance held like a dark wish
fades with the west wind's whipping
as the languor of age beats a steady
retreat from things once held dear.

This, middle ground, equal parts
east and west
burrow and brow
journey and jaunt
clouds the steely glare of
black and white positions.

We cannot be without words
the filing point upon which rests
the sum total of this journey
from base to bone. Yet, these
dull instruments disappoint.
There is more in a handprint
burnt onto a lover's back than
you and I could ever say.

Carolyn Smart

Insomnia at Summer's End

Heavy head upon the pillow,
that and the music, hissing,
running on. It will not stop
though I grit my teeth to halt it.

Outside, one cricket rubs and rubs.
There is no rhythm there.
Why can't I find a place
to fit my limbs tonight?
The bed's an uproar
and my brain ticks, sharp as tacks.

Summer's gone.
I am what I wanted to be:
grown-up, no more than that.
If I told myself the story of my life
it would sound like lies, believe me, now.

I forgive so little,
lapse back into that fast, cold song.

Kirsteen MacLeod

Monsoon

Caught in a summer storm:
the lake roils, pines thrash, and
you just told me who she is.
I won't take shelter, wait
in the torrent for release.

I'm back on Kovalam beach,
where the rain is born. I wore a silk sari
of inky-grey cloud, and you, a white *kurta*
that whipped in the prelude winds.

The sea frothed, palms bent to the sand,
and we rocked in the blasts with the others:
sky-watchers, seared in torrid heat.
Crows blew away, dark clouds flew toward us,

and when the rain finally burst,
we blessed it with open arms,
danced and embraced and kissed
people we didn't know.

Tara Kainer

The Reading

Coming into the bookstore to browse
you stumble upon it by chance, ask me
afterwards (shy & awkward in your
unkempt clothes, your wife slouching
sullenly behind you), whether we are authors
too, confess you'd thought about writing
a book yourself once, the story
of your great-grandfather
a stonemason in the mid-1880s who'd blasted
great chunks of stone into perfect, clean-edged
blocks, hauled them out of the quarry to build
churches & stately homes along King Street

You'd describe him as a boy, tell
how he & his friends hid out
in the bushes on Montreal Street behind
the now-collapsed train station, lying low
with their fishing poles smeared with honey
to capture the wild, golden canaries, they'd pop
them, singing! into homemade wooden cages
to sell at the market on the waterfront lot

You talked & the memories quickened
into stars in your eyes, they blazed
with the understanding that
there's a poem inside of
you too, embodying your
great-grandfather's antics –
a boy with his buddies marching
proudly together down to the lake
with their melodious loot

Sage Pantony Irwin

Little Cat

We're kids and our mornings are filled with xylophone lending, pennywhistle practice, water painting, and no parents. Then lunch, where we run around in the woods fighting children's wars over the biggest forts.

We all have "nature names": Dustin is Hawk, Alice is Squirrel, Liam is Chip, Jeremy is Coyote, and I am Tiger. The latter was inspired by my hair, a colour the adults call strawberry blonde. I think it's orange, though. Orange like a tiger.

Eventually, Pine calls us in for an afternoon lesson where we learn about animal tracks, fur pelts, and scat. Then we head out to the trails, searching for paw prints in the mud or wearing our highest wellies for pond dipping.

I remember finding a salamander under a rock, the taste of sap, being dared to ski down the steepest hill.

I remember testing frozen ice and crouching behind prickly bushes.

I remember learning to climb trees, being told it was dangerous, and doing it anyway.

I remember running so fast that I couldn't stop – the fwoosh sound of the wind on my ears, the pride at winning a race, how I felt I could take off and fly.

I remember "take only pictures and leave only footprints", endangered turtles, and my best friend Alice.

I remember my first crush, two pairs of worn-out jeans, and pretending I was tough.

I don't remember it ending.

Amber Potter

September

the wind moves through my heart,
sweeping out cobwebs of love
and though it is never a new start
the freshness lifts me above

I'm moving, unknowing where I go
tumbling forward, no way to stop
an acrobat in a circus show,
hoping that i end on top

i remember when it was black and white
and now it's all shades of grey
to what is, solid i hold on tight
what has past will fade away

people, like stars, move in circles
slightly changing along the way
each breath we take is a miracle
and life's gift is every day

Tim Murphy

This Heart Against Reason

These arms'd take form
That's not yet theirs to take.
These lips'd press mouth
That may not say those words.

These eyes look for signs
That'll not be erected.
This chest against one
That is locked from my heart.

These desires exist
Without a rich culture.
These desires disperse
Like rocks in the sea.

These desires might intend
To break a stone heart.
These desires'd grow
Like a tree through a stone.

These arms leave the form
That they wouldn't take to suffering.
These lips leave the mouth
That's mute to their call.

These eyes look away
To a mountainous plain.
This heart, against reason,
Lets pebbles fill veins.

Rich Tyo

Chilly Winds

I'm headin' where the chilly wind blows
I don't care if it snows!
I'm heading out 'cause I dream
And you know what I mean.

Words form the wise:
Don't stay inside;
Roam the country side

Relax your mind;
There is still time
Climb the hillside glide.

I may be outta my head
But it's still being fed
By the streets that I stroll
And the people who know:

They're passin' through;
Right into you
Take the hilltop view!

See from the top
Feel from the ground
Find what can't be found.

And we never knew when
This life would come to an end
But you can treat it like gold
To live a life that 'aint sold.

Combine your eyes,
Try not to buy
The life that gets you high

Go from within
We can all win
A prize we all supply

Leah Murray

Migrations

Ok...the north.
My Dad a Royal Canadian Air Force
Radar Technician, DEW Line concerns.
Faint memories still in mind of
Quebec postings, geodesic radomes
teed up in the forests –
never heard of
mini-golf
there.

Our houses
Stilted on cement
At balmy southern James Bay,
West shore of Hudson's Bay
between Moosonee, Ontario
and Churchill, Manitoba.
My childhood's memories
were built on the northern edge
of boreal forest and
the southern edge
of tundra.

You know:
Spring muskelunge and pike,
Summer Cree and Inuit visitors,
Fall belugas, narwhales,
Winter seals, mukluks,
sled dogs, snowshoes, snowmobiles –
the usual stuff of childhood.

Spring breakup,
river moaning all night,
shrieking, grinding past the banks,
crashing, crushing like
bad weather traffic in express lanes –
a dustless demolition
derby.

In early May serious melt begins
Snow banks crackle
shrinking, water
splashes, rustles,
gurgles off sidewalks
down streets – to the
boardwalks
or sink
out of sight
in the mushy surface;
don't walk off roadsides –

Waterlogged snow,
Like quicksand,
Swallows once.
Morning rounds by the bug truck,
fogger belching DDT
into the ditches and
incidentally, my
peanut butter –
Showed me the

White insides of its clouds,
the base hospital.
Other kids
fare less well
facing black flies
and mosquitoes and deer
flies all at once, infections
rampant, scarring their skins
And psyches.

Tall boots all summer —
ground's spongy up top
but you hit permafrost
a foot down.
Sink in that
running and you
can break an ankle.
Mom gardens anyway.
We get carrots, tiny,
Poppies, large,
Jokes about

Opium farms. Creek water so cold
it's a freon-free fridge for
Orange Crush — On the
hottest summer day,
your hands ached
holding it to drink
one hour later.

At 11PM, sunset – dawn
comes at three. Grey night smells
of willows – acrid and sharp
like aspirins. Noon hours
taste of red and black
currents, wild
gooseberries,
acorns and hazelnut,
fresh fish, river delta water.
Marsh marigolds swim
Underwater, unscented flowers magnified.

My Dad,
Boat Taxi driver –
extra cash between St. Charles and
Moose Factory. I crewed. Without tourists,
I slept, all my four feet
Stretched, didn't cover centre bench
in his freight canoe returning
to gover'mint dock – fetch
another load.

Mischief-makers:
Ouisquejaak (camp robber jays)
Coyote, Wolverine and Windego.
A thousand skeins of
thousands of Canada geese
gaggle, gossiping, overhead in
spring and fall migrations.
The great hunters – Nanook,
The grey wolf, arctic fox and snowy owl –

Are back again, snow flying among them
at September's end. Cold, pitiless sun glaring
down on hard pack, white miles in every
direction by November – watch out, sudden
snow blindness.
White winds so dense as to prevent
sight of mittens hung on strings
down your outstretched arms.
Christmas carols sung under
the Star of Bethlehem –
Dad said No, it was the pole star.

Frozen cheeks, burned lips, hot chocolate.
A feast of seal, walrus, caribou,
with dancing, woodsmoke, sweat,
arctic char in the firepits.
Groceries running thin.
Trains can't get through,
Planes grounded by weather.

Not sure the presents will get here
in time, but they do. We have many books
beneath our tree: it's a long time 'till spring.
One afternoon we leave school at three,
get home before dark and then
the back of the bitter season
has broken.
Sunny March and mild
April breezes follow each other
across the snowfields. Before the river
can bellow its annual anguish they tell us

we are leaving, going south. I protest, then howl –
people go south, I think to die. I keep it up for weeks,
salt tears are scoring my face
like the melt waters are
cracking the roads.
We moved then
To the Gateway of the North.

I growl because they got the direction
wrong and it's a city.
Huge. Buses not
Bombardiers.
I am lost in
tropics
S(h)tunned.

I run away often heading north
never getting home again.
They keep
taking me south
Another twenty miles
And I'll be on foreign ground
Acclimatized, tropicalized.
Assimilated. Homesick
Like the Cree girls.
Troubled, warm.
Ok...the north.

Jason Heroux

Camouflage

I love lying awake at night
listening to the leftover scraps
of birdsongs warmed up
in a tree's microwave

the sound of easy-going traffic
drinking the road's smooth wine

happiness sits still, blending in
perfectly with its surroundings

a gentle breeze parks its limousine of joy
the world may not look beautiful but it is

gillian harding-russell

Pluperfect intensified: Trip west '78

On the hip of a lake's
promontory, larch and alder's long-legged
reflection in stippled water's silver mirror
ripples towards the pebbled shore
and dark slice of land before

it is pulled back by the moon, bodiless
in darkening blue skies amid head and shoulder-size
boulders gazing up. Later you sleep on a rock-plated
incline facing the lake on the north-west

towards fighting dreams – try to wake up from
driving west, you know you must not drive like
this in your sleep a voice in your head that resembles
your mother's tells you it's dangerous – crackling of
branches outside the tent at midnight, and an animal
rubs antlers on your forehead, you frown
at this phantom thought while
sinking farther yet, into sleep...

You wake up in the shadow of the earth
at dawn, to bird talk and filtered green light, aware
that wetness seeps inside your sleeping bag under
the same full moon whose vestiges are nickel
small in some nether part of the morning sky at the back
of thought when a squirrel flashes its red tail
among the big leaves outside the tent flap.
Someone half stands up in the canvas-stale air
ducks out into sweet-warming freshness of forest
walking along its winding dirt paths, at last
arriving back where you busy yourself
with twigs and a match that strikes
a thought in your head about the not

quite forgotten country of your mind
recovered in sleep, dream frame with a cougar dipping
his rugged jawline at the lake's edge while a woodpecker
rat-a-tat-tats in your memory of the branches
overhead... Now a man with spruce and wolves
and moose in his three-week beard comes
forward to lend you firewood.

Bethmarie Michalska

Tufa

Near a spring, in first love's prime we built our hope on Varty's shore,
Dug the whole by hand down to bedrock – limestone,
Keeping the copse intact.
With pick ax, shovel, wheel barrow – clearing space,
Blessing the crags, swept with brooms,
Adding mortar to our concrete blocks–
4 by 8 foot wall, then, 2 by 8 foot window,
Ten of each interspersed, when finished.
By day, 'stonehenge' amid the trees,
By night, a spaceship, oil
lamp radiating light through cedars ,
the bullfrogs' swamp chorus
gazing in wonder – a 'hippie' home – off the grid.

No Canadian shield protecting our hearts, we made wild love
In sun-warmed fields, on hot stone
Forever this, forever bliss
Pulsing skin, taut and streaming joy
Maritime girl and British boy – organic–
Brand's "Whole Earth Catalogue", our guide,
Growing our garden shared with rabbit, and gopher alike.
Inviting artistic, and politico friends
To potluck feasts, to dance at the solstice dawn,
Take naked dips, canoe the marsh, fish pike, if inclined.
Bach's Brandenburg ecstasy through 12-volts
Glistening across the air, warming near the ingle;
Recharging it all on Sundays.

Earning our keep in Kingston, commuting hydrocarbons daily,
past stone mills into the basin where the river meets the lake,
Seeking science plus philosophical truth at Queens,
We grew together.
Playing out parental fantasies too –
Unknown to us, this particular family pattern,
Until later.
Evaporation of the spring insidious
Somehow, after a time the passion left,
Buried under academic toils perhaps,
Or gone with the tightness of fulfilling someone else's dream,
Or lost in the seduction of a drunken night's fling –
Generational myths revealed – no one willing to forgive.

Jennie McCaugherty

Voice of god

Spread it like thighs to lust
Anger
Frustration
Manipulation
All the things you can't see
Everything you don't want to be
But are
Or were
Or could be, if one moment in time were to shift
If you were sitting here alone
Wishing on a phone,
a computer screen, a falling star for things to change
But they are, they always do
Sometimes it takes a river of tears to lead you back to you
Words knock you down 'cause you're not sure
You were ever enough smart enough, you were her
The quiet girl in the back row
Walked past
Passed by
Spit on in the halls
Wishing you could die
Cause that feeling of alone that comes and goes
Is here again
You are here again wishing it would end
Feel the distance in the voice of
God
Mother
Father
Sister
Brother
Imaginary lover
The distance that lends pain to alone
Like water over me, pulls me down
Removes me from me

In the supposed to be, not this time
Right and wrong
Black and white lie
My energy is low and i want it back
Not forever
Happily ever
After that it fell flat
I want real
Raw and not afraid to feel
I think i better find it first
That's probably the deal

James D. Medd

The Meeting

Two streams of pale
Entwine and rise toward
The unlit horizon

Ashen breath
Clouds the cast of light
Where the chanteuse seeks
Her audience without resolve

Their words are quiet
But apprehension
Hangs in the smoky haze

Roger Dorey

Fourth Avenue

You didn't need name tags
To know who your neighbours were
Back then
With at least five kids per family
Running through the streets
Running through the back yards
Running through the houses
Tripping over each other
In the park, the schools, the churches
Made for great hide n seek
Then one day
I'm not sure who was IT
But when they started counting
Steam boats
They should have been counting
Moving trucks
For when they said
"Ready or not here I come"
Everyone was gone
If you came back to the street now
You would need name tags

Theodore Christou

Near Syndenham, winter

There was a smokestack on the crest of a house; it was not a stack, however, it was more of a pipe. In the winter air, the smoke was beautiful. Like breath it danced. This was furnace breathing, not fire, not logs. If the house were a boat and the frosted snow that on the yard and driveway slept were waves, the smoke might have billowed similarly.

There is a solemn sadness in the loneliness of this vision. It is as if I were blind; my eyes do not see. There is a necessary isolation in imagining. The moon, looking at us in the clean but biting icy air must feel like me. I find no consolation in this thought.

Through an open window, I spy pencils in the snow. They defy the principles of schooling, though there was a sparkle in the eyes of the students who leaned over each other's backs to add to the disarray and to marvel at the image.

I am alone again, observing.

Were this a song, this snowy isolation would be my chorus. Perhaps it is the absent soundtrack that I'm lamenting. Music has a way of being understood, while words are skimmed over and shattered.

Joanne Page

Taking Inventory, Garden Island

Cabins among the trees.
Doubles either side of the path
for shipwrights, carpenters, machinists and clerks.
Boardinghouses and shanties for the rafters,
half-breeds and Frenchies five hundred strong.

In the sail loft, by candlelight, he is counting:
two hundred and twenty-six yards
of cotton duck, eighty-four life jackets,
a gross of patent grommets, Number Nine,
toggles, a thousand and five.

Fen is perched on a stool.
He turns from the count.
Now he is bent low,
hunched over his journal,
his exquisite copperplate hand writing verse.

He would be Virgil of the Island,
his epic *Poems of the Earth*.
He has finished *Lake and River*.
This one is *Forest* and will be
fine grained as the tongue of language allows.

His table pine, all the furniture is pine,
The walls of the sail loft are board and batten.
Here at the foot of the island
lumber is piled up everywhere
for wooding-up the steamships,
floats and traverses for the rafts
that move the season's harvest to downriver.
Irregular lengths and cordwood in perfect stacks,
all pine. Fen's whole life is constructed of pine,
much of it he is responsible for, and so you might wonder
why he is trying to build it into verse:

I would have gazed through riven mist,
Before the axes' sound,
timbers piercing heaven's brow
With all their needled crowns.

Forest is the poem lost when we made the axe.
We chopped the poem down.
Before the cut, pine in the St. Lawrence Basin
stood two hundred and fifty feet up,
seven feet around.

Woodlands knew unbounded sheltering dark.
The cone-topped steeples of the white pine
crest like green waves in the wind,
swelling, soughing, sighing,
soft flesh destined for figureheads and masts,
untouched, unseen, unheard,
felled by their own weight.
Light lying in sun flecks on the forest floor,
throws bark into deep fissured relief.
Massive trees, liquid-filled.
Balance of wood and water struck, held.

Engraver of trees, calligrapher.
At his feet a sheaf of inked pages
fisted into pulp.
Woodcuts, wordcuts onto the paper,
nothing like good enough.
Too heavy, the weight.
Too late the night.

Michael Casteels

Four Seasons in a Hospital

Winter

Visiting hours are over
the sun exits the sky's waiting room.

A sharp wind disposes itself
in a box meant for needles.

A sheet of white paper
spreads over the examining table.

The sound of
footsteps in the snow.

Spring

Songs play over the intercom
to let you know that a baby is born.

The silence in between
lets you know someone is dying.

Summer

The nurse hums
like a mosquito.

She says
you'll only feel a pinch.

Autumn

The songbirds
chirp intermittently

beeps on a monitor
in a quiet room

where a tree
is losing its leaves

and the hands of a clock
move as steady as a surgeon's.

Kin Man Young Tai

Season:

Spring 2011

Zero has the fear of a dissolution, but only if I miss
the circle and what it divides
the alcohol red has no end of the sparrows' thrill
with the red cloud stretched across the trees
nor the crows, announcing what may be;
and the tree line, the events of warmth.
Already the clouds are lightening, blue between,
emerges around the Firs and Spruce
the buds in the Maple are like notes on staves
ready to erupt into music
the forsythia, the purple sand cherry
are slow, with no fire brimstone preacher around.
Steam drifts and rises over the roof of the school,
never going far beyond the other roof
the robin tweet tweet rolls over the grass frosted
on Duncan`s lawn
here crocuses, behind the bricks and a low cedar
watch a grass not as coated.
The tulips that Siu brought from Holland years ago
return around the apple trunk arch
the sheep head log from the same tree
nestles its nose in the creeping thyme over the sand
long and sharp another answers the distant robin
and sweet, the sparrow overwhelming both.
The cast now has the sun emerging
between a roof and the evergreen behind the fence
three bundles of cuts and last year`s growth
beg a task beyond my will in this cold.

Late Spring 2011

Time so limited seems more precious with beauty
as I age
green returning with names, the azalea
with poison and grace
beautiful the sight of Oleanders and strong,
the Rhubarb leaves.
This robin is ahead of me with the Sun,
trilling to no end
what is he so insistent about,
what would this backyard be without me
questions beyond my time, because
what I started yesterday needs a completion.
Sunshine making golden
the William Baffin, is a poor man's joy
not in acres, but alone in a spot that it had assumed
over the years
the Forget-me-Nots in pools highlight the green
with blue and a touch of pink.
The grass left alone has the beauty of youth,
fresh and here to overcome
the recovered Cedar has now signalled
its old intention to attain stature
there it will stay as would the Japanese Willow,
no more the thrill of relocation.
The sunlight lays out a fine gold out of reach
of my pockets
so much, in small measures comfort a soul
hungry for the infinite.

Early Summer 2011

Flipped over, the Maple leaves continue
their sun exercise
breathing the air they must know of others
around and related
knowing sometimes, gets around vision,
through joy, a blind can relate.
Neruda wrote in his memoirs, a poetry
feeding off poets in cafes
each carrying rivers and trees of a country
and engaging in literary claims
greatness is the light of their star, and smartly
he did not argue his case.
My exercise brings a joy within the burn of a sun,
in the repeated songs of a Robin
for a spell my body hosts a soul lost in an unknown
that is useful
time is a green rising in a blade of grass; a flower
opening to light.
This is my country, a backyard where colour
and form return me a past
the tulips and peonies with a country`s indulgences
crystallize a read
the primroses insist with a strong butter yellow
as the Spruce advances to their roots.
The pit has the failure of Thai Basil,
my stomach in midsummer, less anxiety
I will wait with the leaves for the stir
To decide on what to revise.

Late Summer 2011

This morning I wake to the Spruce tree needing to speak,
the Maple with its audience of green
the William Baffin gathering a scatter of pink flowers
to view the world from its top
the white Phlox in the hedge has retreated,
the Helenium yet to open up its prayers.
There was a Butterfly Monarch here to visit
the Butterfly weed
noticeably few are the Borages,
though early this year there were bees
the Coleus viewed gives me Shylock
slowly stepping through, with an inspection.
A buzzing riding over the crickets with cicadas
comes from a few yards away
is it insisting on a tree or machinery set to dig;
the Maple leaves flutter, the oval swings
The Japanese Willow no longer permits a view of flowers
near the wooden fence.
Caught in stride between the roofs, the Ash
has directed a closed fist at me
a conversation follows about the closing of distance
between living
the water in the pond near the Spruce
ripples over the reflected clouds.
The Hibiscus has managed an arrangement
between size and green
the Rosemary in quick days has thickened
its embrace of a twisted stem.

Sadiqa de Meijer

What Crows Say

Vendors of mornings, pitching
raucous, vernacular, lurching from lilacs
to eavestroughs, gurgling tuneful intimacies,
scolding cats, croaking elated
over crabapples –

kaa! the glimmer in your pocket-full of words

– some days, their calls bluster over
the stroller like proof; what I told you
is true. On others, the truth is them mutely
traversing the sky, bird-shaped holes
in the cloak of the world.

Anne Graham

Black Knight

I WON'T GO BACK into that darkest hole
that sucks out energy and clouds my mind.
I will not entertain the fantasy
Of black despair and paralytic fear.
Are you trying to seduce me with hope?
Hope of eternal rest? Should I believe ?
I see your evil eyes, laughing with joy
as I slide, trying to resist, towards
the endless darkness that beckons to me.

Please take me entirely, my evil friend.
Free my mind, expunge the weakening hope.
Shut out voices saying what might have been.
Let my hope be for quick oblivion.
I have no trust that time can sometimes heal.
Why offer words of comfort, then turn away
If not to make the loss more bitter still?

Hold me, dark knight, tightly in your strong arms.
I know your foetid breath, fear you instil.
Take me to the realms of forgetfulness
With you I will sleep safely all alone.
It is soft emotions that hurt my soul;
I know this now, despair is certainty,
not wounding as deeply, as one kind word.

K.V. Skene

Migratory Animals

Cold leaves let go, fall.

Snow shrinks the horizon
to nothing but ...

Caribou walk. Canada geese
fly.

Anyone can
download the rest of their life
into an old duffel: sweater, socks,
shampoo, toothbrush ...
                                  Zip.

Anyone can rent an uptown flat,
stock it with champagne, candles,
CDs and surrogate singles
(safe sex a phone call away).

Staying is down-to-work, DIY,
overdrafts, mortgages,
in-laws and out
to lunch everyday
after day

the same two mugs
leave coffee-brown rings
side by side
on the kitchen table.

Gary William Rasberry

Pre-Winter Bleak

Hard to even scratch out a line across
this country, the wind blowing
like a son of a bitch, ground
hard and dry, waiting for whiteness
to cover all sins.

Barns, ravaged and twisted,
wait around every crook and curve
in the highway, field after field
bleached and beaten, boulder and
stone ready
for harvest.

You see some lights—
Christmas lights, hung
in the shape of a cross, for
Christ's sake.

Wet snow on the windows.
Windshield wiper trance,
bleak metronome gives you measure,
time to think about the grey hills,
blunt sky, jagged
tree limbs dying
for some other season.

John Donlan

Lotus

Today I spent too long breathing the scent
the wind carried across the water:
acres of white water lilies, thousands.
At the far shore

under the forest wall, they're dots;
here, they could be emblems
of enlightenment and perfect peace.
Disordered by their perfume,

I imagine this afternoon unending,
I jump the job, never to return,
while my colleagues drudge
and laugh that I call this work.

That's how far I am from enlightenment
and perfect peace. When I look out again
the lilies have closed against the sun,
fisted in green casings until tomorrow.

White Pine
heidi mack

Index of Previously Published Work

Page 3, Gary William Rasberry, "Finding Form" - Previously published in *As Though It Could Be Otherwise* (Studio 22 Idea Manufactory, Kingston, 2011).

Page 12, David Sheffield, "butchering" – Previously published in *The Link* arts magazine, September, 2010 (Cambellford, ON).

Page 16, Gabrielle Santyr, "In Time the Lake" - Previously published in *Vista* and in *Beastly Metaphors* (Artful Codger Press, 2005).

Page 29, Eric Folsom, "The Lost Road" - Previously published in *'Scapes – Poetry & Company: A Kingston Community Anthology* (Hidden Brook Press, 2007).

Page 31, Joanne Light, "Religion on a Monday Morning" – Previously published in *Seasons' Light*, anthology. (Ann Hart, Ed. Halifax 201), and *The Second Mile*, magazine. (William Pope, Ed. Hantsport 1985).

Page 34, Kelly Rose Pflug-Back, "A Chorus of Severed Pipes" – Previously published in *Goblin Fruit* (2011).

Page 40, Paul Kelley, "Paul Kelley, from *Untimely*" - The poems presented here are drawn from a cycle contained in a new book, *Knock*.

Page 56, Ashley-Elizabeth Best, "The Hot and the Bitter" – Previously published in *Lake Effect V* (Artful Codger Press, 2011).

Page 67, Bruce Kauffman, "rain" - Previously published in the chapbook *Seed* (The Plowman, 2005).

Page 71, Greg Bell, "La Maison D'Eva" - Previously published in *Better Locks and Daylight*, chapbook (Cactus Press, 2011).

Page 72, K.V. Skene, "Walking Percy Street" - Previously published in *Reach*, Issue 141, June 2010 (UK).

Page 81, Lindy Mechefske, "The Arsonist" – Previously published, *Queen's Feminist Review*, 2012.

Page 102, Stuart Ross, "Cobourg, Night" – Previously published in *You Exist* (Anvil Press, 2012).

Page 120, Eric Folsom, "Shaking" – Previously published in *'Scapes – Poetry & Company: A Kingston Community Anthology* (Hidden Brook Press, 2007).

Page 147, Kathleen Moritz, "the pressure" – First appeared on the website *deviantart*, http://this-blue-eyed-girl.deviantart.com/gallery/#/d3lb86v.

Page 148, Joshua Jia, "foetal escape" – Previously published in *TeenInk* magazine (April, 2011).

Page 190, Laurie Lewis, "Sometimes a Dead Poet" – Previously published in *Gas, Grass or Ass, Nobody Rides for Free* (Thee Hellbox Press, 2010).

Page 200, Gary William Rasberry, "Black-letter Stammer" – Previously published in *As Though It Could Be Otherwise* (Studio 22 Idea Manufactory, Kingston, 2011).

Page 219, Steven Heighton, "You Know Who You Are" – Previously published in *Patient Frame* (Anansi Press, 2010).

Page 220, Stuart Ross, "My City Is Full of History" – Previously published in *You Exist* (Anvil Press, 2012).

Page 231, Bruce Kauffman, "cage" – Previously published in the chapbook *Seed* (The Plowman, 2005).

Page 237, John Donlan, "Religion" – Previously published in *Spirit Engine* (Brick Books, 2008), and *The Fiddlehead* (North American First Serial Rights).

Page 246, Vivekanand Jha, "My Poem Falters and Fails" – Previously published in *Mississippi Crow* magazine, *Carpe Articulum Literary Review*, *Mobius Poetry* magazine (all US).

Page 248, Steven Heighton, "The Wood of Halfway Through " – Previously published in *Address Book* (Anansi, 2004).

Page 249, Steven Heighton, "News From Another Room" – Previously published in *Address Book* (Anansi, 2004).

Page 252, Martina Hardwick, "A Tail for Our Times" – Previously published in different form in *The Fish* (an internal newsletter).

Page 291, Kathy Figueroa, "Trees (Ontario, Canada)" – Previously published in *The Bancroft Times* newspaper (September 04, 2008).

Page 311, Gary William Rasberry, "Tired Dance" – Previously published in *As Though It Could Be Otherwise* (Studio 22 Idea Manufactory, Kingston, 2011).

Page 314, Kelly Rose Pflug-Back, "Birch" – Previously published in *Not One of Us* magazine (2010).

Page 361, K.V. Skene, "Migratory Animals" – Previously published in *Lampton Court*, Issue 5, 2005 (UK).

Page 362, Gary William Rasberry, "Pre-Winter Bleak" – Previously published in *As Though It Could Be Otherwise* (Studio 22 Idea Manufactory, Kingston, 2011)

Page 363, John Donlan, "Lotus" – Previously published in *Spirit Engine* (Brick Books, 2008), and *The Antigonish Review* (North American First Serial Rights).

Index of Author Page Listings

(*Listed alphabetically by first name*)

- A. Gregory Frankson – p. 38, 280
- Amber Potter – p. 68, 332
- Andrew Scott – p. 128
- Anne Graham – p. 233, 360
- Anne Nielson – p. 257
- Ashley–Elizabeth Best – p. 10, 56, 159
- Barbara Erochina – p. 22
- Bethmarie Michalska – p. 345
- Bob MacKenzie – p. 69, 259
- Brandon Crilly – p. 276
- Brent Raycroft – p. 23
- Bruce Kauffman – p. 67, 231
- Carla Hartsfield – p. 65, 199, 229
- Carole Tenbrink – p. 194, 260
- Carolyn Hei-Kyoung You – p. 165
- Carolyn Smart – p. 19, 64, 235, 328
- Christine Miscione – p. 177
- Clara Langley – p. 163, 313
- Coreen Covert – p. 47
- Cori Mayhew – p. 48
- D. L. Iffla – p. 14
- David Malone – p. 53, 70, 237
- David Sheffield – p. 12, 176
- Denise Hamilton – p. 52, 162, 234
- Diane Dawber – p. 45
- Diane Taylor – p. 164, 203
- Eliot Kane – p. 121
- Elizabeth Greene – p. 28, 239
- Eriana Marcus – p. 61, 168,
- Eric Folsom – p. 29, 120,173
- Felicity Sidnell Reid – p. 7
- Gabrielle Santyr – p. 16, 258
- Gary Wiilliam Rasberry – p. 3, 200, 311, 362
- Gene Rankin – p. 30, 287
- gillian harding-russell – p. 17, 343
- Gina Hanlon – p. 193, 293
- Gloria Taylor – p. 167, 256
- Greg Bell – p. 71, 285,
- Heather Browne – p. 5
- Honey Novick – p. 179
- Hugh Walter Barclay – p. 171
- Ian Hanna – p. 9
- James D. Medd – p. 156, 310, 349
- Jan Allen – p. 21, 172
- Jason Heroux – p. 20, 342
- Jeanette Lynes – p. 119, 269
- Jennie McCaugherty – p. 73, 174, 261, 347
- Jessica Marion Barr – p. 8
- Joan Wilding – p. 157
- Joanne Light – p. 31, 178, 204
- Joanne Page – p. 32, 118, 352
- Joanne Walton Paterson – p. 155
- John Donlan – p. 236, 363
- John Lazarus – p. 154
- John Pigeau – p. 33, 152, 181
- Joshua Jia – p. 148, 191, 240
- K. V. Skene – p. 72, 361
- Kali Carys – p. 78
- Kathleen Moritz – p. 147, 205
- Kathryn MacDonald – p. 184, 206
- Kathy Figueroa – p. 291
- Kelly Rose Pflug-Back – p. 34, 188, 314

- Kin Man Young Tai – p. 312, 355
- Kirsteen MacLeod – p. 35, 207, 329
- Kristin Andrychuk – p. 74
- Lara Szabo Greisman – p. 55, 116, 185
- Laura Dyer – p. 77, 146
- Lauren Hearnden – p. 262
- Laurie Lewis – p. 82, 190
- Leah Murray – p. 336
- Leeane Betasamosake Simpson – p. 208
- Lee-Ann Taras – p. 186
- Linda Allison Stevenson – p. 122
- Lindy Mechefske – p. 81
- Louise O'Donnell – p. 129, 272
- Lucy Barnett – p. 274
- Lynn Tait – p. 131
- Mansoor Behnam – p. 325
- Martina Hardwick – p. 252
- Matthew Reesor – p. 327
- Matthew Shultz – p. 283
- Matthew Sinclair – p. 307
- Michael Casteels – p. 254, 306, 354
- Michael Hurley – p. 106
- Mieke Little – p. 322
- Morgan Wade – p. 36, 141
- Nicholas Papaxanthos – p. 54
- Norma Chakrabarty – p. 211
- Patricia Henderson – p. 104, 319
- Patricia Sullivan – p. 247
- Paul Kelley – p. 40
- Philomene Kocher – p. 228
- Phyllis Erwin – p. 87

- Rich Tyo – p. 334
- Roger Dorey – p. 85, 138, 350
- Rose Deshaw – p. 245
- Ruth Buckley – p. 150
- Ruth Clarke – p. 213
- Sadiqa de Meijer – p. 88, 359
- Sage Pantony Irwin – p. 89, 331
- Sandra Alland – p. 90, 302
- Sandra J. Walton – p. 216
- Sarah Richardson – p. 92
- Sarah Yi-Mei Tsiang – p. 91, 217, 321
- Shane Joseph – p. 133, 294
- Sonja Grgar – p. 103, 218, 304
- Steven Heighton – p. 219, 248, 249
- Stuart Ross – p. 102, 220
- Susan Olding – p. 250
- Tapanga A. Koe – p. 298
- Tara Kainer – p. 96, 227, 330
- Terry Ann Carter – p. 255
- Theodore Christou – p. 309, 315, 351
- Tim Murphy – p. 303, 333
- Ursula Pflug – p. 97, 221
- Veronica J. Atkinson – p. 225, 308
- Vivekannand Jha – p. 246
- Walter Lloyd – p. 101, 226, 324

Editor's Bio

Bruce Kauffman lives in Kingston, ON and is a poet, editor and writer. He was research editor/volunteer coordinator for a poetry reference manual, the *Poiesis Poetry Guide* (1998). His work was shortlisted in the 1995 Poiesis Poetry Competition. His publication credits include a poetry chapbook, *seed* (The Plowman 2005), a stand-alone poem, *streets* (Thee Hellbox Press 2009) and a book review in *The Antigonish Review* (fall 2010) for John Pigeau's *The Nothing Waltz* (Hidden Brook Press). His poetry has also appeared in a number of compilations, periodicals and two plays, *The Garbage and the Flowers* (2008) and *A Moveable Feast* (2009).

He was editor of and coordinator for this anthology, *That Not Forgotten* (Hidden Brook Press/North Shore Series 2012), and his first full collection of poetry, *The Texture of Days, In Ash and Leaf* (Hidden Brook Press), will launch in 2012.

He has just begun facilitating a series of "stream of consciousness" writing workshops with a spin-off writing group. He hosts a monthly poetry open mic reading series, poetry @ the artel, and a weekly spoken word radio show, *finding a voice*, on CFRC 101.9fm www.cfrc.ca and hosts a blog page around that show at: http://findingavoiceoncfrcfm.wordpress.com/.

Author Bios:

Listed alphabetically by first name

A. Gregory Frankson, OCT, B.Ed. Greg Frankson a.k.a. Ritallin is a Toronto-based writer, performer, arts educator and consultant. He is a graduate of Queen's University and represented Kingston at the 2011 Canadian team poetry slam championships. He has produced three chapbooks, three spoken word recordings and the poetry collection *Cerebral Stimulation*. Greg is a past National Director of Spoken Word Canada and a respected poetry event organizer.

Amber Potter is a former Canadian gypsy that has taken root in Kingston, Ontario. She has always enjoyed writing, using it as a catalyst for growth and self-reflection. Recently, she has developed the courage to share her inner secrets with others. If you enjoy her writing, you can check out more of her musings at www.feathersmarblesandorangemarmalade.blogspot.com.

Andrew Scott is a Canadian Native. He is a reviewer for literature and music on Swaggakings.com and hosts *ReVerse*, an international on-line classic poetry radio program. Andy's eclectic poetry style has been featured in numerous publications worldwide. His chapbook, *Snake With A Flower*, is available now on Amazon.com.

Anne Graham says that "I consider myself a traveler, an observer and a writer. Making my own original writings, in my own way. I feel I have lived many lives, and cannot settle into one perspective; I love to explore and examine many changing possibilities, as I live. I am a singer and a poet / I am "different" and I know it. / AND I am: / 65% oxygen, 90% water + hydrogen, / nitrogen, calcium, and Phosphorous. / Yes, indeed I am. / Anne Graham.

Anne Nielsen has been writing poems, articles and short stories for over thirty years. Her whimsical style makes her writing amusing to the reader. She and her husband live in a small community in the Rice Lake area.

Ashley-Elizabeth Best is from Cobourg, ON, Canada. She has been published in Stuart Ross's anthology *529*, by Carolyn Smart in *Lake Effect Five*, *The Changing Image*, and *The Antigonish Review's Poet Grow-Op*. Recently she received an honourable mention at the Dorothy Shoemaker Literary Awards in Kitchener, and was on the poetry shortlist for the 2011 Matrix Litpop Awards. She blogged for *Kingston's Writerfest* and during the fall of 2011 interned with Mansfield Press. Currently she is completing her BaH in History and English at Queen's University. Lake Ontario is her ocean and she doesn't think she could live anywhere more enchanting than Kingston ON.

Barbara Erochina is a writer, a believer and a lover. Working for social justice and reconciliation, Barbara serves progressive faith communities in Toronto sharing her gifts of passion, faith, mentorship and the written and spoken word. Her history with the North Shore area is comprised of ten glorious and life changing months as a military partner, a Queen's Theological College student and a Kingston cycling enthusiast.

Bethmarie Michalska, born in the Canadian Maritimes, is a 're-emerging' writer who works as a psychotherapist, and educator in Kingston, Ontario. Her poetry has been published in the *Queen's Undergraduate Review*, and in *Quarry Magazine*, where she was an assistant editor in the 1980's. She feels privileged to have experienced motherhood in a peaceful country where woman may own property, and have a fair chance at fulfilling life goals. She may frequently be found staring into space with wonder, and sometimes takes pleasure in creating or voicing text.

Bob MacKenzie's poetry has appeared in many publications, including *The Dalhousie Review*, *University of Windsor Review*, and *Ball State University Forum*, and in numerous anthologies. He has seven published books of poetry and prose, poems represented by visual artists and sculptors, an entire visual arts exhibition dedicated to his poetry, various awards for his writing including an Ontario Arts Council grant for literature. Bob performs his poetry live with original music and has released six albums.

Brandon Crilly – Originally from Burlington, ON, Brandon has been living primarily in Kingston since 2007 while he attends Queen's University. He has become very attached to the life and history of Kingston, finding a unique feeling in the city that can't quite be found anywhere else. He also owes a great debt to the friends he has made in the local writing community, for their ongoing guidance and support. Departing Kingston someday will be bittersweet at best. For more on Brandon's work, visit brandoncrilly.wordpress.com.

Brent Raycroft lives with his partner and their two children in Sydenham, north of Kingston. He works from home as an editor of legal publications and writes poetry when he can. He grew up in Prescott, on the St. Lawrence River.

Carla Hartsfield is a classically trained pianist, singer, writer and visual artist. Her first book, *The Invisible Moon* (Signal Editions/Vehicule) was short-listed for the LCP Gerald Lampert prize. *Your Last Day on Earth* (Brick Books) was longlisted for the B.C. Relit Awards. Carla's long-sequenced poem, *The River*, appeared from Rubicon Press in 2011, and her poem *Seven, Seven, Oh Seven* made the Best Canadian Poetry longlist in 2010.

Carole TenBrink took an MA in creative writing at McGill, and, from her thesis, published a book of poems, *Thaw And Fire*. She continued to publish poems in literary magazines, but at some point, began to feel that was too intellectualized. She wanted to engage with the audience, melt poetry with story, drama, and primal rhythms; eventually, she found Spoken Word Poetry. In 2011, she attended Banff's Spoken Word Poetry residency, which gave her important direction. Now calling Kingston home, she performs regularly there and in the surrounding area.

Carolyn Smart's fifth collection of poems, *Hooked – Seven Poems* was published in 2009 by Brick Books. An excerpt from her memoir *At the End of the Day* won first prize in the 1993 CBC Literary Contest. She is the founder of the RBC Bronwen Wallace Award for Emerging writers, and since 1989 has taught Creative Writing at Queen's University. You can contact Carolyn at – carolynsmart@kos.net

Carolyn Hei-Kyoung You holds a Master's in Theological Studies from Queen's Theological University. She is a breathwork practitioner and poet who lives in Kingston, Ontario.

Christine Miscione was born and raised in Hamilton, Ontario. She has completed her Honours B.A. in English Literature at McMaster University and her M.A in English Literature at Queen's University. She has been published in *This Magazine* as well as *529: An Anthology* (Proper Tales Press). Christine was also the recipient of the 2011 Hamilton Arts Award for Best Emerging Writer.

Clara Langley is a grade 12 student at Regi who enjoys running, writing and listening to/playing music. Clara started writing in 2008 after being encouraged to do so by another writer in the anthology, Denise Hamilton. She is greatly influenced by the music she listens to and hopes one day to be able to incorporate poetry into her own musical compositions.

Coreen Covert wrote her first piece of poetry when she was 10 years old, and was a poet in waiting until college when she was first published in a newsletter at Saint Lawrence College. The first published poem was called *Spring*. She has written poetry over many years (approximately 30 years of various entries). She is a mother of two grown children and her inspiration comes from life experience, nature, family and the First Nations people of the Kingston area. My poem *Old Wise Ones* is about the older ones of many races around me and how they live in their time and have contributed to my life.

Cori Mayhew, a Milton Acorn Poetry Award winner, returned to Kingston several years ago. She binds visual art and her writing into a personal presentation. She is presently writing and constructing an interactive book of poetry with hands-on "do your own thing and go for it attitude" art for the reader.

David Malone lives in Kingston. He is married and has a son. He drives a taxi, day-time. He has lived in Kingston for twenty years or so and has family here. His in-laws have lived in the area for generations. He has often hiked or camped by the shores of Lake Ontario.

David Sheffield grew up in the Napanee area but has lived, worked and made a home in Northumberland County for many years. A long-time volunteer with Shelter Valley Folk Festival near Grafton, he's a story collector who believes in community, campfires, and meals shared together. His work in community outreach takes him to the margins of small town life where the human spirit is illustrated in full colour.

Denise Hamilton (born in 1994) is looking forward to a lifetime of writing poetry. Born and (so far) raised in Kingston, she cannot wait to explore broader horizons. Her poetry attempt's to depict real life, as real as it can be. She would like to thank her yellow bird and everyone who has supported her.

Diane Dawber has written ten books (3 non-fiction, 5 children's collection, 2 adult collections) – latest for adults is *Driving, Breaking and Getting out to Walk*, Hidden Brook, 2009. She has been a Veteran of the Banff Winter Cycle Pilot Project in Writing, 1980, Alberta Heritage Scholarship; an educator in the Artist in Community, Faculty of Education, 1983-84; a Ministry of Education writer on Poetry in the Schools, 1984; a veteran of Squaw Valley and Sarah Lawrence College writing retreats, 2006; and has been anthologized in many collections for young people in UK, USA and Canada. She was the organizer of Poetry and Company (2005-2009), ed. of a Kingston poetry anthology, '*Scapes* (2007), and is currently Board Chair, Health Pursuits Reading and Research, an incorporated not-for-profit (1996-present). www.myunderwearsinsideout.com

Diane Taylor lives in Port Hope, is the author of *The Perfect Galley Book*, a memoir of her life at sea, and over forty magazine articles in *Canadian Yachting, Cruising World, The Journal of Palliative Care, Country Connection* and others. She taught English as a Second Language in Toronto and Miami, and worked on a conch farm in the Turks and Caicos Islands. She now gives a workshop in memoir writing, and composes oral histories for elders in families. See more at www.dianemtaylor.wordpress.com

Donna-lee Iffla, since before the Second Punic War, has worked in community arts and development, anti-violence initiatives, and education in China, England and Canada. Despite the notorious slowness of her Muse, she has struggled to keep a foot in the Door of Perception and a finger in the winds of change.

Eliot Kane was born in Kingston ON and quickly realized his life was meant for art, embedding himself in creative activities since. He loves to paint, read and watch movies in his spare time. Writing and acting are Eliot's directions in life and he is currently attending Fanshawe College / Theatre Arts. To keep up to date with his words and art check out noahs-songs@tumbler.com.

Elizabeth Greene has lived in Kingston since 1969 when she began teaching English at Queen's University. She has edited/co-edited five anthologies, including *We Who Can Fly: Poems, Essays and Memories in Honour of Adele Wiseman*, which won the Betty and Morris Aaron Prize for Best Scholarship on a Canadian Subject, and Kingston Poets' Gallery. She has published two collections of poetry, *The Iron Shoes* (Hidden Brook, 2007) and *Moving* (Inanna, 2010). She lives in Kingston with her son and three cats.

Eriana Marcus was born in Kingston, Ontario during an ice storm in 1960. She says "When I was ten years old my best friend told me something that became the philosophy I live by: "Look for the Beauty". I've not travelled much, but every person, every moment is a world of enchanted exploration. I've been writing on scraps of paper for forty-one years; the beauty I find in the journey of living. Someone told me it was poetry... Honouring illuminated moments – Keeping the Beauty Alive!"

Eric Folsom, born in Lynn, Massachusetts, has lived in Kingston, Ontario for the last 37 years. He is the author of *Northeastern Anti-ghazals* (published by Ottawa's above/ground press), *Icon Driven* (from Wolsak and Wynn), and *Poems for Little Cataraqui* (Broken Jaw Press). He is currently the Poet Laureate of Kingston.

Felicity Sidnell Reid is a retired teacher of English, History and ESL. She is the co-author (with Frances Parkin) of a book for teachers, *ESL is Everybody's Business*, four textbooks for learners of English and other educational materials. She now lives in Colborne, with her husband and goldendoodle, where she writes poetry, short fiction and is completing an historical novel for young people set in Northumberland County.

Gabrielle Santyr is a retired teacher and editor (with degrees in Anthropology from McMaster and Education from Toronto), now a freelance writer of poetry, short stories and articles. Her poetry has been published in *On the Threshold* (Beach Holme), *Kingston Poets' Gallery* and the *Queen's Feminist Review* and in her collection, *Beastly Metaphors* (Artful Codger Press).

Gary William Rasberry is an artist-educator. As artist-in-residence, he has worked and played at schools both near and far (Yarker, Ontario to Barcelona, Spain). He offers songwriting and recording workshops at Queen's University. Gary also writes and performs as a solo artist and with the acoustic trio Fireweed. He has published two books, *Writing Research/ Researching Writing: Through a poet's I* (Peter Lang) and *As Though it Could be Otherwise* (Studio 22 Idea Manufactory). His current recording project is a children's record, *What's the Big Idea?!?* to be released in 2012.

Gene Rankin, aka Eugene Cornacchia, says "The plausibility of my romantic back-line story, that I was a Feral Child raised by Northern Pine Squirrels, and that I learned to read-and-write with only the aid of a tattered hardware-store catalogue, has finally worn thin in my estimation. There comes a time in an artist's life when one comes to embrace the simple and indeed comforting fact that one is more ADD than Renaissance Man. My words and music are a simple offering to my fellow travelers. I am but a humble Scribe, charged with the task to Open Eyes, and Slay Lies."

gillian harding-russell has published three poetry collections, most recently *I forgot to tell you* (Thistledown, 2007). A chapbook, *Maya: Poems for the Summer Solstice* (Leaf Press), and a holm, *Stories of Snow* (Alfred Gustav), will appear in 2011 and 2012. Poems are forthcoming in *Carousel, Windsor Review* and have recently appeared in *Front Range*, the *Naswaak Review, The Antigonish Review* and *The Literary Review of Canada*. Also a poem is forthcoming in the anthology with the theme 'Poets on Poets' to be published by Guernica next year. She lives and works in Regina.

Gina Hanlon has lived in Kingston since 1992 and has been active in the arts for the last several years. She graduated from York University in Toronto from Political Science in 1992 and moved to Kingston for further studies. She is also interested in painting and photography with Different Strokes Arts Group as a special interest project and has had several showings including at the Kingston Frontenac Public Library and a silent auction. She has been at CFRC in alternative frequencies for news studies.

Gloria Taylor, a retired English as a Second Language and French teacher, returned for the second year to read 10 of her original poems in the POETRY MARATHON held at Chapters in Kingston. Several of her poems have appeared in *VISTA*, a Kingston magazine for seniors, *Kingston This Week* and in Canadian and American anthologies. Her hobbies include Irish Ceili Dancing as well as Scottish Country Dancing and travelling to visit her granddaughter.

Greg Bell lives in Kingston, Ontario with his wife, Jacqueline, and sons, Graydon and Frank. His work has appeared in *Rhythm Poetry Magazine*, *Misunderstandings Magazine*, *The Puritan*, *Encore*, and featured on *Eyewear*. His chapbook, *Better Locks and Daylight*, was launched in November, 2011. He is working on his first full-length manuscript.

Heather Browne is a lover of water and rivers and currents. She lives on Dog Lake, Ontario with her husband, David, and the faith of her father. The quotation in *Faith of Our Fathers* was her dad's expression.

Honey Novick is a singer/songwriter/voice teacher/poet. Her collection *Ruminations of A Fractured Diamond* was published by *lyricalmyrical* in February, 2012. Her poem *White Squirrels of Queen Street West* is included in an eponymous anthology, October 2011. She directs the Creative Vocalization Studio, is the song facilitator of Sheena's Place, music consultant to Friendly Spike Theatre Band and sings with bill bissett and SAMA Music. She will sing on a recording of Rumi poetry set to music. www.honeynovick.com

Hugh Walter Barclay is a retired Orthotic consultant. He has presented some 20 scientific papers and published 10-12 journal articles. He did develop several orthotic devices including the invisible scoliosis orthosis, developed and pioneered wheelchairs with dynamic tilt, and established Advanced Mobility systems in 1988 - sold in 2003. Hugh established Thee Hellbox Press in 1981 and, there, has published some 47 titles, 30 of which were authored by himself. The press has also produced a good number of broadsides and countless ephemeral pieces.

Ian Hanna is a local poet who divides his time between the big city busy-ness and the peaceful quiet of his woods just to the north. He enjoys pondering the semiology and science of swamps and other low laying emotions on frequent long walks with his dog. Ian also enjoys light domestic chores on occasion and collecting typewriters. Sometimes he also writes poetry. Ian has published in a handful of reputable places and is currently working on a collaborative project with a visual artist. The dog heartily applauds the long walks.

James D. Medd is an occasional indie musician who first began writing songs and poetry in his teens. He holds degrees from Carleton University and McGill University, and is ambivalently employed as a health sciences research professional in Kingston.

Jan Allen, a writer and curator, moved to Kingston in 1972 and has been held in its orbit ever since. Her critical and non-fiction writing has been published widely. Allen's first book of poetry, *Personal Peripherals*, was released by BuschekBooks in 2006. Chief Curator/Curator of Contemporary Art at the Agnes Etherington Art Centre, she is also an assistant professor in the Department of Art and in the Cultural Studies Program at Queen's University, Kingston.

Jason Heroux is the author of two poetry collections, *Memoirs of an Alias* and *Emergency Hallelujah*, both published by Mansfield Press, and a novella titled *Good Evening, Central Laundromat* (Quattro Books, 2010) which was shortlisted for the 2011 Relit Novel Award. His work has appeared in chapbooks, anthologies and magazines in Canada, the US, Belgium, France, and Italy. He lives in Kingston, Ontario.

Jeanette Lynes is the author of five collections of poetry and one novel. Her sixth book of poems is forthcoming in 2012. She is the Coordinator of the MFA in Writing at the University of Saskatchewan. Kingston is her second home.

Jennie McCaugherty was born on June 24, 1979 and grew up in a small town. Her poetry really took off during the years she spent in Vancouver. There was a lot of soul searching, a lot of healing in those years. She loves art and music and words, and spends most of her free time either in her head or creating something.

Jessica Marion Barr is an artist and educator who is in the second year of her Ph.D. in Cultural Studies at Queen's University. Her work focuses on forging links between visual art, elegy, ecology, ethics, and sustainability. Recent exhibitions include *In Power: Out of Control* at Union Gallery, *With This Land* at The Artel and *The Rough Edge of Beauty* at Modern Fuel Artist-Run Centre – all in Kingston, Ontario.

Joan Wilding is a relative newcomer to Kingston. After living for seventy years on the prairies, her curiosity about Kingston's long and colourful history led her to write this ballad. As a teacher of high school English, she enjoyed helping students become competent writers and readers.

Joanne Light lives in Halifax and has had three acceptances to the Banff Centre's literary studios. There a colleague, Judy McFarlane, wrote of the 2010 Wired Writing Program at the Banff Centre "...one of the real highlights...hearing Joanne Light read/perform... her poems grabbed my attention, held it throughout, made me laugh, cry, moved me more than I thought possible ...insightful, honest, funny, and, in my opinion, brilliant." Joanne is presently working on a book of non-non-fiction stories revolving around her life as a traveller.

Joanne Page is a visual artist and author of three books of poetry, contributor to numerous anthologies, and editor of a book of essays by her friend, Bronwen Wallace, entitled *Arguments with the World*. Her poetry has been short-listed for the CBC Literary Awards. *Watermarks*, Joanne's most recent collection, was a finalist for the prestigious Trillium Book Award in 2009. "These astonishing poems show Joanne at the height of her powers," says Molly Peacock. "She uses her characteristic wit, insouciant intelligence and wide-roaming interests to make worlds we can enter with delight."

Joanne Walton Paterson is a recovering high school teacher. She currently resides in Ottawa with her husband John, where she strives to marry her passion for all things literary with her concern for inclusion issues. As a native and lover of Kingston, Ontario and graduate of Queen's University, she knows from first-hand experience that The Sleepless Goat cafe on Princess Street in the Limestone City has the best vegan brownies around.

John Donlan is an editor with Brick Books and a librarian at Vancouver Public Library. His books of poetry are *Domestic Economy* (Brick Books, 1990, reprinted 1997), *Baysville* (Anansi, 1993), *Green Man* (Ronsdale, 1999), and *Spirit Engine* (Brick Books, 2008.) He spends May through October writing at his property in South Frontenac. In fall 2012 he will be the Barbara Moon Fellow Writer and Editor in Residence at Massey College at the University of Toronto.

John Lazarus is a playwright who has taught in the Drama Department at Queen's University since the year 2000. He was born and grew up in Montreal, where he attended the National Theatre School, graduating in 1969. He then lived for 30 years in Vancouver, working in theatre and broadcasting, before moving to Kingston.

John Pigeau is the owner of Backbeat Books, Music & Gifts in lovely Perth, Ontario, the founder of the First Edition Reading Series, and the author of the acclaimed novel *The Nothing Waltz*. His second novel, *The Journals of Templeton Speck*, will be out in the summer of 2012.

Joshua Jia grew up dreaming of making the NBA, playing football and trying his best to be a high school sports star. His inspiration comes from recovering from a neuropathic injury he suffered from when he was 16. Today, Joshua is a fourth year Commerce student at Queen's University aspiring to build a career in finance while writing poetry as a hobby. His proudest accomplishment is recovering from his injury, and he believes this would not have been possible without poetry.

K.V. Skene was born in Sault Ste. Marie, Ontario, raised in Lachine Quebec . She lived in Toronto, Colborne and Port Hope before moving to a houseboat in Victoria B.C. In 1993 she departed for England where she lived (except for a year in Ireland) until recently. Now repatriated, she writes from Toronto. Her publications include *Love in the (Irrational) Imperfect* (Hidden Brook Press, 2006) and *You Can Almost Hear Their Voices*, 2010, Indigo Dreams Publications (UK).

Kali Carys, called Kingston home for the most formative 5 years of her life so far, before running off to the east coast and joining the circus (seriously: look it up). In Kingston, she lived in a lot of houses, and was involved in creating a lot of beautiful things. Many of these were theatre and performance pieces, or cupcakes; she has yet to combine the two -- in public. She was also a founding member of the High Voltage Burlesque troupe.

Kathleen Moritz began writing poetry when she was ten years old. Six years later she stopped rhyming, with the vague, misplaced notion that it made her a 'poet.' She had the wonderful opportunity to do her first reading at the Thrive Reading Series in Kingston, Ontario, in April 2011. Kathleen now writes in the scantily-lit hours of the day in between studying at the University of Waterloo.

Kathryn MacDonald's poetry collection, *A Breeze You Whisper*, was launched in 2011 by Hidden Brook Press. Her novel, *Calla & Édourd*, was published in 2009, also by Hidden Brook Press. Essays on farm life, along with recipes, were published in *The Farm and City Cookbook* (Second Story Press, co-authored with Mary Lou Morgan, 1995). Kathryn earned a B.A. from the University of Windsor and an MPA from Queen's University, Kingston. She teaches literature and writing online through Loyalist College, Belleville. When not wordsmithing, Kathryn silversmiths, creating original jewellery using gifts from the earth.

Kathy Figueroa is a poet, freelance writer, and photographer in the Bancroft area. She credits, 'Flowertopia,' which is comprised of her numerous flower gardens, and the rugged wilderness that surrounds it, for much of her inspiration and this is reflected in her work. Since 2006, her poems have frequently appeared in the Bancroft area newspapers and her articles and photos have been printed since 2004. Kathy has published nine small collections of poetry in illustrated chapbook form.

Kelly Rose Pflug-Back grew up on a farm outside a town called Norwood and spent a number of her teenage years hitch-hiking on Highway 7. She got to know that highway like you would an old friend. She has been a number of things in life, including a squeegee kid, a political prisoner, and now, against all odds, a university student.

Kin Man Young Tai, of himself and his work, says "I was born in 1950 in the West Indies of Chinese parents, migrated in 1994, and now live in Kingston, Ontario. Here I have worked when I could, a backyard and a voice to add to the countless, as eager for poetry. The demons of poetry continue to chase me, with demands I was never schooled to deliver."

Kirsteen MacLeod has lived beside Lake Ontario for much of the past 25 years. Her poetry has been published by *The Malahat Review*, and is forthcoming in *Contemporary Verse 2* and *The Toronto Quarterly*. *Island of Witches*, a Brazil story from her book-in-progress, *Spirit Geographies*, was nominated for a Canadian Broadcasting Corporation Literary Award in creative non-fiction in 2006.

Kristin Andrychuk is a longtime Kingston writer. She graduated in English and philosophy from Queen's University. Three times she has been the recipient of scholarships to attend the Banff Centre's writing studios. She has two published novels: *The Swing Tree* (Oberon Press 1996 and *Riding the Comet* (Oberon Press 2003.) She is currently working on another novel.

Lara Szabo Greisman is an independent cultural producer based in Stockholm, Sweden and a former collective member of the Artel Artist's Accommodation and Venue in Kingston, Ontario. She works in diverse artistic disciplines looking at representations of identities and histories as well as the deocratisation and accessibility of culture. The pieces in this anthology were mainly written during her residency at the Artel and nod to Kingston as a formative and supportive community she had the pleasure to learn from.

Laura Dyer spent the first eighteen years of her life in the stretch of farmland tucked in between Kingston and Gananoque. After spending most of those years escaping rural life by hiding in Kingston she now lives in Toronto where she is completing a degree from Ryerson University.

Lauren Hearnden studies English Literature, more or less, at Queen's University. She is from Colborne, Ontario where there may be a few cornfields. In the future she hopes to spend a few years bumming around.

Laurie Lewis is a Fellow of the Graphic Designers of Canada and is editor and art director of Vista, the magazine of the Seniors Association in Kingston, Ontario. Her written work has been on CBC and has been published around and about, including *Contemporary Verse 2*, *Queen's Feminist Review*, *Kingston Poets' Gallery*, and *Queen's Quarterly*. A chapter of a memoir was shortlisted for the 2007 CBC Literary Awards in Creative Non-Fiction. Her memoir *Little Comrades* was published by The Porcupine's Quill, June 2011.

Leah Murray is a rural- based photographer, writer and small business owner in Hastings, Prince Edward and Northumberland Counties, Ontario, Canada. She started her photography career in her teens as an adjunct to her established writing habit. Leah's personal work focuses on documenting rural and small-town Canada along the shores of the Great Lakes in the post-millennium years.

Leanne Betasamosake Simpson is a writer, activist, story-teller and scholar. She is a citizen of Kina Gchi Nishnaabeg-ogaming and is a member of Alderville First Nation. Her third book, *Dancing on Our Turtle's Back: Stories of Nishnaabeg Re-Creation, Resurgence and a New Emergence* was published in May 2011 by Arbeiter Ring. Leanne lives in Nogojiwanong (Peterborough), Ontario.

Lee-Ann Taras grew up in Prince Edward County on the Bay of Quinte. Kingston has been her home for over 20 years. Taras is particularly interested in the power of art making as a means for self-expression and transformation. Her mixed media art practice tends towards abstraction yet it is often evocative of landscape/cityscape. Her work, of late, has been examining concepts of individuality and kinship, an ongoing exploration of the uniqueness of one within the solidarity of many.

Linda Allison Stevenson was born in Henderson, Kentucky and began writing poetry when she was 10 years old. Her mother and biggest influence pushed her to write more. Writing many short stories and poems throughout middle and high school, each time throwing them away, her mother would go behind her and pick them up. For that she was both then and is now very grateful. She is 32, married, to a wonderful husband, Riley, and has an adorable five year old son, Connor. The poem included herein was written while she was in labour with her son.

Lindy Mechefske is a freelance writer, editor, photographer, and Associate Editor of the Queen's Alumni Review. Born in the U.S.A., she has lived in England, and Australia, and currently makes her home in beautiful Kingston, Ontario. Lindy is author of *A Taste of Wintergreen*, and the forthcoming travel–memoir, *Going Down Under*.

Louise O'Donnell was born and educated in Toronto (York University) Eng/creative writing and moved to Wellington, Prince Edward country in 1990. She has worked with prominent authors across Canada (Di Brandt – Sage Hill, Linda Rogers – Mentorship Programme/The League of Candian Poets, Carolyn Smart – Queen's Univ. Summer Writing Progamme). Her work has appeared in magazines and journals in Canada, the US and Australia, and has two published collections: *Shuffling into Place* and *Infinite Horizons*.

Lucy Barnett is a writer, photographer, farmer and mystic who divides her time between the rolling Northumberland Hills and the Big Smoke. Often scolded for talking too much, she decided to use her wordy powers for good and started to write.
My tie to the area was an impulsive purchase of an old school house north of Campbellford 7 years ago. It is truly a marvellous obsession and I feel myself release tension as soon as I come home (except when the pump's frozen).

Lynn Tait is an award-winning poet/photographer living in Sarnia Ontario. Her work has appeared in *Contemporary Verse 2*, *Windsor Review*, *Feathertales*, in eight Ascent Aspiration publications and in over 60 Canadian and American anthologies. She is a member of The Ontario Poetry Society and The League of Canadian Poets.

Mansoor Behnam immigrated to Canada in 2006 and completed an MA in Comparative Literature at the University of Western Ontario (2010). Over the years, he has gained extensive experience (for more than fifteen years) in experimental writing and filmmaking while he also worked as theater director, instructor, freelance writer, translator and researcher. He is currently a second year PhD student in Cultural Studies at Queen's University, working simultaneously on his research about Iranian independent cinema and his experimental novella entitled *"This Is the Way I disappear."*

Martina Hardwick arrived in Kingston in 1992 to attend Queen's University and formed a serious attachment to the town. She can't imagine ever living anywhere else and loves its limestone, waterfront, and ferries.

Matthew Reesor lives in Kingston with his wife and two sons. His poetry most often appears in mixed medial collaborations with his sister, Sarah Reesor, a painter currently living near Orillia, Ontario.

Matthew Shultz was born somewhere between here and wherever the Earth was a few decades ago, knows you'll have trouble finding that on a map, and hopes to keep it that way as he has trouble finding the time himself and would be embarrassed if anyone else found it first. Like most humans he's been writing since attaining basic literacy, however due to undiagnosed neural abnormalities this was inflicted earlier in life than is usually the case and he has been struggling with this ever since.

Matthew Sinclair is 32 years old and was born and raised in the North Shore geographical area. He grew up in Cobourg, Ontario and finished high school there before moving to the Quinte region for his post secondary education. He is now a Manager in the Developmental Services field and resides in the lovely Kingston, Ontario. His writing has definitely been shaped and influenced by his experiences gained through growing up in this beautiful area of Canada.

Michael Casteels was born in Cobourg, Ontario and has lived along the north shore of lake Ontario for the majority of his life. He has self-published 11 books of poetry and artwork through Puddles of Sky Press. He lives in Kingston, Ontario where he works as registered massage therapist, and occasionally writes in the third person.

Michael Hurley, a resident of Kingston is a poet, graphic novelist wannabe & prof at RMC were his motto is the old Celtic saying, "Never give someone a sword who hasn't learned to dance." He's also done occasional stints over the decades as a stand-up comic, clown, cartoonist, community volunteer/activist, prison farm arrestee & spiritual runt at retreats led by Tibetan lamas, Buddhist monks and nuns, Hindu pujaris, Sufi whirling dervishes, Zen fools, aboriginal elders, and assorted non-denominational wise guys.

Mieke Little is a second-year Phys Ed student at Queen's. She started writing when she was in grade 12 for a Writer's Craft course. Her greatest inspirations in lyric writing are John Prine, Dan Mangan, and an array of other amazing artists. Writing is the greatest way she feels she can express what goes on in her mind. To quote Mieke; "I really think poetry is something that should be without rules, because everyone thinks differently"!

Morgan Wade lives in Kingston, Ontario with his wife, a son, and a cat named Mabel. His short story, *The Solitaire*, won an honourable mention in the Niagara Branch of the Canadian Authors Association 2010 Short Story Competition, and published in their *Ten Miles High* anthology. *Truth*, another story, was published in 2011 in the *Quarc* issue of *The New Quarterly*. His first novel, *The Last Stoic* (ed. Helen Humphreys) was launched in June 2011. When he isn't writing, he is learning the difference between a genoa and a jib.

Nicholas Papaxanthos was born in Vancouver, but grew up in Lefkosia, Cyprus. He moved back to Canada to complete an English degree at Queen's University, and is currently in his fourth year. He has been published in the anthologies *Lake Effect 5*, *529*, and recently put together a chapbook, *Teeth, Untucked* with Proper Tales Press.

Norma Chakrabarty, while attending St. Lawrence College, fell in love and married her very patient husband Buddhadeb. Although she lives in Kingston, her home will forever be in the rolling hills of her youth in Northumberland County, where she ran, played and gathered strength in the footprints of her ancestors.

Patricia Henderson is a Kingston writer and the owner of Writing By Design. A graduate of Queen's University and the National Theatre School, she worked as a stage manager at the Stratford Festival and Expo '86 before going to work with CBC Radio as a writer/broadcaster. Patricia has awards from Writer's Digest Writing Competitions (magazine feature) and the Writer's Union of Canada (short story) and is the co-author of 3 plays. Writing By Design has just celebrated 15 years of writing.

Patricia Sullivan, born in London, England, immigrated to Cornwall, Ontario as an infant. She studied English at York University before living in Amsterdam, the Netherlands, for two years, then returned to York to study Art History. She received her Master's in Art History from Queen's and has worked in public art galleries ever since, first at the Art Gallery of Ontario, and since 1999 at the Agnes Etherington Art Centre. In her last ten years in Toronto, she lived close to one end of the lake and now I see the other end of it every day.

Paul Kelley's poems, plays, translations, performance works, prose pieces, and scholarly essays have appeared in both Canada and the U.S. He has taught courses in Literary Theory and Canadian Poetry at Queen's University in Kingston. His most recent book is *Matter's Music* (Buschek Books, 2010). The poems presented here are drawn from a cycle contained in a new book, *Knock*.

Philomene Kocher lives in Kingston, Ontario where she explores poetry and photography. She has been living in Kingston since 1988.

Phyllis Erwin, born in Winnipeg, Manitoba, studied Interior Design at the University of Manitoba, and Fine Art and Design at the University of Michigan. Then in Toronto, as a colour consultant and part-time interior designer, she painted and became interested in pottery. She and her husband now live in the Northumberland Hills north of Cobourg. As a ceramic artist, her work appears at the OENO GALLERY in Prince Edward County. Currently she is writing a memoir of a half year period living in rural France in the 1970's with her husband and their five-year-old son.

Rich Tyo moved to Kingston three years ago from Ottawa. He was writing before that, but since moving to Kingston, his writing has increased significantly. He now writes songs, poems, stories, makes zines, and is working on his first novella. He works in the mental health field.

Roger Dorey is a singer/songwriter and spoken word poet based in Kingston, Ontario. He has previously released a collection of poetry, entitled *You're an Easy Kill Standing Still: Urban Blues Poetry, to defend your soul against the impending domination of globalized indifference to personal emotions*. He has also recently released his EP titled *55 Ain't no Limit*. He can be contacted at www.rogerdorey.wordpress.com

Rose DeShaw has been frequently anthologized, written national columns, published in England, the U.S. and Canada, short-listed for the CBC and Star literary competitions, had song lyrics produced, sold poems and writes a weekly blog, *Slices Of Now*.

Ruth Buckley is a retired professional who lives in Kingston. She has been writing sporadically since 1952 when, as a school girl, she won a provincial award for her essay on Queen Elizabeth's Coronation. Her muse has followed her closely throughout the years and continues to prod her to write more often. She writes poetry and short stories.

Ruth Clarke is the author of five books of non-fiction. She has recently completed an historical novel and is working on another, this one steeped in magic realism. She is a resident of Northumberland County and a descendent of one of the notorious Cavan Blazers.

Sadiqa de Meijer's writing has appeared in a range of literary journals, was short-listed for the CBC Literary Awards and included in *The Best of Canadian Poetry 2008*. She is currently working on her first poetry manuscript.

Sage Pantony Irwin, a prophetic poet, oft' considers her visions more of a curse than a gift. Wishing to live the life of a hermit she finds happiness unlikely so long as thousands line up to read her "Poems of the Future". The only solution to this problem is a good old fashioned escape to Europe, where she hopes to achieve peace and enlightenment – as well as a small cactus for her room.

Sandra Alland is a writer, performer and intermedia artist. Her previous publications include *Proof of a Tongue* (McGilligan Books, Toronto, 2004), *Blissful Times* (BookThug, Toronto, 2007) and *Here's To Wang* (Forest Publications, Edinburgh, 2009). She currently collaborates with Y Josephine in the multimedia band, Zorras. http://www.blissfultimes.ca

Sandra Walton was born and raised to the Kingston area and except for a few brief stints elsewhere, remains here. As a teen she became enamored by the solace Lake Ontario afforded and it became her muse in her expressions of poetry where life and the lake are analogous. This will be the first time Sandra has anything in print, as sharing her work is a new phenomena; one that will hopefully continue. *Where* is one of her first saved writings, written while mooning over the loss of a "first love" while being dazzled by the sun.

Sarah Richardson is from a small town called Erin, Ontario. Sarah loves to play with her imagination and lives for the infinite characters, places and images that writing provokes. The inspiration, special people and the strong writing community of Kingston are all instrumental in keeping this writing journey alive.

Sarah Yi-Mei Tsiang is the author of *Sweet Devilry*, (Oolichan Books) as well as two picture books with Annick Press, *A Flock of Shoes* and *Dogs Don't Eat Jam and Other Things Big Kids Know*. She has two new books forthcoming with Annick Press, *Warriors and Wailers, 100 Jobs in Ancient China that you might have relished or reviled* (non-fiction), and *The Stone Hatchlings*. Her work has been published and translated internationally, as well as named to the OLA Best Bets for children 2010, nominated for the Blue Spruce Award, and shortlisted for Book of The Year.

Shane Joseph is the author of three novels and a collection of short stories. His work *After the Flood* won the best futuristic/fantasy novel award at the Canadian Christian Writing Awards in 2010. His short fiction has appeared in international literary journals and anthologies. His latest novel *The Ulysses Man* has just been released. For details see www.shanejoseph.com

Sonja Grgar is proud to have called Kingston home for the period of thirteen years. She continues to be mesmerized by the many layers of life in this town, and by the complexity of the many communities who inhabit the city. Although she as of recently no longer lives in Kingston, she carries its lake-kissed limestone shores tenderly with her wherever she goes. They have nurtured her, challenged her, and inspired her for a lifetime. She is currently working on building a career in media and writing, and resides in Surrey, British Columbia.

Steven Heighton's most recent books are *Workbook: memos & dispatches on writing* and the novel *Every Lost Country*. His 2005 novel, *Afterlands*, appeared in six countries; was a *New York Times Book Review* editors' choice; was a best of year choice in ten publications in Canada, the USA, and the UK; and has been optioned for film. His poems and stories have appeared in many publications—including *London Review of Books*, *Poetry*, *Tin House*, *The Walrus*, and *Best English Stories*—and have received four gold National Magazine Awards. He has also been nominated for the Governor General's Award and Britain's W.H. Smith Award. He lives in Kingston, Ontario.

Stuart Ross is a poet, fiction writer, editor and writing coach. His most recent books are *You Exist. Details Follow.* (Anvil Press), *Snowball, Dragonfly, Jew* (ECW Press), and *Dead Cars in Managua* (DC Books). Stuart is the Fiction & Poetry Editor for *This Magazine* and he has his own imprint, "a stuart ross book," through Toronto-based Mansfield Press. He was the 2010 writer-in-residence at Queen's University. Stuart lives in Cobourg, Ontario. He blogs at bloggamooga.blogspot.com.

Susan Olding's *Pathologies: A Life in Essays* won the Creative Nonfiction Collective's Readers' Choice Award for 2010. Her poetry and prose have appeared widely in magazines such as *CV2*, *Event*, the *L.A. Review of Books*, the *New Quarterly*, and the *Utne Reader*. She lives with her family in Kingston.

Tapanga A. Koe lives in Northumberland County with her husband and three children. After family, she loves growing food and reading. She has been a part of a local fiction workshop through Loyalist College, taught by author Ursula Pflug.

Tara Kainer grew up in Knoxville, Tennessee and Regina, Saskatchewan, moving to Kingston, Ontario to attend Queen's University in 1988. She is the author of the poetry collection, *When I Think On Your Lives* (Hidden Brook Press, 2011). Currently, she lives and works in Kingston.

Terry Ann Carter is the author of five books of poetry. *A Crazy Man Thinks He's Ernest in Paris* was shortlisted for the Archibald Lampman Award. *Lighting the Global Lantern: A Teacher's Guide to Writing Haiku and Related Literary Forms* was published by Wintergreen Studios Press, in 2011.

Theodore Christou lives in Fredericton, New Brunswick with his wife, Aglaia, is an Assistant Professor at the University of New Brunswick, and completed his PhD at Queen's University in 2009. He has worked as a public school teacher in the Toronto District School Board, as an adult educator in the Durham District School Board, and as a Greek teacher in the Toronto area. He is the author of two forthcoming books, one prose and one verse, titled *The Problem of Progressive Education* (University of Toronto Press), and *an overbearing eye* (Hidden Brook Press).

Tim Murphy was born in Kingston in 1967 and has lived here three times, 27 years this most recent round. He has been writing, according to his mother, before he could actually physically write, by dictating a story. He gave up dictatorship before kindergarten, though, and has been writing in one form or another ever since. He was once told he wrote for forty-year-old teenagers, which is a reasonably good summary of his life, though, unlike most teenagers, he didn't have a boyfriend back then. He has been making up for it ever since, though only in small monogamous bursts.

Ursula Pflug, author of the highly praised novel *Green Music* (Tesseract Books, 2002), lives south of Number Seven Highway, on the Ouse River. Her internationally published, award winning short fiction has been collected in *After the Fire* (Tightrope Books, 2008). A new collection, *Harvesting the Moon*, is forthcoming (Britain's PS Publishing). A novella, *Mountain*, has been sold to 40K Books in Milan. Pflug freelances as a book reviewer, editor and teaches short fiction at Loyalist College. She has lived in the Norwood area for over twenty years. http://ursulapflug.ca

Veronica J. Atkinson is a graduate of Humber School for Writers. Her family has been avid fishers of Rice Lake for generations, starting with her great-grandfather, who was part Native Indian.

Dr. Vivekanand Jha is a translator, editor and award winning poet from India. He is the author of five books of poetry. His works have been published in more than seventy five magazines round the world and his poems have been chosen and published in more than fifteen poetry anthologies. He has more than twenty articles published in various anthologies and journals. His works have been published in more than sixty magazines round the world. Apart from that his poems have been chosen and published in more than fifteen poetry anthologies. He has more than twenty research and critical articles published in various national and international anthologies and referred journals.

Walter Lloyd says "The north shore of Hay Bay shaped my bones and taught me to love the water. Grew up in and around Napanee then moved to the metropolis of Kingston. There I work as a carpenter and live with my lovely wife and children."

Artist bios:

Cover Artwork: "The Light"

William Weedmark is a professional photographer and graphic artist with 35 yrs. experience. He has worked on magazine assignments as well as exhibited in public galleries. His photographic work reflects a sense of place and time, of things lost and found, left behind or discarded. Yet these things contain a history and significance unto themselves, which he finds compelling. His tie to this area is familial. His parents met, married, retired and passed away in Kingston. For the past 12 years he has called this city his home, establishing a broad network both professional and personal.

Section Artwork
Listed alphabetically by first name

David Woodward is currently in his third year of the BFA program at Queen's University in Kingston. He works primarily in painting, drawing and printmaking, and has shown at the Gladstone Gallery, the John B. Aird Gallery, Modern Fuel Artist-Run Centre, Agnes Etherington Art Centre and Union Gallery. David's figurative paintings, prints and drawings reflect his interest in the honesty and, ironically, the deception of the human body. Influences include Rembrandt van Rijn, Tom Thomson, Lucian Freud and Ryan McGinley.
Ed. note – David's artwork, "Lakeshore Road in Winter", introduces Section III.

heidi mack works and goes to school in Kingston and has a home here, but she "lives" in an off grid cabin north of Sydenham in the shield... In preference to a traditional bio, she offers this–

these paintings and photography
emerge
from water
and trees
from music and poetry
which I devour
like pistachio gelato

I am trained by wind and granite
blessed with a fearless spirit
and have painted and taken photos
since dodge and burn days
since tempera and smocks days

they are my light:
part spectrum
part food
part
dance

visual artist solo mom phd student therapist poet scholar teacher
Ed. note – heidi's artwork, "Showshoe Moments", introduces Section I; "Frontenac Sky" introduces Section IV; and "White Pine" heads Section VI (Index/Bios).

Meredith Westcott was born and raised in Kingston, Ontario and proud to call the limestone city her home. As a mom of two wonderful children and wife to a fantastic husband, she purchased her first digital camera in 2007 in an effort to capture those precious family moments. In no time at all a serious passion for photography was born. Her "toy" began to occupy every moment of her spare time. She found herself quickly graduating from point and shoot to SLR, and something inside her clicked like she was always meant to be doing this!

She completed an interesting photography class at St Lawrence College, eventually inspiring her to pass on her skills to others in nature workshops that she now hosts. She really enjoys the creative and expressive sides of photography, and pushing her camera's limits has encouraged her to see things in a new way. Mundane objects, no longer, and ordinary is now extraordinary!

She has been fortunate enough to have had her photography featured in Our Canada Magazine, Doors Open Ontario paraphernalia, local newspapers and local businesses. If someone were to ask her what she loves to photograph the most, the answer would be easy, EVERYTHING!

Ed. note – Meredith's artwork, "Rock and Flow", introduces Section V.

Milenko Grgar is a film director by training, and photographer by passion. He specializes in 19th century heliographic processes, such as gum bichromate print, oil print, and cyanotype, just to name a few of his favourite methods. He relishes the skill and the focus required to practice these time consuming early photographic methods, but most of all he adores the complexity and the painterly quality these alternative techniques bring to the images. He has exhibited and won prizes for his work in British Columbia, New York, and Richmond, Virginia.

Ed. note – Milenko's artwork, "The Lake Will Never Forget Us", introduces Section II.

Ohter books in the North Shore Series

Find full information at
– http://www.HiddenBrookPress.com/b-NShore.html

First set of five books

— M.E. Csamer – Kingston – *A Month Without Snow*
   – Prose – ISBN – 978-1-897475-87-2
— Elizabeth Greene – Kingston – *The Iron Shoes*
   – Poetry – ISBN – 978-1-897475-76-6
— Richard Grove – Brighton – *A Family Reunion*
   – Prose – ISBN – 978-1-897475-90-2
— R.D. Roy – Trenton – *A Pre emptive Kindness*
   – Prose – ISBN – 978-1-897475-80-3
— Eric Winter – Cobourg – *The Man In The Hat*
   – Poetry – ISBN – 978-1-897475-77-3

Second set of five books

— Janet Richards – Belleville – *Glass Skin*
   – Poetry – ISBN – 978-1-897475-01-0
— R.D. Roy – Trenton – *Three Cities*
   – Poetry – ISBN – 978-1-897475-96-4
— Wayne Schlepp – Cobourg – *The Darker Edges of the Sky*
   – Poetry – ISBN – 978-1-897475-99-5
— Benjamin Sheedy – Kingston – *A Centre in Which They Breed*
   – Poetry – ISBN – 978-1-897475-98-8
— Patricia Stone – Peterborough – *All Things Considered*
   – Prose – ISBN – 978-1-897475-04-1

Third set of five books

— Mark Clement – Cobourg – *Island In the Shadow*
   – Poetry – ISBN – 978-1-897475-08-9
— Anthony Donnelly – Brighton – *Fishbowl Fridays*
   – Prose – ISBN – 978-1-897475-02-7

— Chris Faiers – Marmora – *ZenRiver Poems & Haibun*
  – Poetry – ISBN – 978-1-897475-25-6
— Shane Joseph – Cobourg – *Fringe Dwellers* Second Edition
  – Prose – ISBN – 978-1-897475-44-7
— Deborah Panko – Cobourg – *Somewhat Elsewhere*
  – Poetry – ISBN – 978-1-897475-13-3

Forth set of five books

— Diane Dawber – Bath – *Driving, Braking and Getting out to Walk*
  – Poetry – ISBN – 978-1-897475-40-9
— Patrick Gray – Port Hope – *This Grace of Light*
  – Poetry – ISBN – 978-1-897475-34-8
— John Pigeau – Kingston – *The Nothing Waltz*
  – Prose – ISBN – 978-1-897475-37-9
— Mike Johnston – Cobourg – *Reflections Around the Sun*
  – Poetry – ISBN – 978-1-897475-38-6
— Kathryn MacDonald – Shannonville – *Calla & Édourd*
  – Prose – ISBN – 978-1-897475-39-3

Fifth set of three books

— Tara Kainer – Kingston – *When I Think On Your Lives*
  – Poetry– ISBN – 978-1-897475-68-3
— Morgan Wade – Kingston – *The Last Stoic*
  – Novel – ISBN – 978-1-897475-63-8
— Kathryn MacDonald – Shannonville – *A Breeze You Whisper*
  – Poetry – ISBN – 978-1-897475-66-9

Anthology

Changing Ways is a book of prose by Cobourg area authors including: Jean Edgar Benitz, Patricia Calder, Fran O'Hara Campbell, Leonard D'Agostino, Shane Joseph, Brian Mullally. Editor: Jacob Hogeterp
  – Prose — ISBN – 978-1-897475-22-5

CPSIA information can be obtained at www.ICGtesting.com
Printed in the USA
LVOW090613150812

294334LV00004B/4/P